THE BATTERED HEIRESS BLUES

A Novel

LAURIE VAN DERMARK

Copyright © 2012 by Laurie Van Dermark

Cover model and author portraits courtesy of Godwin Photography / godwinphoto.com. *The Arlington Home, Birmingham, Alabama* photo courtesy of Katie Hallmark Photography. Cover design by Caitlin Carroll Graphic Design / caitlincarrolldesign.com.

ISBN: 0615579914
ISBN-13: 9780615579917
Library of Congress Control Number: 2011962877

CreateSpace, North Charleston, SC
Please visit the author's website at **www.laurievandermark.com**

For Noah and Izzy

Acknowledgments

⸻

A wise man once directed me to the writings of Gustavo Gutierrez, who says in part, "Neighbor is not he whom I find in my path, but rather he in whose path I place myself, he whom I approach and actively seek." I have met many along the path who have contributed to the work in progress that is Laurie Van Dermark.

First and always, praise and glory to my very patient God.

Thanks to my dear parents for their support and encouragement.

Nothing but love for Michael, my quick-witted brother, for our verbal sparring. Spending time with you is like going on a mind vacation. Thanks for the trips.

My precious children who are so loved. The years have flown by since your adoptions in Guatemala. Your cooperation and humor have made this book a reality.

Jacy, I feel bad that other people don't have you as a best friend! You are the real deal- selfless and present. No matter the time or request, you are always there- no excuses. You are a rarity in this world.

While living in New Zealand, I was fortunate enough to meet some truly stellar Kiwis. I would like to express a special thank you to Maureen and Daniel Tustin. The kids and I will always be in your debt. You taught me the meaning of Kia Kaha.

Additionally, being in the presence of the following people has enriched my life so greatly: Shane and Jen Waters; The White family; Fr. Gerard Boyce; Hector Bosse for introducing me to humanitarian work; Monsignor

Richard Lynch for our chats in Chimbote; The Bookalam family; Donna Estes; and Katie Hallmark.

I met Fr. Jack Davis and Sister Peggy Byrne in 2000 when I answered a call to experience the life of the poor in Chimbote, Peru. While our missionary group was bringing tangible goods to help the poorest of the poor, living outside the mission walls, we received far more than we could ever give. Jack and Peggy work tirelessly to try and meet even the simplest needs like food, water, and shelter, which most of us take for granted. Watching a large family crowd into a one-room estera shack with dirt floors, no roof, food, running water, or bathroom facilities is appalling. Not only do these heroes of humanity struggle to give the poor the dignity and care that is their God given right, they also work to raise funds for healthcare and education; without which, the next generation doesn't stand a chance for a better life. Every time I travel to Chimbote, I leave a piece of my heart there. Please visit www.friendsofchimbote.org to help.

John Tinney, my legal representation, for dealing with the distractions. I am blessed.

PROLOGUE

———⧉———

Sissy was the smallest black woman I'd ever laid my eyes on. What she lacked in stature, she far made up for in gumption. Her bark wasn't worse than her bite. Her words, spewed forth with clear fervor, made white men tremble, but the bite- well my father shed more than one tear on her account. My nana often called her the greatest gift she'd ever given my mama, as if Sissy was of the character to stay where it didn't please her most emphatically. She was four feet ten inches of pure stubborn power with micro braids down the length of her back. In so much as John Spencer felt he was the head of his own household, Sissy worked for Nana and no other. Father worked diligently to have her dismissed, but she never departed the mansion and never left my mama's side for a second. Where one went, the other followed. When I came along, she became my devoted guardian, hiding me beneath her protective wings from John's indifference to the birth of a daughter. In Sissy's eyes, I was the grandest and most treasured gift she had. This shelter continued as my mama bore John a son- my brother, Thomas.

Mama had grown tired and slept for stretches of time. Sissy made excuses, but I knew that all was not well. My father began making time in his busy schedule to take her on multiple shopping trips to Atlanta. I was young and naïve, but not stupid. Mama hadn't been well since she turned up pregnant with Tommy. For all of Sissy's convincing and her infinite planning to keep me busy, I saw Mama wither like a delicate rose on the vine at the end of a glorious season. Though she became a prisoner to her carved wooden bed, she seemed at any moment to arise and entertain the high cotton sort that was Savannah royalty.

John blew through abruptly and left just as quickly, never staying longer than a night, unable to face the gravity of losing his beloved Grace. Thomas and I held vigil at her bedside daily until Sissy would muster the energy to half carry and half drag us down the hall to our beds. Mama had become a shell that housed multiple tubes. One snaked down her nose, one in her arm, and another in her chest. She'd wake briefly and shower us with smiles before drifting off again. Thomas was too small to feel the sharp sorrow that pierced my heart. She was larger than life to me.

"I don't want a sick Mama anymore, Sissy," I cried, watching the nurse adjust the tubes that made the most beautiful woman in the world a human pincushion. Turning away, my body found its haven in the arms of my shadow. Pulling me close to her bony chest, she brushed the dark unruly curls back over my shoulders.

"You wipe those tears dry, you hear? You're a lucky girl, Julia Spencer."

"My mama's dying. That's not lucky," I whimpered, burying my face against her.

"Well, God sure didn't see fit to give me a mama like yours. My mama was as mean as a cottonmouth snake. She used to make me pick my switch before she beat me with it. Your mama is an angel. Now, look at her. Is she not the finest woman we know?"

"Of course," I replied softly, shaking my head in agreement, as I turned to see the pile of bones under Sissy's homemade quilts. Only her head was visible, displaying the exquisite ebony silk that sprung forth from her scalp, meticulously coiffed by her old friend.

When the nurse left, Sissy laid out a picnic blanket at the bottom of Mama's bed and presented Thomas and I with a basket of food to explore. He thought Mama was merely sleeping but we knew her silence was from the stuff that flowed through the tubes- the medicine that kept her quiet and free from pain. Sissy grabbed our hands, blessed the food, and prayed over Mama for healing before we broke bread. We talked about the blue water that stretched out into the horizon just beyond our backdoor and made plans to swim in the morning. Sissy handed out her special chocolate chip cookies and fruit punch that we held tightly while she sang old hymns. The sound radiated beautiful tones that filled the room- almost visible. She didn't miss a note as she spied my brother's body beginning to slant in the direction of the soft mattress. Rescuing the glass from his tight grip, she placed it on the vanity dresser where Mama once sat and brushed her hair.

Footsteps pounded heavily against the wooden floor in the hall, getting louder as they approached the bedroom. The melody stopped mid-phrase. Suddenly, the door flung open and my father filled the space between us with anger and rage, sucking life's air out of the room like a vacuum. His face was as red as the inside of a watermelon. He walked with determination to where Thomas lay and grabbed him harshly, disappearing from our sight. The cries of my startled brother became more muffled as Father stormed further down the hall. Only moments passed before he returned and instructed me to leave with haste.

"I'm not leaving my mama," I said defiantly.

"Oh yes you are, young lady, and I mean directly," he replied, pointing to my exit.

Sissy took a step toward me, volunteering to incur his wrath on my behalf.

"You best stand back, Sissy," he said, shaking his fist in her direction.

Looking to her side and then the other, followed by a lingering glance behind, she responded with an equal amount of hostility, "Just who do you think you're talking to? You see a slave in this room? You forget yourself, Mr. Spencer."

"You're fired. Leave."

"Well, you've already fired me one hundred and thirty-five times and I am still here. I'll still be here tomorrow, and the next day, and the next day after that. I don't work for you. I work for Nana- the one who bankrolls your business and bought you this fancy house. Grace is my best friend. You have no authority over me. Collect yourself before you scare your daughter."

Opting to go around the mountain instead of through it, he slipped by her to the opposite side of the bed and started to pull my right arm with conviction, causing the red juice to splash against the ivory quilt.

"Look what you did. You let that child loose," she demanded.

"Or what? Your benefactor is not here, is she? Run along, Sissy. Go tell Nana."

Father was committed to his present course of action, but a scrappy African goddess who was part sugar and part salt raised me. I wouldn't go down without a fight and I had absolutely no intention of being removed from my mama's presence. "Leave Julia. Now," he yelled, making Mama flinch, though her eyes remained closed.

"The hell you say," I responded, grabbing hold of Mama's hand that barely fell below the edge of the quilt.

Both Father and Sissy said my name in unison, in its entirety, the very second the profanity left my lips, "Julia Grace Spencer". Just as quickly as they came together on common ground they receded back into their corners.

"I am sleeping in Mama's bed again tonight and I'm not leaving," I said with resolve.

Father scooped me up from behind, breaking my connection to Mama, and began making forward progress toward the door, but my hands found the wooden posts at the end of her bed. He pulled and pulled until the sweat began to gather around my fingers, causing me to lose grip. Catching the doorframe as we passed through it, I recommitted to my cause. Sissy began speaking with wild contempt at a speed that no mere human could understand, cursing him to be sure. Thoroughly frustrated and impatient, John finally grabbed my hands and ripped them across the metal doorplate, sending a stabbing pain straight through me. Blood spattered across the planked floor and Sissy spun into action, removing the scarf from around her neck and winding it around my hand.

"You're wicked. You've done gone crazy, John Spencer. Get out of here. Go on, you hear? Your heart has turned as black as the night. You're no good to no one."

Father looked at me with both hostility and remorse. He was as broken as the woman that was bound to her bed. I had one parent dying of cancer and another dying to share her fate. Thomas and I weren't enough to keep him engaged in reality. We were reminders of the life he had envisioned with a beautiful Southern sorority girl all those years ago.

He left that night and didn't return from New York, until the day that Nana signed the papers to shut off her only child's life support. After the funeral, I rarely saw Father, with the exception of holidays. Sissy died soon after Mama in a terrible car crash, leaving me disillusioned and jaded. No doubt, her exit was planned all along to reunite her with her dear white sister Grace. Nana did her best to trudge on in Mama's place, giving Tommy and me many years of happiness and affection before leaving to join those rowdy women in heaven.

But I was heir to the Spencer fortune. There had been no contingency for sorrow. Weakness wasn't an option. I grew up, only sure of one thing- my father and I were done, forever.

Slowly surrendering to the fate of dying alone, I struggled to keep my eyes open. The clinic's light swung overhead casting shadows on the dusty floor, making me question whether he was gone. A strange voice, angelic in nature, commanded me to remain still. As my body shivered with each shallow breath, the warm red blood pooling under me was oddly comforting. I was cold.

An eternity seemed to pass in silence. No one came, but I remained obedient to the voice that made me motionless. In the distance, I heard the faint sounds of crying, but my mind was too detached to assign a sense of familiarity to the voices. I was slipping away. I welcomed the end.

There she was- the African goddess of my childhood, sent to protect me. I felt my body move upward and find its rest in her small lap. Leaning toward me, the braids brushed over my beaten face and the smell of my blood was replaced by the fragrance of a hundred honeysuckles. My guardian had returned to keep me safe. I called and called to her in a loud whisper, still fearful that my attacker was not quite done, but she never answered. Sissy only began to sing as she stroked my matted hair. *His Eye is on the Sparrow,* filled the room- its notes forming a cocoon around my frail and lifeless body. The song became harder and harder to hear until the melody and my angel disappeared altogether. I was alone again, but no longer afraid.

Peace washed over me. My mind displayed a montage of life experiences- small triumphs and heart wrenching losses. The images appeared one right after the next until a strong kick summoned me, with a fortitude that no longer matched my own. Clutching my belly, I let out a guttural scream. I'd forgotten him. I was dragging him into this abyss. He was an unwilling participant; his kick reminding me that our fates were linked. Climbing out of the quiet, I found my voice. "Help me. Please help my son." With my strength fading, the tenseness in my body relaxed and my eyes closed. My body was becoming his tomb.

Chimbote was a far cry from the privileged life I led in Manhattan. Fleeing to Peru was my most masterful escape to date. John Spencer the third, my father, labeled my trip a vacation. He related stories of me traveling in style to tourist destinations like Machu Picchu, neglecting to share that my departure was precipitated by finding my husband in bed with his associate. Somehow, disclosing that information would have embarrassed the family. I was certain that he blamed some inadequacy on my part for Jackson's little indiscretion. And so, I broke through my shackles and outran the search parties. The only person to eventually locate me was Henry. He was the only man I had ever loved. He was my *Tru*.

Henry Truman Walker was my father's right hand man. He was his lawyer, confidant, and all around errand boy. I had no doubt that my father would play upon our past, in asking Henry to find, and persuade me to come back to the States. He hadn't taken into consideration that I was my father's daughter. As much as I despised John, I could be every bit as stubborn as he.

Henry had it all- a Harvard law degree, stellar relations, and the good looks to match his English pedigree. He came to our family business as an intern, but quickly surpassed the skills of John's upper level executives. You couldn't help but be dazzled by his charm and dedication.

Deep down, I knew that Henry would have insisted on coming. College sweethearts- we were now the best of friends. I preferred his empathy to my father's work the problem mentality. We had a history. He was the first person I called when Jackson cheated on me. Henry was the clear choice. The priest in Tommy would have instructed me to pray, and my father would have cautioned about the impending scandal, but Henry just wanted to kick his ass. I loved that about him.

I felt his warm touch as I tried to open my eyes, squinting to shield them from the bright, harsh lights of the hospital room. I'd lost time. My body felt very heavy.

"Jewels." There was an apprehension in his greeting.

"Tru?" My head was pounding and my stomach uneasy. The room began to turn circles as if I were looking through a kaleidoscope. I tried to focus on his eyes.

He rose over me and kissed my forehead. His image was clearer now as I adjusted to my surroundings. "Thank God you're awake." His delivery was solemn, as he sat next to me on the bed. He was never very good at disguising truth- it just poured out of him.

"What's the matter?" I said, becoming keenly aware of the immense pain in my abdomen as I reached to greet him.

"You'll be okay, Jewels." He stroked my forearm without meeting my gaze. His evasiveness betrayed him and I began to panic.

Memories flooded back into my hazy consciousness. *I was stabbed. My baby. My Conner.* My hand slid down to my belly and anxiety swept over me. "Where's Conner? Take me to him," I demanded angrily.

His head dropped and after a long pause, he whispered, "He's gone."

"What? Gone where? I don't understand. Just take me to him." My mind wouldn't allow his words to register- self protection. I would find my son alone, if need be.

Struggling to get my body upright, Henry braced my torso and pushed me back down on the bed. I fought against his hold to no end. I was too weak. He placed his arms under my neck and drew me to him, whispering in my ear, "He didn't make it Julia. I'm so sorry. There was so much damage. The knife severed the cord. The baby wasn't getting oxygen. The doctors worked on both of you for such a long time…"

I couldn't process what he was saying. My breathing became erratic. There wasn't enough air. Hysterically, I grabbed my throat. Instinctively, Henry pulled me forward to the edge of the bed and placed my head between my knees. The nausea was overwhelming. Pushing by him, my hands secured the trash can. The familiar sensation of warm fluid pooling beneath me startled him and he began to yell for help as my stomach purged itself of the remaining anesthesia. Succumbing to my irrevocable state, my head surrendered to the coolness of the tile floor.

I couldn't hear the noises that must have accompanied the staff entering. My view became the shoes that scurried in and out of the room. I was alone with my mind. I had my silence back. My only desire was to become smaller until I disappeared.

Henry protectively crouched down at my side as countless hands grabbed at my body. His face appeared in my line of sight speaking words with no sound. Pulling my body onto his lap, he motioned for the hospital staff to stand aside. A nurse steadied my arm and added medicine to the intravenous line. The heaviness of my limbs returned, but he easily lifted me as the nurses kept their instructed distance. I felt the softness of the bed before the medication overtook me.

A surgical resident woke me in the early morning hours to examine my incisions. He spoke very little; just mentioning insignificant details like how much fluid had collected from the tubes that were protruding from my abdomen. I couldn't blame him for the lack of conversation. What do you say to a woman who has lost her mind? – Whose baby suffered a tragic death? He uncovered me, lifted my gown, admired his handiwork and expeditiously left, waking Henry who had fallen asleep in a rocking chair across the room.

"Hi love." He walked over to the bed and helped me prop my back up on the pillows. Sitting down next to me, his fingers traced the colorful bruises on my face that I had only then discovered as I caught a glimpse of myself in the mirror. They stained my otherwise pale complexion. He pushed a stray piece of my long dark curls behind my ear. Tears began streaming down my cheeks, having no control over them. His jaw tightened as he tried to stifle his anger. My hands found his and I tried desperately to pull myself together. Learning to compartmentalize my emotions would be a necessary tool if I were to survive the days ahead.

"How did you know about all this?"

"The Bishop called your brother's parish. Tommy phoned your father. We were in a meeting. I came straight away." He busied himself out of nervousness, taking the water pitcher off the table and pouring me a glass. When I didn't eagerly accept it, he placed it in my hand.

"You didn't have to come." He looked away as if I had injured him with my low expectations, but I quickly recovered. "I'm glad you did." I took a sip of the water and placed the glass down.

"Where else would I be?" Pulling me forward, his embrace was delicate and full of compassion; an effort ruined by the words that were to follow. "Your father wants you home...immediately. I've made arrangements." Henry pulled a thick ivory colored envelope from his jacket pocket and held it in front of my hands, subconsciously willing me to grab the correspondence. "He asked me to give you this. John sends his love."

I grabbed the letter and placed it on the bedside table, with no desire to read it. "I need some time to figure out..."

"Everything will get sorted." He paused and I could tell that he was unsure of how to proceed. "Julia, there is a matter we need to discuss."

His business-like approach made me feel uneasy.

"The police would like a statement. You shouldn't be alone for something like that, so I'd like to stay." The attorney in him needed to tie up loose ends- anything that would restrict my ability to leave the country. "Are you up for that?"

"I need to see my son, Tru. I need to hold him. Can you find him for me?" My arms came to rest on his shoulders as our eyes met. "It's important."

He nodded, not in agreement, but acceptance, pulling my hands down to his. "Let's talk to the police and get that over with. Then, I promise I will find Conner. I'll bring him to you. You have my word." He walked to the sink and wet a washcloth; returning and wiping dried blood from my hairline.

"I won't think about that night. I can't." I turned away from him toward the window, losing myself in the vastness of the sky, angry that he was pressing me to participate in remembering the attack.

"You have to tell them what you know. There is nothing more important. He has to pay for what he did to you and the baby."

"I can't...talk about this...ever." My eyes began to well up with tears, but I held onto them as best I could.

"They're not going to accept that, Julia. The embassy wants answers on why an American was attacked. They won't let this go."

"I don't remember anything. I don't know who did this."

"I don't think that's true."

"What will the truth bring me? My son is dead. There's nothing to tell. You tell them that. It's done. I'm taking him home. Make the arrangements."

Henry could sense that I was fragile. He didn't push against my defiance. He reluctantly shook his head in agreement.

"I'll tell them that we'll send a written statement in a few weeks, once you're home and you've had some time to reflect on the importance of justice."

"Get Connor...there is nothing more important," I replied, my tone unkind.

"In here?"

"Yes. Can you help me into the rocking chair?" I said, trying to pull my body up into a seated position.

"Of course, but wait- let me help you," he insisted. Henry walked over to the rocker and placed it alongside the bed, carefully pulling me to the edge and down into the chair. The discomfort was evident on my face.

"Thank you," I muttered, trying to catch my breath.

"Are you sure about this, Jewels? Is this a good idea?"

"Probably not, but I was supposed to deliver him, in this very hospital, next week. I have to hold him, Henry. Please."

While his judgment softened, the expression on his face was one of worry and premature regret. "Then I'll be back in a few minutes. Will you be okay alone?"

"Yes," I responded as if asking a question.

After he left, my mind returned to the day of the assault. I grew concerned wondering if Maria and her family were safe. Helping them had cost me everything. As I reached for the phone to make inquiries, the door opened and a nurse cautiously pushed a bassinet toward me.

There was my son, swaddled in a white blanket with a blue cap pulled down over his head. His eyes were closed and his face was very pale, but the corners of his mouth seemed to hold a small smile. He looked as if he were simply sleeping- like any loud noise would startle him and prompt a crying spell.

Henry knew me well. Dismissing the nurse, he asked that no one disturb us. I was thankful for that- for him being with me. He reached in and picked up Connor, pausing to steal a moment before gently placing him in my arms. That's when it happened. A mix of emotions overwhelmed me so completely. I was happy, but sad. I was enraged, yet at peace. He was finally in my arms, but unable to respond to my voice or touch. Our roles had reversed. As a mother, the job of comforting my child was meaningless. Connor comforted me now.

Henry stood over me as I began to rock my baby. His discomfort was palpable. He wasn't a man that was accustomed to not having the answers or perfect quip to alleviate an awkward moment.

"Do you want me to go?" he whispered.

"Do you want to stay?"

"Do you need me to stay?"

"No," I replied, letting him off the hook.

"I'll go get us some coffee. Would that be okay?"

"Okay? Yes." I became keenly aware of the remarkable talent I had for clearing a room.

We were alone at last. With Henry gone and the promise of no interruptions, I began humming a lullaby- mostly for me. I wasn't so far gone that I expected to soothe my dead child, but I needed a moment of normalcy. Unwrapping him as we rocked, I counted his fingers and toes. He had ten of each. This was the time that Connor should have gripped my finger. He didn't.

My hands were drawn to his cap. Tugging at the fabric revealed dark, thick hair- so soft. This was too much. He was only sleeping. There were no visible wounds on his perfect body. All I could do was press him to me and rock.

As I moved back and forth in repetition, warm liquid ran down my chest, wetting my gown. My milk had come in; only there was no baby to receive it. I cried over what should have been. Even my body was deceived.

Henry returned without the coffee. My sadness must have drawn him back to me. You could see the conflict in his eyes as he struggled to find the right words to speak.

"Do you want me to call the nurse? Get you a new gown?"

"No," I quickly responded, knowing that the nurse would likely snatch Connor.

"Shall I take him then?"

"No. Where would he go- back to strangers?"

"Jewels, I've made arrangements for Connor to be flown back to Savannah. I assume that you want him to be buried next to your mum?"

"I hadn't given it much thought."

"I can make alternant plans if you like."

"No. Of course, you're right. He should be in Savannah with Mom. Thank you."

"The doctors won't release you for another week. They are insisting on keeping you here until the drains are removed. They're worried about an infection. I think it's a good idea. You could use the time to regain your strength. Anyway, people will need time to travel to Georgia."

"People? I don't want anyone else to come. Just us…okay? Tommy will say the funeral Mass."

"I'll apprise John of your wishes."

Continuing to stare at Connor, I conversed with Henry, barely taking my eyes off my son. "Has the house been opened for the summer yet?"

"It's being taken care of, Julia. Don't worry yourself with those details."

"I want Connor to have the blue blanket that I knitted for him. Also, he should wear the white christening gown hanging in the nursery closet. It's all in my New York apartment. Can you send someone over to get them?"

"I'd be happy to."

"I should donate his furniture and toys to the women's shelter. There are some clothes in the drawers. They are welcome to them as well. I can't go back to that nursery, Tru."

"I know. I know. Let me take him now, Jewels. You need to rest."

I laid him in my lap and wrapped him in the same manner I found him, tucking the edges in like a package. I was a natural. A stray lock of hair poked out of the blue knit cap and my fingers were drawn to the curl.

"Can you find a pair of scissors for me?"

He left and quickly returned, offering the scissors and a handkerchief from his jacket pocket. He knew what I was after. Snipping the brown curl, I carefully wrapped it in the embroidered cloth and stared at that beautiful face awhile longer, kissing my son's cold cheeks. He didn't have that baby smell like I expected. He smelled sterile, like his surroundings.

The nurse knocked on the door and walked in front of me with outstretched hands. She didn't speak, but I knew exactly what she expected of me. The exchange felt like it took place in slow motion. She was kind and patient as he lingered in my arms. Once relinquishing my hold, she whisked him away before I could change my mind. He would soon be on his way back to the States, without me.

My belly remained sore, but the doctors were pleased with the progress. After removing the drains, they marveled at how the incisions were neatly sutured. The chief surgeon gave me instructions about refraining from lifting for another month and cautioned about physical intimacy for a while. Then he delivered grim news. My uterus had suffered a serious insult and was weak. The chances of being able to sustain a future pregnancy were slim. He encouraged me to seek the advice of a specialist when the time was right. In my view, there would never be another time. They should have removed it when they took Connor.

Our days in Lima were spent roaming the hospital halls. The doctors lamented about the necessity of being mobile, instructing me to make daily laps around the surgical ward. At first, walking was dreadful. When I stood upright, my abdominal muscles and the underlying sutures felt like they were tearing me in half, causing a great deal of pain. I saw very little reason to venture out and comply, but Henry was a serious task master- a real masochist. Within a few days of his regimen, I was no longer hunched over. The exercise stayed off the blood clots that would have tried to form in my legs had I remained in bed.

Henry slept in my hospital room night after night, refusing to go to a hotel. Once Connor left, he gravitated toward lying in bed with me. I looked forward to this time every night when his arms built a protective barrier between me and the rest of the world. In the morning, he would walk me to the shower and assist in washing my hair. After helping me dress, he'd sweetly brush my curls out, before making me comply with his carefully devised exercise program. With lunch digested, we'd participate in the beautiful custom known as the siesta, watching one of the English speaking channels on the television until I drifted off. There was a short period of time, between CNN and REM sleep, which left me anxious, thinking of Connor alone. I wanted to crawl out of my skin or peel it off altogether, but I didn't want Henry to know I was troubled. I didn't want to burden him further. I would solve my own problems. A Spencer shouldn't need to be rescued. I found myself counting backwards from one hundred slowly, usually making it to thirty-four, before my consciousness shut down and I was alone with my son. In my dreams, we played together. He laughed and smiled. The visions felt real and fulfilling. Waking only led to great disappointment because it ended the fantasy.

Over the course of the week, with little else to do, I began to notice how the nurses adored Henry. They paid me very little attention, but offered to have his clothes laundered and food brought in from local restaurants. If I weren't so sad and tired, I might have minded. What they didn't realize was that Henry was one of those men that didn't know how attractive he was. Flirting was wasted on him. His mind was typically occupied with business. They would have to be much more direct in order to garner a longer than usual glance from him.

Waking up first, on our last morning in Lima, I took the opportunity to appreciate the blessing of having Henry back in my life. He lay beside me still, exuding that sweet peace from his sun kissed face. Henry was a ruggedly handsome man. He always looked like he just stepped out of a GQ magazine. His hair was precisely messy with every strand perfectly out of order, yet still in place. His five o'clock shadow was always sexy. His style was effortless, whether he was in a Hugo Boss suit or casual khakis and a button down.

Then there was me- battered Jewels. I was not particularly put together. Henry always referred to me as a fine mess. I was his Picasso- bold and beautiful, but with an unpretentious quality that made me the girl next door- evidently, the messy girl next door. My long curly hair was unruly unless I made a concerted effort to tame it and look refined. I felt most at home in jeans and a t-shirt, but would make the sacrifice to dress properly if the social event dictated better attire. I appreciated fashion, but loathed shopping. I wasn't your typical socialite. My trust fund deserved a more dedicated social climber.

Looking at Henry still gave me butterflies. I had always known that he was my destination. The trip, up to this point, had gotten a little muddled. I learned a very difficult lesson about ultimatums. After asking Tru to choose between his career and me, a terrible fight ensued and no one won. He stormed out and Jackson stormed in, literally. After too much wine and the loss of good sense, Jackson and I stumbled in to one another at a party. I made the mistake of asking him to walk me home. When Henry came to apologize the next morning, he witnessed Jackson leaving my apartment. That was that. We never discussed the end- it just happened. He continued to work for my father and I married the worst mistake of my life. At the time, it seemed like the thing to do- to prove Henry's judgments about me correct. I was a fine mess.

My hands found his hair and I toiled until he woke up. Before his eyes opened, that gorgeous, knock your socks off smile greeted me. His confidence was intoxicating.

"How long have you been awake?" He rolled over on his side, facing me, and swept his hand over my cheek.

"Not long. I'm ready to leave."

"Me too. I've had enough of Peru to last a lifetime. Have you had breakfast?"

"No, but I'm sure one of the nurses would be more than happy to get you something," I scoffed, making fun of his groupies.

"Funny," he laughed with fake bravado, sitting up and turning towards me. "We could always eat on the plane."

"Sounds like a plan. Let's go." I started to unravel the sheets from under me.

"Can I get a shower first?"

He didn't need one. He smelled great and looked even better, unlike me. "Do you need help?"

He started to walk toward the bathroom, but looked back, flashing that devilishly gorgeous grin of his. "Don't trouble yourself. I'm sure one of those dedicated nurses would be more than happy to wash my back."

After successfully dodging the pillow I threw in his direction, he disappeared. With the sound of the water started, I decided to make haste and be ready to go, calling the nurse to remove my intravenous line and prepare the paperwork for my departure. She reviewed the discharge instructions left by the doctor and exited the room.

Henry had bought a few choice outfits for me to wear over the past weeks that included jeans and sweats. Though longing to wear the jeans, the thought of buttoning them and applying pressure to my waist made me quickly decide to choose the pink sweats. Hopefully, they were the absolute last things available in my size. Why would he choose such an obnoxious color, knowing my gravitation toward all things neutral?

The mirror didn't lie. I was hideous. Without makeup and a real will to achieve beauty, there was no way to remedy my appearance. Pulling my hair up into a knot on the top of my head, I pinned it tightly. One solitary curl fell down at the side of my face, which I didn't bother to readjust. The long tress fell across the last of the yellowing bruises and seemed to provide a bit of camouflage. The sound of the water ended and the bathroom door opened, revealing Henry bare-chested with a towel wrapped around his waist.

"Can you hand me some clothes out of that bag?" he asked.

He should be in marble. I felt very plain next to him. I walked to his weekend bag and sifted through the options.

"What should I wear?" he thought aloud.

"You sound like a girl," I protested.

"I'm asking so you feel comfortable, considering I bought you a leisure suit."

"Well then, where is yours? That would make me feel more at ease."

"They were out. I guess I'll just go with the Abercrombie and Fitch."

"You bugger. Hurry up. I'm ready to go."

Nodding, he dressed, tussled his hair, and we were on our way home- to Connor.

2

⁂

The plane ride was long and uneventful. We'd bought some food on the way to the airport, but the gravity of the day diminished my appetite. Henry tried to persuade me to take advantage of the darkness and sleep, but I knew what the morning was going to bring. After our arrival at dawn and the drive home, I would only have a short time to change and emotionally prepare for Connor's service. The quiet I was enjoying would soon be stolen by well meaning strangers.

Henry, on the other hand, had no trouble sleeping. Stretching out with a full stomach, he became lifeless, except for the occasional turn from one side to the other. The captain's announcement of our impending landing woke him. Becoming very attentive, he prodded me to eat and drink some juice. Looking out the window, I prayed for strength to make it through the day.

I must have nodded off in the car, only waking when the vehicle came to a screeching halt at the gate to my mama's house. Transferring ownership to me after her death, the house had remained well maintained and very stately. A tall red brick wall surrounded the property line at the road. Two black iron gates with an "S" scrolled into the design had been a gift from my father to my mother. Stopping at the black box to type in the security code, the gates slowly rolled away from one another, revealing a tree lined drive to the main house. I put down the window to take in the salt air. I felt like I was finally home.

The big white house was all-abuzz with workers coming and going from the front door. The old Southern mansion had real charm with huge verandas on both levels. The rocking chairs on them were inviting, but no one had time to sit a spell on this day with tasks to accomplish before the service. Florists were delivering peace lilies and white roses. Catering trucks cluttered the circular driveway making it impossible to park at any close distance to the house. Tables and chairs were being unloaded and brought inside.

The car came to a stop and I paused, reluctant to open the door. Henry gave my hand a squeeze, signaling his support. I tried to smile in return.

"What is all this? I thought we were having a quiet, private ceremony for the family?"

"I told your father about your wishes, but you know how he is. I'm sorry."

He exited the car and stood stoically, looking around at all the commotion. Shaking his head in disapproval, he walked around to help me out.

"Why don't you rest for awhile? I'll take you upstairs."

"No. I'm going to the chapel. -Alone...to pray. I'll be back. How much time do I have before people start showing up?"

"Two hours. No more. You'll need time to get a shower. I had my assistant buy a simple black dress and heels. I hope they'll be okay. They should be upstairs in your room. Are you sure you want to go alone? I can sit with you."

"No. I'm sure Tommy will be there preparing for the Mass. Don't worry."

"-Easier said."

I gave him a hug and my best look of having it together before walking toward the path that led to the small white chapel. Someone had tied ropes of white roses around the tree trunks that lined the path. The gesture wasn't charming or sweet- just weird. This was a funeral- not a wedding. There would be no happiness today. If I could have tinted them all black to match my mood, I would have done it. The chapel doors were open and I could see the tiny casket sitting below the altar. Unlit candelabras were at the end of each pew, along with those ridiculous flowers. Sprays of floral arrangements with cards attached filled every available space.

Connor was alone and I was thankful. Stepping in the doorway, I closed it shut behind me. My feet ran forward, stopping the instant my hands found the wood. I tried lifting it to see if I had the strength to carry it over to the first pew. I did. The muscles in my abdomen silently screamed in pain, echoing the noises in my mind. Sitting back slowly, I rested him on my lap. The tears that had disappeared over the last week, returned in full force. I couldn't look at the casket and think of him in there. I just imagined that I was holding my son as I did in that hospital room, fixing my eyes on the cross ahead. We sat together for some time before I heard the chapel door squeak open. Unable to bring myself to look back, I suddenly felt ashamed for having taken Connor from the stand. People wouldn't understand me holding him like this. I wasn't sure I cared.

"Hi." My brother knelt down beside me trying to ascertain my mood, placing his hands upon mine.

"Hi." I was happy to have Tommy with me. He and I had been inseparable since childhood. The loss of a mother and alienation of a father made us cling to each other as if becoming our own life raft. Tears silently paraded down my face and he reached up to wipe them away.

"I love you...so much. I'm so sorry for all this."

"I can't do this, Tommy." My panicked eyes found his.

"You can. For him, you can. You're the strongest person I know."

"Stubborn and strong are two different things. It's not supposed to end like this. I had plans for us. We had a future."

"You still do, Julia. You just can't see it now. God will..."

"Don't start with the God crap." He pushed the wrong button. I wouldn't stomach his allegiance to any deity that would take my baby. "Where was your God, Tommy...the one you pray to every night? -The one who you asked to protect us during your nightly prayers. He doesn't exist. A good God would never have let this happen. Please..." My head lowered in defeat.

"I'm sorry. Can I just sit with you?"

I shook my head in agreement; embarrassed for the tongue lashing I had given him. His intentions were honorable, but I still didn't want to hear it, even if it was coming from my brother, the priest. We sat silently until Henry came to retrieve me. He looked a little perplexed, seeing us holding Connor's coffin in our laps.

"Uh, you need to come and get ready now." He stood, stumped about what else to say that would elicit movement toward the chapel door.

Tommy got up and asked with his eyes if he could take Connor from me. I moved my hands off the top of the wood to signal my approval. He

15

placed him back on the stand and took a step back. Walking forward, I stroked the lid, and left.

Our walk back to the house was silent. Trucks were starting to leave and ahead of me, on the porch, stood my father, waiting to greet me. My stomach soured. If Henry hadn't been at my side, I would have walked around to the back to avoid him.

"Julia." His arms were outstretched and I had little choice but to walk into them. I couldn't bring myself to return the embrace. My arms remained at my side as he half hugged me, equally uncomfortable

"John," I replied, emotionless.

He broke our embrace to look at me. I could feel his disapproval of the pink leisure suit. Turning to Henry, he commanded, "Does she have something more suitable to wear?"

"Yes Sir. She's going upstairs to change now."

His attention turned back toward me. "Take a shower. Your hair..."

"I will. I'll be presentable. Don't worry."

"I'm not worried, Julia. You are always presentable."

I pulled away and brushed by him to enter the house. As expected, Henry remained with him. Climbing the stairs to my room, I shut and locked the door, figuring that Henry would try to sneak away to check on me and I was mad. I didn't want to see him now if it meant cheating on my father.

The hot shower felt relaxing. I tried to focus on the task at hand, hoping to keep my mind from wandering beyond scrubbing my body and washing my hair. The dress that lay on the bed was simple and elegant. I put on the black slip and decided to dry my hair. The grooming products he left for me helped as I twisted my hair up into a loose bun. Opting to forego eye makeup, I decided to just add a little color to my lips and powder to my face. The dress fit perfectly and the heels were a manageable height. Looking in the mirror, I thought that I seemed presentable- the thought more a question than a statement of fact. Let the misery begin.

The house had come alive again after a year of no visitors. My father had hired a caterer to provide the food for his guests. The funeral had turned into an event; a networking affair for the who's who of the business world.

I'd lost Henry again to a formidable adversary. When my father beckoned, he ran to his side like an old faithful lap dog. The sight of them together still made me cringe, despite the somberness of the day. Their partnership was a constant reminder of an entirely different kind of loss; for the heart keeps a different space reserved for romantic love, even when we have lost all hope.

Tommy delivered a beautiful service for Connor. I sat alone and motionless, in the first pew of the chapel, through the readings. Little could be said about a life that never came to pass. My brother spent most of his homily talking about my qualities and how my son missed out on a great mom; if only that were true. Hindsight painted another picture altogether. I would have said, *"Here is a sad, scared woman, who, in fleeing from her life, placed her helpless, and innocent baby in harm's way. Before you, a selfish and broken woman sits, devoid of all faith and joy."* That condemnation would have been far more accurate and refreshing to those in attendance, for I figured that most held the same skewed thoughts as me. At the very least, I was certain that my father held me accountable. I could feel his glare burn the back of my neck, from the row behind me, during the service. On this day, no one could hate me more than I hated myself.

With the closing prayer, my father stepped out of the shadows to invite everyone to the house for food. The small chapel began to empty and I was left alone. Tommy was busy shaking hands while Father led the parade to the refreshments.

I had asked that no one attend Connor's internment. I'd barely made it through the ceremony, knowing that all these strangers were watching me. I refused to allow them to be present when his precious body was laid forever in the cold ground. That moment belonged to me. Hearing footsteps behind me, an outstretched hand came over my shoulder. I opened my eyes and turned to find Henry, standing beside me with tears collecting in his eyes.

"May I carry Connor for you?" His voice cracked as he worked hard to hold back his emotions. His objective for the day was to lend me his strength. He wouldn't be happy if I had to console him.

I stood with tears streaming down my face and managed to reply, "Would you please?" My face began to feel strained as I tried to refrain from crying, but I wailed out in utter despair when I stepped forward and leaned across my tiny son's casket, pushing the blanket of roses off onto the floor.

"My baby. My son."

The sounds of the chapel door closing behind me shook the panes of the stained glass panels. Tommy was adamant about maintaining my

17

privacy, despite my father's party planning. He appeared at my left side and grabbed hold of my hands. They trembled as I embraced the dark stained wood.

"We're going to make it through this. Just let it out Julia. No one is here, but us. Say your goodbyes."

He had given me the permission I needed to unload the world from my shoulders. Henry moved to my right and grasped my waist. I could hear their muffled sniffles as my sobbing came and went.

I had cried for so long and so hard that I suddenly found myself quieted and at peace just holding the coffin. I didn't know how to let it go. I wasn't sure I could, knowing that the next step was to tangibly let them put him in the soil that was calling him to rest.

Tommy slowly loosened my fingers from the casket and I stepped back slowly. My body felt weak and I started to fall, but Henry caught my waist and sat me down in the pew.

Sitting beside me, my brother whispered, "Connor's with Mom, Julia. She's looking out for him. He's at peace. He feels only joy in the presence of God."

"Screw your joy and peace."

Tommy knew the importance of forward progress. "We should finish the service now, okay?"

Waiting for my approval, I could only offer a nod. There were no words for this. He walked back to the chapel door and opened it, asking the funeral home workers to carry the flowers to the grave. I waited and watched as they removed the countless flowers and sprays that lined the altar and aisles. When they collected the last one, I stood of my own volition and drew a long strong breath. Tommy extinguished the candles and the chapel became dark. I could have stayed in that dark chapel with my son all day.

Henry walked forward to the small coffin and lifted it off the stand. I could still smell the incense burning that Tommy had used during the Mass. We processed into the day- Tommy, then Henry holding Jackson's son, with me staggering behind.

The last time I had made this walk was to bury my mom. Parents should die before their children. We're programmed to expect this through old age or illness. No parent should suffer the loss of a child. Grieving a child is unnatural. No mom or dad should have to place a piece of their own heart in the ground. My son was my heart. He was my future. I was as good as dead inside.

The walk felt long, but the cemetery garden sat just behind the chapel through an iron gate, which the funeral director held open for us. Large mature crepe myrtles sat at the four corners of the space. My father had planted cypress hedges around the exterior so people couldn't see him mourning my mother. I grew up thinking that he was emotionally twisted because of this, but I was now thankful for the privacy. In the center stood a beautiful fountain and an old weeping willow, whose feathery branches relayed a sense of peace. The sound of the water was calming as I approached the grave. My mother was buried on the left and Connor would rest to her right. I had requested no tent or chairs. I didn't want others to feel invited to attend this goodbye.

Henry placed Connor on his grave and then walked toward me, grabbing my hand. The throbbing in my chest made me feel as if my heart would explode through my skin. With my legs beginning to fail me, I could barely hear Tommy. The tight hold I had on Henry's hand was slipping.

"Get her a chair, now," Henry barked at the workers. Within a minute, one materialized under me and he was pushing me gently down. A beautiful red cardinal caught my attention as it rested on one of the tree limbs that hung over Connor's sacred space. Seeing such beauty distracted my sorrows for a brief moment. My hearing slowly returned for the final *Amen*.

Tommy walked over and held out his hand to urge me up on my feet. Handing me a rose, he took the lead in placing one on Connor's coffin. I held the white rose, unable to release it, but Henry covertly opened my fingers and I watched it slowly fall to the wood below.

"Let's go, Julia," Tommy insisted, pulling me away as I protested.

"I want to stay for this." I turned back toward Connor.

"No. You can come back later. Let's go greet your guests and get a bite to eat."

"I'm not hungry."

"Come now, Jewels," Henry instructed, holding my hand and pulling me to him.

They were trying to protect me from what was coming next. They would lower my sweet baby's body into the dark depths of the dirt and no one he loved would be keeping watch. I would give in for now, while I was under their scrutiny. The funeral director offered a simple condolence before we walked in silence back to face the guests I hadn't invited.

The house was overflowing with people I didn't know. It felt like a bad socialite party- terrible company, insincere sentiments, and lots of empty promises. As we approached the front steps, Henry squeezed my hand and then vanished into the crowd. I felt many hands touch me as I passed and words were exchanged that I paid little attention to. I simply didn't care. All I could do was shake my head as a thank you for what I assumed were kind words. Hopefully, people knew better than to engage me with questions that required a true response.

I finally made my way to the guest bathroom and locked the door behind me. The mirror portrayed a grotesque picture. My face looked unrecognizable. The person looking back at me was so full of misery and sadness. I had never allowed myself such moments of heartache in the past. I was a pick herself up by the bootstraps kind of girl- a mentality drilled into my head by my father. My nose and cheeks were a blistering red and my eyes were swollen from crying. Turning away from that stranger in the glass, I slid down the door until finding a resting place on the floor. I began the comforting practice of counting ceramic tiles. For some reason, counting eased my anxiety. I had a good five minutes alone before people started knocking to either use the toilet or perhaps look for me- probably the toilet. Truly, no one wanted to be here.

Reaching up, I grabbed the marble vanity and pulled myself vertical. That same strange woman was eyeing me again. Turning on the faucet, I splashed my face with cold water and then pulled out the hair pin, allowing my long dark curls to provide some shelter from the staring eyes beyond this safe room. I could do this. For a few more hours, I could keep it together.

Making my way to the drawing room, I found solace in a single chair that was set off to the side. From that vantage point, I could see the show. Henry was smack dab in the middle of the festivities, shaking hands and dispensing opinions under the watchful eye of my father. He barely glanced at me during the long drawn out afternoon. We hadn't touched at all since our return to the house and I longed for one gentle, reassuring caress to remind me that the future held some small amount of happiness. Around him, I always breathed in a sense of hope, but it appeared that this day would not allow such luxuries. He would never so blatantly cross my father.

In the fight for Henry's affections, I was always the loser. Business always seemed to come first.

Father had made it abundantly clear to Henry during college that any opportunity with his firm came with a prerequisite. He must end his relationship with me. At the time, I estimated that the decision was a no brainer, but the cards were heavily stacked against me. John had contacted the other firms interviewing Henry. Despite his wicked talent, my father persuaded the various companies to pass on offering him a position. John made certain that he would have no alternative but to work for Spencer Industries. How could I compete when all I had to offer was me?

After an hour of mindless small talk, I rose to my feet and excused myself, feeling drawn to my mom's portrait that hung in the foyer. With my hasty retreat to Peru, I hadn't studied her face in months. Oh, how I longed for her today. I needed someone to prop me up and tell me that life would continue- or even that I wanted it to. I had no one. John had been an absentee father since my mother's death. He became instantly disengaged, a prisoner to his own sorrow. We were a constant reminder of her and so he stayed away from us as much as possible, making appearances at birthdays and holidays. My nana had influenced our rearing, and though lovely as she was, no one could replace our parents. In one fateful day, my mother and father were both lost to us.

Henry was deliberately avoiding me in this public forum. I felt very alone until my brother walked around the corner.

"She was so beautiful," he remarked.

"Loving, warm, and yes, very beautiful. I can still close my eyes and feel her brushing out my curls."

"I miss her too." Tommy's face was covered with regret and shame; the very emotions my father had brainwashed him into thinking over the years since her tragic death. The cancer grew rapidly during her pregnancy and to spare Tommy, the treatment was delayed. One life was given and another was taken away, in an instant. My father placed the blame on Tommy and with that our lives were altered.

I noticed John watching us as we stared at Mom's painting. Tommy turned his head to take in my view. He grew uncomfortable.

"He's led a bitter life. I wish things were different. I've missed having a father."

"Never mind that now," I said. "We have each other." I pulled Tommy out of the room and onto the veranda where we found respite in two rocking chairs. We rocked, eyes closed, holding hands, two against the world, like it always had been. The sound of people leaving was the only thing disturbing us.

"Here you are." Henry was doing his best to be both charming and apologetic.

"I've been *here* all day." I didn't bother to open my eyes.

"Your father is about to leave."

"Okay," I said indifferently.

"I thought you'd want to come and say goodbye."

"Not really."

"Julia." His voice was condemning.

I opened my eyes to face his accusatory tone. "If he's leaving, he'll be going through that door, right?"

"Yes. But…"

I cut him off. "Then I'll say goodbye…to you also."

"I wasn't going to leave."

"Weren't you?"

The peacemaker interrupted a long pause. Tommy was God's own human instrument. "How about something to eat? You haven't had anything all day."

"Sure. That would be nice. Thanks."

Tommy left his chair and entered the house, leaving it rocking back and forth. Henry decisively stopped its swinging and sat down. "What's the matter Jewels?"

"The matter?"

"Yes."

"Well, let's recap shall we? I buried my son today. Does that suffice for what's the matter?"

"I'm sorry," he responded, embarrassed for asking such a silly question.

"About what exactly?"

"You're upset?"

"Yes."

"Have I done something…?"

"No. You haven't done anything," I coolly replied.

"What does that mean? Why are you picking a fight with me?" Henry leaned forward and stopped my chair from rocking. His close proximity was intimate.

"Careful now- my father is afoot," I teased.

Without warning, John walked through the door, as if he had some sixth sense that we were talking. Henry quickly stood up and took a step backward.

"I'm ready to go Henry." John walked toward me, but stopped.

Henry searched his pockets for his phone and started dialing. "Very good, sir. I'll call the plane." He walked to the end of the veranda and started squawking instructions into his cell while my father grew impatient.

"Where are you headed?" I asked, completely disinterested in his answer.

"New York." There was a long pause. "...unless you need me to stay." His invitation was a rouse. He had no intention of staying. I had no intention of being hospitable.

"Have a good flight. Thanks for coming and bringing so many mourners- it really made the day seem all about Connor."

John was visibly aggravated. He made his way to the steps while I took the opportunity to chastise him.

"By the way, how is your son doing...or haven't you bothered to inquire? Time is ticking away, John. You are in control of most things, but not time. Look at me. Don't end up like this...full of regret...with a child in the ground who never knew your loving touch or kind words."

Descending down the stairs, without looking back, he said, "I'll be in New York." That was that. He fell out of view. I heard a car door slam in the distance. There had been no great sentiment over my loss. This was classic John.

The house was quiet. The last of the guests had finally made their way to the airport. Everyone had felt so damn sorry for me. Truth be told, they would have left after the final prayer if etiquette had not contradicted their departure. Most were hoping for an *Amen, good to see ya, sorry for your loss, and goodbye*. Their discomfort began to wear on my nerves. I wasn't feeling particularly kind. If I had not been so sad, I would have made it a point to talk to each of them as long as I could tolerate, in hopes of prolonging their agony. Broken glass for everyone- stomach it and run. Misery demanded company. Unwilling to participate in my descent to hell, the captives were eventually freed, practically causing a stampede exiting the house once my father disappeared. The only remaining hostages were my brother and Henry.

Henry placed his cell phone back in his pants pocket and walked toward me. "What was that about?" questioning John's earlier retreat.

"Just saying goodbye- like you wanted."

"I have to get him on the plane, but I'll come back…if you want me to…"

"Really?"

"Of course. Give me a few hours." He looked around before leaning down to kiss my forehead.

Tommy returned with a plate of food and placed it on the table between our rockers. "Are you leaving Henry?" His attention quickly turned to me. "Eat," he instructed.

"Your sister doesn't need me hanging around." Shamefully, Henry was lying to a priest.

"When will we see you again?"

"Definitely Easter. I'll come hear you say Mass. Kate will be sorry to have missed you."

"Your sister? How is she?"

"She's flying here from London tomorrow afternoon on holiday to make mischief with Jewels."

"Good. She needs the company."

Henry shook his head in agreement with my brother's assessment.

"Don't talk about me like I'm not here."

Tommy smiled. "I could always put off leaving until Kate turns up."

"Don't be silly. I'm exhausted. I'll probably sleep straight through until her arrival. The caterers have stocked enough food to survive a famine. Really, I appreciate the offer, but I need some alone time- some quiet. Please. Feel free to irritate me with phone calls, okay?"

"Can I drop you at the airport, Tommy?" Henry seemed in a hurry to falsify his departure.

"Yeah. Let me grab my bag." My brother wandered into the house.

Henry knelt down and ran his hands through my hair before they rested on both cheeks. "You've been very brave today around these strangers. I don't buy any of it. You don't have to be so strong all the time." He leaned his forehead against mine before standing up in anticipation of seeing Tommy.

From the other room I could hear him. "I've left my number at the parish by the phone in the kitchen." Within seconds he was lifting me out of the rocker and squeezing me. I held him just as tightly.

"Thank you so much for today- for Connor. I love you, Tommy. I'm sorry if I was harsh."

"Don't think of it again. I love you too. I'll try to give you some space, but check in with me from time to time so I don't worry. Will you do that?"

I broke his hold and gave him an obedient smile. "I promise." He threw me a skeptical look that I passed on to Henry. "Seriously, some of us can't lie to a priest."

He smiled and then they were gone. I was alone for the first time in weeks with nothing to do. The staff had cleaned the house and everything was back in its place.

3

I walked a lap through the downstairs trying to find a task for my hands, before stopping at the front door. Feeling compelled to open it; I reached for the knob, knowing what lay on the other side of the ornately carved wood. Slowly, turning the knob and pulling the door back, I could see the chapel in the distance and imagine his grave. My mind immediately posted a picture of the coffin in the ground and my son covered in dirt. I wanted to run to him, to dig him out with my bare hands, but my feet wouldn't allow me to clear the threshold. I couldn't do it alone.

Leaving the door ajar, I stepped out of my black heels, and started making a path through the drawing room, into the dining room, then the kitchen, family room, study, library, and living room. There was the door again. Another lap. The door again. Another lap. The door again. I became obsessive about my new occupation. Eventually, I no longer stopped and looked out toward the chapel cemetery. Finally growing tired of the route, I began to count seams in the hardwood floors. Counting still made me feel calm and in control.

Mental exhaustion finally took its toll and I withdrew to that same chair in the drawing room, sitting and fidgeting with my dress, straightening out the creases over and over again. The wind blowing hard against the house as the sun disappeared rattled the old windows. A storm was brewing. Lightning lit the dark room. My hand nervously twirled a loose curl that had fallen across my face as I rocked back and forth, trying to self soothe.

A car's headlights danced across the drawing room wall. The motor stopped and a door slammed shut. Within minutes, the figure of a man paused in the open doorway. Henry was back.

"Jewels. Where are you, love? Why is the door open?"

He made a reverse lap, hollering my name, as he proceeded through each room, turning on lights. I wanted to answer him, but I couldn't. I just kept straightening my dress and twirling my hair.

The bright light of the chandelier had no effect on me. Henry had a look of panic in his eyes. He knelt down and released my hand from its curling motion as I continued to rock.

"Why didn't you answer me? How long have you been here?"

I couldn't respond.

"Jewels, have you been here all afternoon?"

I wanted to ease his mind.

"It's okay. It's been a long day. You just need some sleep."

I felt Henry embrace me and my rocking. We moved in unison as one hand held my back and the other was cupped around the back of my head. He was in over his head.

Henry mumbled, not realizing that somewhere deep within me, I was in touch with this experience. "Holy shit Jewels…one of us needs medication."

I heard that.

"We need to get you to bed. Grab hold of me."

Forcing my arms around his neck, he lifted me off the chair. Walking to the open door, he kicked it closed before we climbed the staircase to the bedroom.

Once inside, Henry placed me on the bed and unbuttoned my black dress, pulling the sleeves down off my arms and revealing my black slip. Pivoting my body, he slowly laid me back against the pillows, removed my dress, and pulled the comforter over me. Sitting down on the other side of the bed, he took off his watch and dropped his shoes to the floor. He leaned over to kiss me goodnight; his hand pulling the covers up to tuck me in before it gently slid away. I couldn't bear to be alone. Grabbing his hand, I tucked it under my breast. I wouldn't let go.

"I'll stay. I'm not going anywhere. Sleep. I'm here. You're safe." He leaned down and kissed the side of my face- his body coupled to my every curve. I closed my eyes. I was safe. I could feel my mind go blank as I drifted off

Thunder broke my sleep and I awoke to find my slip drenched in sweat. I couldn't recall my dreams, but I doubt that they differed from reality. Henry's hand was heavy on my chest. I turned my head ever so slightly to determine if he was asleep. Thankfully, he was. I wanted to get up and find a dry set of clothes, but I didn't want to disturb him. Instead, I lay there, in wet clothes, counting the evolutions of the ceiling fan that hung above the bed.

After a period of time passed, anxiety set in. I peeled his hand off my breast and slid it down to his side, waiting to see if he would move. He simply made a noise and turned over, giving me the escape I needed. I was almost free.

Quietly, I opened the door that led out onto the upper veranda. The night sky was a mix of thunder, lightning, and a fine mist of rain. A lightning strike lit the yard and my eyes were once again drawn to the chapel.

The scared feelings that gave me cement shoes before now gave me wings. I yearned to be with Connor. I darted past the bed and down the stairs to the front door, stumbling over a death lily and knocking a book from the foyer table to the floor. I waited, crouched down, listening for footsteps from above. The house remained quiet except for the low rumblings of thunder. I fumbled for the light switch and flipped it on, but nothing happened.

Setting out across the soggy lawn, I sprinted toward the cemetery, as the rain began falling more heavily. I paused, scanning the sacred space for his headstone. The heavy gate slammed shut behind me. Mountains of floral arrangements covered his grave. Descending to my knees, the lighting illuminated his name: *Connor Truman Spencer, beloved son, June 15, 2008.* Meticulously clearing the flowers, I drove my hands into the dirt, clutching the earth that held him down below. The soil ran down my arms and onto my slip.

All I could do was lay on top of him in a move of protection from the elements. The cold rain pelted my back, but my mind was occupied, playing images of times I would never know: first words; first steps; first day of school; and his first game. In that moment, I was privy to all of them. I was happy. The comfort was quickly replaced by rage. Rising to my knees, I screamed out in anguish to a God that had deserted me.

"How dare you take him from me? He was mine. You had no right. Where were you? Why didn't you help us? I hate you. Do you hear me? I hate you." My anger was cathartic- it felt good. I threw floral arrangements and rocks at the statue of Christ as I yelled my blasphemies. With one last scream, I fell back to my knees on the loose soil.

I suddenly became keenly aware that I wasn't alone. A hand lightly touched my shoulder. I must have awoken Henry.

Looking back, I found a strange man staring at me. The rain was beating against his hooded jacket, partially obscuring my view of his face. I should have been afraid, but I wasn't. I cared little about what happened to me.

"Are you okay, Mam? I heard you screaming."

"Jewels. Jewels..." Sounds of yelling demanded my attention from the direction of the house. I turned myself toward the gate and then back to the stranger, but he was gone. I looked around the cemetery, but he had disappeared.

The gate slammed shut and Henry was beside me, pulling me to my feet. Grasping my arms, he gave me the once over to determine if I was injured. He pulled me tightly to his chest, smothering my breath.

"You could have been killed out here. What are you doing?"

"I'm angry." I held him crying. "I'm sorry."

"Don't be sorry. I'm angry too." He made it a point to pull me back so that I could see the sincerity in his eyes. "But maybe we can be angry inside the house...away from this lightning, huh? Can we go? Let's go."

Henry held my hand as we made our way back to the house. My eyes searched the grounds for the stranger as we trudged back. He was nowhere in sight. Henry flipped the light switch and discovered that the power was out.

"I'll get some candles. Wait here." He pointed to the very spot I was standing and repeated his command loud and slowly, as if I were impaired in some way. "Wait right here."

"I'm sad. I'm not deaf."

He returned with a towel. "You need a hot shower. You're freezing. Up you go."

Climbing the stairs felt like the walk of shame. He was the guard. I was his crazy prisoner who got caught sneaking off.

I sat on the side of the tub as he lit candles and started the shower. He turned to me and lifted my arms above my head, pulling off the wet slip that clung to my body.

He knelt down in front of me pulling my panties to the floor. There was no embarrassment. We had a physical history together. I didn't have the mental capacity to feel vulnerable about my nakedness.

"Tru, I don't know what I'm doing?"

"You think? You're starting to scare me, Jewels. I don't know how to help you. God knows that I'm doing a piss poor job. A tragic thing happened to you, to be sure, but you've got to get a grip. You can't put yourself in harm's way like this. You're too important to me."

I took his face in my hands. "How do I get a grip? Tell me and I'll do it." I was desperate for the one answer that would heal this hurt.

"Let's start with a shower. We'll figure the rest out." His tone was reassuring.

He led me into the shower and then removed his soaked suit- the one he had worn to the service and fell asleep in earlier. He walked in behind me. The hot water ran down my body. Henry gently caressed my skin, removing the soil before lathering my hair with shampoo. When he was done, I turned to face him.

"I will be okay. Tell me I'm going to be okay," I demanded.

"You will be. We'll get through this together. Give yourself some time. Be patient."

Henry held me under the water until it turned lukewarm. After drying off and slipping into my robe, he led me back to bed.

"Get some sleep. It's almost morning. Kate will be arriving soon."

I nodded while he pulled the covers over me. The image of the stranger popped into my head. I became curious regarding his identity.

"Who was that man in the cemetery?"

"What man?"

"You didn't see him?"

He looked puzzled and concerned. "No."

"There was a man. I may be a little off the reservation, but I'm not seeing things."

"Okay." Henry tried to sound affirming.

"Okay." I closed my eyes before I had to see his disbelief.

"Love you." He left.

I woke from the first restful sleep I had had in months. Rolling over, I hoped my arms would find Henry, but my bed was empty. I pulled myself to the clock- ten. Kate would be arriving shortly.

My feet found the floor. I went into the bathroom to view the damage, expecting to find my face swollen and distorted, but I was pleasantly surprised. Besides the two saddlebags under my eyes, I could pull off plain- not spectacular, but adequate. I surveyed my hair, pulling stray curls vertical, pinning them up to wash my face and brush my teeth.

The knock on the door was measured- Kate. My heart lightened. She slowly pushed it forward as I aggressively pulled it back, landing her on top of me as we fell to the floor.

"Well, that's quite an entrance," I roared. "Ouch. My belly."

We laughed loudly. It was the first ounce of joy I had truly felt. My best friend had arrived, ready for the day in her swimsuit.

"I don't do anything half-way," she announced proudly.

She noticed me looking beyond her into the hallway. She answered my question before I had a chance to ask it. "He's gone."

"Who?" I wasn't a girl who played dumb well.

"Who? Whatever. Suck it up. You're so transparent. *He* gave me marching orders and left for New York. My brother will be back in three days. Deal." She pulled herself up and jumped on the bed. "Which rules shall we break first?" She seemed excited at the prospect.

"Was there one regarding alcohol?" I asked.

"That was number one so it should be the first to be broken, don't you think? Ah…it's good to see you." She pulled me up beside her and surveyed my stability.

"It's good to be seen. Your brother must have told you that I've gone mad."

"He did instruct me to hide the butter knives and toss the razors. Looks like its mushy food and hairy legs for you."

"I haven't been myself."

"He mentioned that. Why don't we picnic at the beach? Put your suit on. I'll pack a hamper full of food and booze."

"I don't have a suit."

"Henry told me that, yes, you do have a suit. He instructed me to tell you to look in your drawers and I quote, 'Don't make excuses about leaving your room'. So, chop, chop. I'll be downstairs."

Kate was my polar opposite in looks and style. She was shorter than me with shoulder length, dark blonde hair, which was stick-straight. She was into fashion and always looked polished whether she was going to sleep or like now, in an expensive bathing suit cover-up that probably came from a couture house in Paris. She was every bit Henry's sister. The entire Walker family had the look of royals.

I was so thrilled to have Kate in the trenches with me. She busied my thoughts with mindless talk about mutual friends and acquaintances. Our five-minute walk to the beach was filled with immense laughter. She took her role as best friend very seriously, vowing to keep me occupied until Henry returned.

The sky was overcast. After we laid the blanket down, and set up the umbrella, we spilled out the contents of the picnic basket. Disappointment washed over my face.

"Beer?" I was thinking of something a bit harder.

"Pace yourself, Jewels. It's only lunchtime."

"How long are you staying?"

"Indefinitely."

"Sounds perfect. How can you manage that?"

"I'm in between jobs."

"What happened to the magazine gig?"

"I got sick of writing about mundane shit." She paused and struggled with finding her words. "Who cares? It's silly stuff, really- of no consequence...nothing to burden you with."

"Please, burden me. The statement I promised to write for the Chimbote police is due tomorrow. Until then, I don't want to think about my crappy existence. Let's talk about your crappy life."

"Well, when you put it like that, I feel much better about having told my boss to sod off. It seems like the right decision now...getting fired and all."

"You did what? Does Henry know? He got you that job."

She shook her head as fear flew across her face. "And you better not tell him either. Same rules apply as they did in college. We take secrets to the grave."

In an instant, Kate realized what she had said to me. She was speechless- not an easy accomplishment for her. I broke the ice by raising my beer to hers.

"-To the grave." I hit her brew with mine and her face relaxed a bit.

"I'm an idiot. We know that about me. I'm sorry. What I meant was..."

"I know what you meant. Stop stressing. I can't have you editing yourself around me. Not you. Everyone else does that right now, but not you. Agreed?"

"So I can say stupid things?"

"Yes, be yourself."

"Ah, touché."

We heard the wind snap and our heads turned to the sound. A man and a child were on the boardwalk, near my old, weather beaten, cottage, flying a kite. The beautiful colors of the dragon with its long tail whipped through the air, turning left and then right. The boy's face was blank- disconnected.

"Who's that?" Kate inquired.

I was intrigued. "I have no idea."

"They're on your property. Are you still renting out the cottage?"

"Yeah, that must be it. The realtor didn't call, or maybe she did, with me away, I don't know. Should we go over and introduce ourselves?"

"No. I think no," she said.

"He's waving." Now I felt awkward.

"Maybe he's hot. It's too far to tell."

Kate turned back toward him and waved her best beauty queen wave. I tried to study his face as I returned his glare. He seemed vaguely familiar, but I couldn't place him.

"You have a one track mind. Someday, one day soon, someone is going to steal your heart right from your chest."

"Well they better hurry before I jump super dad. Do you think he's married?"

"You are too much. You have the hormones of a teenage boy, Kate."

"No. I have the hormones of a thirty something gotta have it hottie. There is a big difference."

"And what's that."

"Experience. I know what I have and how to use it." She looked over to our neighbor. "Ooh, I bet he does too."

I chugged the beer and lay back, pulling my straw hat over my face.

"What do you think is wrong with the boy?" Kate's wheels were spinning.

"Why do you care?"

"I don't…just curious."

"The man probably lives inside of a fish bowl, with people staring at him, using their curiosity as a weapon. It's unpleasant, trust me. Leave him be. Lay back."

"I didn't mean it like that."

Kate felt the disgust in my tone, which I found hard to disguise. We were best friends. She could take it. I moved the hat to the side so she could see my face.

"I know. Everyone is well meaning. It's just hard living in a glass house when so many people are on the outside holding stones. Not you, but everyone else. You're the best. You're outside the glass house with alcohol. Now, lay back. Let's sun."

Kate slowly relaxed, turning on her side, pretending to read a magazine so she could spy on them. She thought she was in stealth mode, but her attempt was clumsy. I glanced over and made note of their interactions. The boy didn't respond to any of the man's conversation. He didn't show any interest in flying the kite. He sat on the sand, staring into the liquid blue that filled his mind's eye. He was trapped somewhere else. I sympathized with his broken compass. The man, however, had a look of genuine contentment on his face, like he wished for nothing better- at least nothing different.

"Are you sure you don't want to introduce yourself?"

She answered, casually flipping through the pages, "No. He probably has a wife."

That was that. They stayed for another twenty minutes and then vanished. We didn't even notice their departure. That was probably the alcohol kicking in. The rest of the afternoon was spent drinking, laughing, and splashing in the wake of the waves.

Henry called to check up on us under the guise of giving Kate a message from her mom. I wasn't fooled and neither was she. I was pretty sure that he was onto us for breaking rule number one. The conversation was circular like he was trying to trip me up. He felt it necessary to remind me of the statement I had promised to prepare. I brushed him off and changed the subject, but he was adamant that I have it ready and so I agreed- again. Kate was the last to speak, hanging up on him mid sentence, but it mattered little to me. I didn't have a care in the world.

As the sun went down, we tried to gather our things. Either the sand was very uneven or we were very intoxicated. We stumbled as we walked back to the main house, leaving our stuff just inside the front door. Unanimously deciding to skip dinner for sleep, we pulled each other up the stairs and collapsed in my bed.

"Bloody hell, I have to pee," she announced.

I started to push her toward the edge of the bed, but she fell off, causing a loud thud that was only trumped by the hideous laugh that ensued.

"What the hell, Jewels?"

Her head poked up above the covers and she looked like she was seeing double.

"Sorry. I didn't want you to wet my bed. I was trying to be helpful."

"Well now I've peed myself so piss off."

"Don't be like that- it was an accident." I pulled myself to the edge of the bed to make amends, not suspecting that she was out for revenge. The next thud I heard was me being pulled over the edge and crashing onto the hardwood below.

"Now I'm not mad," she said with a grin.

"Why is the floor wet? Awe Kate."

Banging and screaming roused us from bed. My mouth felt like it was stuffed with cotton balls. Leaning over the side, I hoped to find a bottle of water, but no such luck.

"Who is making that racket?" You don't wake Kate in this manner. Ever. "They are going to wish that they never stepped foot on that porch."

"Stop yelling." I covered my head with a pillow. I was officially hung over.

"I'm not yelling. They're yelling. Get up."

"They'll go away," I insisted.

"They're still banging."

"Just call 9-1-1."

"And say what? Annoying Americans are knocking on a door? Get up. This is your house. You're coming with me."

She pulled the covers off and threw a robe at me. I took no notice that I was still wearing my red bikini- Henry's selection. I begrudgingly reached for the white, terrycloth bathrobe and stuck my feet in garden boots before following Kate downstairs. She had made the extra effort to find pajamas last night and was in a better state to entertain company. She looked through the sidelights of the door and turned back with eyes the size of tea saucers.

"What's wrong? Who's here?" I inquired.

She stood in front of the door, her body making the shape of the letter "X".

"Let's go back to bed." Kate grabbed my arm and started to pull me toward the staircase. I turned under her hold and headed back to the door. She quickly caught the back of my robe and yanked me to a halt, jumping back in the lead.

"Whatever you do, I need you to promise that you're not going to freak out."

"Kate, you're being ridiculous. Why would I freak out?"

"On the other side of this door is…" she hesitated.

"Go on."

"Promise me that you'll behave first."

"My head hurts and I'm really tired. No games. Who is it?"

"Judas." She stared back through the sidelights, angry.

"Priest?" I was too hung over to play word association.

"Not the rock band, genius; the lying, cheating, traitor that should be hung from the nearest tree kind of Judas."

The edgy New Yorker rose up within me. I had a gut feeling who was behind the damn door.

"No way. He wouldn't be that foolish, right? Jackson is here? -At my house? -On my property?" I dismissed the assumption and shook my head in disbelief.

"Yes he would- he's Jackson."

I started to walk towards her with an agenda. "Step aside."

"I don't think that's such a good idea."

I turned and walked back into the drawing room and took the shotgun from above the fireplace. Kate followed me, managing to keep her body between the door and me.

"What are you doing? Let's just think about this for a minute," she implored.

"Step aside, Kate."

As we found ourselves in a stare off, Jackson's voice broke the tension.

"I know you're in there. I can hear you. I've called the police. I just want my car."

Kate was pissed. Her plea to behave civilized was null and void. "No he did not just say that- after everything that's transpired."

She spun around and charged the door herself, violently pulling it back, sending it crashing into the foyer wall. Scared, Jackson cowardly shuffled back until he fell off the veranda. Kate continued her forward attack to the edge of the porch.

Hesitantly, I walked to the door, catching the first glimpse of him in ten months. I thought I'd be sad, but I only felt relieved that he was now my ex-husband. He looked like the same old loser, wearing his ridiculous banana yellow windbreaker.

In the moment, I couldn't recall why I ever had married him. Average looking, he was too short and scrawny for my usual taste. He had no muscles and was devoid of a butt and proper calves. I never could figure out how he kept his socks up. His graying hair was like wire that matched the patches poking out from inside his ears. His tobacco stained front teeth were pushed together. When he ate, he resembled a rabbit gnawing food. The clothes he wore were always mismatched and rumpled. He was the polar opposite of Henry. Perhaps, that's why I chose him. My heart would never be stolen away by someone like Jackson.

Looking at him now, I was actually repulsed. I didn't care that my criticisms seemed hypocritical, considering my current choice of wardrobe. I had potential when I tried really hard and no matter what, he would always be a mean prick with no style. I was a good person. I had that going for me. I wasn't condescending in my interactions with people. I treated strangers with kindness and respect. He was always frigid and hostile. Bring him the wrong order or question him and he'd make you feel like the most insignificant person in the room. He was never wrong. He was never accountable. He was the world's most dedicated narcissist and I was done.

"Why are you here?"

"For the car, Julia- I just want my car and I'll leave."

"But our son...Why didn't you come...he's buried behind the chapel." My eyes began to water, but I wouldn't cry in front of him.

Kate jumped off the veranda, stopping within a foot of him. He gave his typical sour smirk to let us know that he wasn't afraid of two weak little girls.

"You're here for a car. Seriously? Your son was buried this week, you wanker. Where in the hell were you? What could possibly be more bloody important than that? A car? There's no hope for you. You'll always be a self-absorbed bastard with no heart." She threw her arms up in the air, moved five feet away from him, and looked back to cheer me on. "Shoot him."

The shotgun rested across my body, finding a home on my right shoulder. Jackson looked at me puzzled and decided that laughing was a good emotion- bad choice.

"Get off my property."

Kate disappeared into the house returning with a golf club. Jackson still maintained his annoying grin

"Look, I don't want trouble from you scary women." He was mocking us now, waving his arms back and forth above his head. "Really Julia, are you gonna shoot me? You don't have it in you."

"Care to test that theory?" I pointed the gun above his head and pulled the trigger. He cowered, momentarily, shielding his face, but regained his composure and stood erect.

"Jewels, you missed. Try again," Kate announced with a dedicated look on her face.

"The police are on their way. Just give me the car. It's mine." He fell back to the other side of the circular driveway.

"Not so much- anymore."

The sound of a siren got louder as it made its way down the long drive, pulling in between Jackson and me. I walked back into the house to locate my gun permit in anticipation of what was to come.

Kate followed me around, nervously. We went from room to room rifling through drawers. The faint sounds of Jackson's annoying voice could be heard, but the distance filtered it. I'm sure he was delivering a 'woe is me speech'. He and the truth were like oil and water. I was sad to be missing his performance, but first things first.

"Maybe it's in the foyer?" I walked back toward the front door talking to myself. No one was in sight. My attention turned back to Kate as she walked up behind me. I was feeling more defiant as each minute passed

"I don't care what donut eating cop they send out. This is my property. That's my car and here- here is the permit for my gun. Ha." I looked up at Kate feeling very proud of myself, but she had that deer in the headlights look about her. She moved her hand to her chest area and nonchalantly pointed with her index finger in the direction of the door. The wind was knocked out of my sails. I couldn't move.

"The donut eating cop is behind me, right?"

All she could do was shake her head yes. Before slowly turning in his direction, I mouthed the words, 'get the car' to Kate. There he was- the mystery man, wearing the same coat as that night in the cemetery. Turns out, I wasn't crazy after all. He walked toward me with his hands raised in front of him, his eyes glancing up and down my body, taking in my strange attire.

"I'm not going to shoot you." I didn't appreciate his theatrics.

"Thanks for that. I would miss all those donuts," he jabbed.

"What can I do for you, officer?"

"This man claims that you have a car in your possession that belongs to him."

"Not true. I own the car."

Jackson walked up on the veranda, spouting off, "It was a birthday gift."

I pumped the gun and the officer waved him back.

"Your car. My car. Semantics. My name is on the bill of sale and title. Would you like to see them?"

"That would clear things up from my perspective."

Kate pulled the red Porsche out of the garage and parked it next to the cruiser.

"Bring the title from the glove box, Kate."

She was still carrying the club as she stopped in front of the officer, delivering the paperwork to him.

"I'm sorry. I didn't catch your name." Kate was hitting on the officer. She had impeccable timing.

"Sheriff Gabe Martin."

"Sheriff," she repeated slowly, looking back at me. Kate was impressed. I was annoyed.

"That was you in the cemetery the other night?"

"Yes. I'm very sorry for your loss. I read about it in the newspaper. I heard you screaming. I'm sorry to have intruded." His eyes were compassionate, full of understanding and sympathy.

He was very unassuming; the type you would pass over in public without realizing just how good looking he was unless your gaze lingered on his face. He had worry lines around his eyes and on his forehead that gave away his hard life. My eyes thanked him and we shared a moment.

Jackson cleared his throat.

"This isn't a sympathy call. I just want my car." He was still an asshole.

Kate was beside herself. Before his very last word made it to my ear, she walked over and slapped him across the face. "Shoot him."

"I'll take that." Gabe intervened, requesting my weapon.

"I have a permit."

"Just the same, your friend really wants you to shoot him." He reached for the gun and I complied.

"Of course I do. Someone needs to. That low life is the father." She gave Jackson a scowl. "I use that term in the biological sense only. You really couldn't attend your own child's funeral?"

"Julia knew she was on her own. I never wanted a kid."

Gabe looked dismayed and handed the gun back to me.

"What are you doing?" Jackson said perplexed.

"She has a permit. She can lawfully own that firearm. Fact of the matter, sir, is that the lady has asked you to leave her property. You're trespassing."

"I'm not leaving without the car."

Straw. Camel. The back was broken. I'd had enough. I aimed the gun at the Porsche and fired, spraying the hood with pellets. Kate joined in, smashing the windshield with her golf club.

"You have to arrest her." Jackson was becoming unglued.

"She destroyed her own car. I can't arrest her for that. It might be wise for you to go. I'll give you a ride into town." Gabe looked back at me. "No more guns. Lay off the noise. You have neighbors."

Kate stepped in between us and offered her hand to Gabe.

"Thanks for coming by. Don't be a stranger. We have lots of donuts."

Gabe shook her hand out of politeness and escorted Jackson to his vehicle.

"Smooth, Kate."

We turned to walk into the house, glancing back to watch their departure.

"He'll be back. Nice outfit by the way. You look like a mental patient."

After tidying up our mess, from searching for the gun permit, Kate retreated to her room to take a nap. A shower was necessary to humanize me before trying to tackle the police statement. Seeing Jackson had unsettled me. I couldn't shake my anger about the fact that he wasn't angry. I couldn't understand how he had no emotional attachment for his own child. How is a man like that allowed to draw air?

I loafed around, busying myself with mundane tasks, trying to delay the recollection of that terrible night. I was clean and dressed. The house was tidy and quiet. I finally convinced myself that I had no more excuses.

Walking around downstairs, I tried to determine which room would be suitable for the grueling job at hand. The drawing room was too open and the kitchen too communal. I couldn't afford distractions. Choosing the study, I closed both doors and sat at my mother's desk. The frame with her picture inside was welcoming and calming. I took out some parchment paper and began to write.

To Whom It May Concern:

> *I'm an idiot.*
> *I killed my child.*
> *I'm the one who should be punished.*
> *I'm the one who should have died.*

> *Regrettably,*
> *Julia Grace Spencer*

I stared at the words on the page with frustration, finally, crumpling the paper and tossing it to the floor. –Again, deep breath.

To Whom It May Concern:

My name is Julia Grace Spencer. I am an American citizen that moved to Chimbote in December 2008 to serve as legal counsel to the mission and assist its parishioners with free legal aid. This help usually consisted of land transfers, hospice arrangements, managing education funds from donors, contracting endowments, and being a liaison to missionaries in other countries, regarding the needs of the facility.

In February 2009, Maria Costelano, a woman from a nearby barrio, showed up in my office, requesting help. Her husband, Hector, had been beating her and their four children. Before periods of abuse, he would steal the money she had saved from cleaning houses and disappear, leaving Maria with no funds to satisfy her bills or feed her children.

I advised Maria to move into the battered women's shelter that the mission ran, but she refused, stating that Hector would find and kill her if she left him. He'd threatened to harm the children if she went to the police. I told her to bring her money to me and we would open a bank account without his knowledge. She agreed to leave some money in their quinta, to dispel any suspicion he might have, and would deposit the remainder in the new account for safe keeping.

Hector Costelano continued to beat Maria. In May, she required an overnight hospital stay to assess the probable diagnosis of having a traumatic brain injury from a blow to the head. He waited for her outside of the hospital with the children, in an act of intimidation, to persuade her not to file a grievance with the police, as I had insisted she do. Due to her fragile state and his custody of the children, she agreed to go home with him.

That violent act necessitated the need for a plan to be put into action, making Maria and her children safe. I contacted a doctor I knew in Lima, urging him to allow them to live in his clinic apartment in exchange for cleaning the clinic and cooking his meals. He agreed, after I made a hefty donation to his practice.

We waited until Hector was in a drunken stupor before making the escape. They left all of their belongings and boarded a bus for Lima in the middle of the night, fleeing for safety and harboring dreams of a better future.

When Hector awoke from his drunken state, he came to my office demanding to know their whereabouts. I dishonestly told him that I wasn't aware of where they had gone and suggested that maybe Maria had taken the children to see her sister in the mountains. He threatened me, saying that if I had any part in him losing his children, that he would be back to take mine from me. I was thirty-four weeks pregnant at the time.

At first, I didn't take his threats seriously. However, later in the week, I began to notice that he was following me to and from the mission. I asked Father John if he knew of two men that I could hire to escort me from my quinta to the church each day, until Hector found a new hobby. Juan and Miguel shadowed me for the better part of a month. This show of force seemed to have detoured retribution, scaring him off. Hector seemed to have moved on and was no longer visible in the community.

Our paths crossed again during the Feast celebration of Saint Anthony of Padua. People had lined the streets for the procession of the sacred statue. Many of the children had gathered around me as we sat, waiting for it to pass, enjoying candied apples. A pick up truck with men in the back crept by our location. I saw Hector's face for the first time in weeks. He looked at me with contempt and slowly drew his finger across his neck and repeated the gesture across his waist. I lost my breath. Some of the people saw his warning and ran to the church to get Father John, who came immediately. He insisted that I move into the dorms at the mission until Hector could be apprehended.

I filed a complaint with the police, but Hector once again disappeared. The following week was my 35th birthday. The traditional celebration of being woken up to Mariachi music at midnight took place. They led me down from my bedroom to the mission courtyard where everyone was gathered under a canopy of strung lights. I had made many friends over the months and we enjoyed a special time of fellowship, food, and dancing.

During the party, a man, who seemed out of place, caught my attention. He walked through the crowds, vanishing behind partygoers and reappearing at will. I scanned the courtyard for him, but he was gone. After my friends sang to me and I cut my birthday cake, he reappeared suddenly, pausing briefly to pull something from his pocket. He placed a black statue in my hand, closed my fingers around the object, and walked away. I didn't understand its significance and placed it in my jacket pocket, assuming that it was a birthday present.

Later, one of the cooks saw me dump it in my suitcase, and panicked, quickly leaving the room. She returned with Father John and some of the men who inquired after the object. When they saw it lying on top of my clothes, they told me I had to leave Peru. After explaining to me that I had received a death amulet, signifying my intended murder, I became angry, knowing that Hector was behind the statue. I thanked Father for his concern and agreed to leave for Lima until the police could capture Hector. I packed my clothes and prepared to leave on the evening bus.

I was anxious to say goodbye to my friends. Most came throughout the day and wished me well. They prayed that I would have a quick return to Chimbote.

An hour before my departure, I received a correspondence from one of the families I was assisting. I had been trying to get their daughter, who was dying from cancer, into the hospice program. The note read "Cecilia will die tonight. Please come to the clinic now." I didn't hesitate. I searched the courtyard for Juan or Miguel, but no one was around. I waited for a short time, but decided to go on alone in order to have time to visit before my bus arrived. My pace was slow. I felt thirty-nine weeks pregnant. The streets were deserted, with the exception of my little friend Daniel. He was waiting for me outside of the mission walls.

We walked along, holding hands and laughing about the numerous dogs that had taken to following us. I stopped to buy him dinner from a street vendor, before we continued on to the clinic. We arrived, expecting to see Cecilia's parents waiting to greet us, but the lobby was empty. We proceeded in and sat down. No one ever came out so I instructed Daniel to wait while I walked back to the exam rooms. The clinic was eerily silent. The floors were dusty. Lights hung from cords above, swinging gently in the breeze. My search of the rooms yielded no results. Finally, I saw an open door with a light on. A shadow moved across the wall. I pushed the door in and entered. A blue curtain was drawn shut and I assumed that Cecilia was resting behind the drape.

Suddenly, I was startled by the door being slammed behind me. I turned back to find Hector standing in front of it with a knife. Clutching my belly, I began moving back to put some distance between us. The door opened behind him and Daniel ran across the room to my side. I yelled for him to go away, but he stood, motionless and afraid. I pushed him behind me and told Hector to leave. He laughed. He was drunk. The note had been a trap.

I whispered to Daniel that he should move with me and be ready to run. We walked in unison around the edge of the room, hugging the wall, as Hector advanced toward us. I angled my belly away from him, as he lunged toward me, grabbing me by the throat. He slammed me into the wall and began choking me, raising the knife to my cheek. I reached around, struggling for air, trying to find a weapon of any kind. My hand felt an open glass jar of some sort. Gripping the glass, I hit Hector with as much force as I could muster, releasing his hold on my neck. He dropped to his knees. His knife fell to the floor.

I gasped, trying to catch my breath, as I scanned the room for Daniel. He remained in the far corner, paralyzed with fear. The door was within my reach. Safety was at my fingertips, but I couldn't leave Daniel alone with him. I knew he'd kill him. I had no option but to stay.

I screamed at Daniel to break his trance. He tried to run to me, but Hector caught his shirt as he brushed by him, throwing him back into the far wall. Hector ignored me and began to walk toward Daniel. In an effort to draw his attention, I threw another glass jar at him, striking his head. He recoiled, swung around, and came at me, leaving Daniel alone. His fist hit the side of my face with such force, that blood sprayed his dirty white shirt. The side of my body crashed against the dusty floor. I was gagging on the blood that I couldn't help but swallow.

Daniel rushed to my side. He wasn't hurt. The blood seeping into my eyes had clouded my vision. I told him that he must run and not look back when Hector came at me again. I pulled myself up as he taunted me with how he would torture us.

A shiny object caught my attention on the table next to me. I reached for the scalpel. Hector laughed as he picked up the long knife from the floor, realizing that he was better equipped for our final battle. I looked at Daniel and yelled for him to run as I sprinted forward. I saw him clear the door as our weapons met their targets. I thrust the scalpel into Hector's neck, while feeling a burning tear in my body as I watched him fall to the floor. I looked down and saw the knife sticking out of my abdomen. My hands were drawn to its rubber handle. I pulled it out and stood watching blood pour out of my belly. The handle became slippery. The blade fell off my fingertips, clanging against the concrete. Within a minute, my legs buckled. My body fell hard.

A gargling sound was coming from my mouth. I tried to spit out as much blood as I could to aid in breathing. I was helpless to move. I saw Hector pulling himself to the door- the scalpel still in his neck. He disappeared around the corner, leaving a blood trail. Every shadow, cast by the swinging light made me worry that he was returning to finish me off. I grew very cold and tired. I heard the sounds of crying before losing consciousness.

These are the events that led to the death of my son, Connor. I urge you to find Hector Costelano and prosecute him for his crimes.

Julia Grace Spencer

I folded the pages and slid them into an envelope. Acknowledging my part in Connor's death made me feel sad. If I had only stayed at the mission, my son would be alive. One poor decision had robbed me from experiencing life though the eyes of my child. After placing the envelope against the picture of my mom, I pushed the chair away from the antique desk, and decided to leave my troubles behind for a walk on the beach. The crisp air always helped to clear my mind. Perhaps, Kate would be up by the time I returned.

Reaching for the flip-flops that rested by the front door, the wood creaked as I opened it, startling Sheriff Martin who was dropping an envelope onto the monogrammed welcome mat.

"Sorry. I didn't mean to disturb you," he nervously offered.

"You didn't," I said puzzled. "I haven't done anything else wrong today, have I?"

He chuckled, "No. I'm just here for the donuts."

"Right." I felt a smile break the tension that paralyzed my somber face.

"I'm just leaving the rent check."

"Rent check?" I was confused.

He pointed in the direction of the cottage, down the path, beyond the chapel.

It all came together now. He was with the boy on the beach. I was his landlord. Kate would be sorry to have missed this.

"You were flying the kite?"

"Yes, me and my son Mattie."

"The cottage holds many special memories for me. I haven't been inside it for several years." Thoughts of long afternoons, lying in bed with Henry, listening to the surf crash against the sand, made me wish I could turn back time to my college days. Life was simpler then.

"Are you heading out? I won't keep you." He started to move back toward the steps as I followed him.

"I was just going for a walk."

"Would you like to see it...the cottage?"

"Really, I wouldn't be intruding?" I could use some distant happy memories to replace the recent images engrained in my mind.

"No, not at all. We don't get a lot of visitors. I'm new here."

"Let me leave Kate a note. I'll be right back."

I scribbled my whereabouts on a pad resting on the foyer table, intentionally closing the door loudly to awaken her as we left.

"It's just the two of you?" I asked.

"Two against the world." He grinned nervously as we made our way down the path.

"I know exactly how that feels. My brother and I practically raised ourselves."

"Did you live here?' He motioned back toward the main house and seemed intrigued to get to the bottom of my past.

"I wish. This was my mom's house. Cancer took her not long after my brother was born. My father kept us in New York after my nana died. I was forced to leave my Southern roots behind and live the life of a chameleon. We spent some wonderful summers here though. I counted the months, each year, until the last day of school. Tommy and I would have our bags packed and ready to go at the sound of the afternoon bell. I would get butterflies in my stomach as the car approached the tall gates. Driving under the canopy of trees to the main house felt like being transported to a new world- a happy one. We'd go room to room, taking the white sheets off the furniture. We had our silly rituals."

"That sounds nice."

I was lost in the past as we walked in comfortable silence. He inquired about the history of the house and the construction of the chapel, as we passed by the cemetery. I couldn't look to my left, knowing that Connor was just over the tall cypress hedges.

Within a few minutes, we turned down the walk toward the cottage. Henry and I used to ride bikes from the main house to claim some hours of privacy, away from the visitors who had accompanied us from Harvard. We'd race. Somehow, I always seemed to win. The fix was in and I always claimed my prize.

"Does it look the same?" he asked.

The cottage stood in all its old glory; the keeper of many secrets. The white paint was peeling off the roughened corners, but it was still magnificent. The black hurricane shutters were still framing the windows, with the exception of the one at the end that had fallen and taken rest against the house.

"Remarkably, yes."

"Come in and meet Mattie."

"I'd like that."

He held the door open, motioning me forward.

"Who is with Mattie?"

"A group of women from the church take turns sitting with him from time to time when I have to work or run errands."

"How old is he?"

"He's four. He doesn't speak yet, but I'm hopeful."

"Do you mind if I...?"

"He has autism. He doesn't communicate with words yet, but I have faith that we'll find the right key to unlock his world one of these days. There are some promising therapies that may prove beneficial. I'm trying to educate myself."

Not much had changed in the house. The walls were still a casual whitewash. Most of the same furniture still remained. We stopped in the kitchen.

"Would you like a cup of coffee?"

"Sure."

I sat down on a stool while he busied himself brewing the coffee. The volunteer from church came in to speak to him, trying to ascertain when she'd be needed next. They reviewed his schedule, he thanked her, and she left. Mattie was in the living room, sitting on the floor alone, gently rocking back and forth while the television played cartoons. He left me briefly to hug his son, but he didn't respond. Gabe looked sad, but quickly recovered and entered the kitchen composed.

"Cream and sugar?"

"Please."

He poured coffee into the mugs and handed me the one that read 'World's Best Father.'

"Where's his mom? Oh, sorry, that's none of my business- it's too personal. Really, I'm not fit for public company yet."

"It's okay. I don't have any secrets. Oddly enough, it makes it more real to talk about it, you know? She left a year ago when it became clear that something was challenging our son. She couldn't accept him like this. She wasn't prepared for how she viewed him- as imperfect."

"His own mom?"

"Don't judge her too harshly. I've learned to accept her decision and just be thankful that she gave birth to such an extraordinary boy. Mattie is amazing. She's the one missing out," he replied, looking toward Mattie with love.

"How can you be so forgiving?" My face couldn't hide the contempt I felt for a woman I had never met. I would have done anything to have my child with me and here she is, throwing her baby away, because he wasn't perfect in her eyes. What a monster. I looked down at the half empty mug trying to compose myself. I felt bad for putting him on the defensive.

"Don't misunderstand; I wasn't always in this headspace. I was mad as hell a year ago, but I learned some very important truths about suffering."

"Go on..." I was anxious to get a grasp on that teaching, considering this eternal state of being utterly pissed off with most everyone and everything.

"Suffering and punishment don't necessarily go hand in hand. They're not mutually exclusive. That mentality is a crock of shit; excuse my language."

"What do you mean?"

"God is a loving God. He doesn't look down one morning and decide to afflict a child with a disease, or in your case, take your son from you. It's really kind of arrogant and self-centered to think that He derives satisfaction from our misery or has a need to stick it to us or teach us a lesson."

"You've sure given this a lot of thought."

"I was really angry at first, but what can you do with that emotion- it's poison. It only harms you. My ex didn't care that she was leaving me with a child. The world didn't care that my son was sick. I didn't see the point in being so pissed off after a month of feeling sorry for myself."

"You don't blame God- hold him accountable for your difficulties?"

"Man has some part in it- free will and all. We usually suffer because either we, or someone else, decided to exercise their free will to inflict pain or create disorder. And sometimes, shit happens-there's absolutely no reason for it. Why are you so angry...unless you'd prefer not to discuss it?"

"I got my son killed."

He felt uncomfortable with my answer and disengaged in the conversation. I needed to back-peddle.

"I'm sorry. That was too direct, wasn't it? It's just that we don't know each other very well, yet, and it's refreshing to speak openly about how I feel without having to edit. You don't have any unrealistic expectations about my coping abilities since we've only just met. I can be mad at myself without you trying to convince me that someone else killed my son."

"I read the article in the paper, Julia. You didn't stab yourself."

"No, but I put myself in the situation for that result to occur."

"You can't be responsible for that man's choice to harm you. You're the victim. It doesn't matter where you were at the time. You couldn't have made his choice for him."

Memories flew back into my mind and I sat up straighter, taking a deep breath. I had to be responsible. The pain of that kept Connor present in my mind. Gabe could tell that I was upset by his comments. He shook his head, struggling to find the right words to calm the conversation.

"I apologize. I've had a lot of time to think about why Mattie is trapped inside his body. My conclusions aren't the gospel. They just help me sleep at night."

"I don't mean to sound bitter and hostile. I'm just really angry with God, much to the disappointment of my brother, the priest."

"Oh well, he probably has much better theories than someone like me."

"Not really, he's never faced a crisis of faith. I'd rather hear your thoughts. Please. If you don't, I'll think it was because I was rude."

"I just think that there is this great need to assign blame, in our society. I think that's why my ex-wife struggled so much. She was convinced that it had to be something she did or didn't do. I never thought that for a second, but I was unable to convince her. She blamed everything from having a glass of wine before she knew she was pregnant to an x-ray she had in her third trimester, after a slight fender-bender in the mall parking lot. Blame was so necessary to her that she never allowed herself to imagine that Mattie was truly perfect in his own way, and that furthermore, God thought that we were strong enough to raise him."

"You obviously are. Look at you. A man raising his child alone with no challenges is commendable, but you're doing it…"

"-With a lot of help. Don't be fooled. My mother is the one who organized the church volunteers to sit with Mattie during my work shifts. She comes every other weekend and takes Mattie back to Tybee Island because she says that I need down time. Much to her dismay, I honestly just sit here and watch the clock until he returns Sunday evening."

"Do you date?"

Gabe didn't quite know how to deal with my straightforwardness. He shifted on his stool and blushed.

"Are you asking me out?"

"Heavens no- I mean, you're a great looking guy and a family man, and trust me there's nothing sexier than that, but I'm a mess. I should have little orange cones all around me with caution signs posted. I'm rambling."

I took a big sip of my coffee. I could feel my cheeks flush. They must have been turning a bright shade of red.

"So you're asking in a general sense?"

"Yes. Why don't you date…allow yourself the possibility of happiness?"

"My life really isn't conducive to dating."

"Well that's a cop out."

"I can't envision a woman getting a glimpse of my life with Mattie and being all in. His own mom bolted on us."

"It has to be said, from someone much more emotionally immature than you; she's a moron- a complete jackass, actually. Mothers don't leave their children. Babies are precious. They're a gift. You don't toss the gift just because you don't like the package it comes in. You're too forgiving. There are a lot of women out there that would adore you and Mattie."

Gabe smiled. He obviously wasn't used to receiving compliments.

"Yeah…they're beating down the door to get in."

"First, you have to take the invisible go away sign off the door so they know they're welcome."

"Still, I don't really have an opportunity to meet women."

"I know one."

I smirked and he caught on quickly.

"Not that gun happy crazy Brit? I have enough troubles."

"Her name is Kate and she's amazing- a little outspoken, but she's British, what can you expect? They have a dry sense of humor. You get used to it."

"She is pretty," he thought aloud, "Why is she here?"

"Her brother and I...well, he and I are involved. It's complicated. Kate and I are best friends. We all went to college together. She came in after the funeral and is staying here indefinitely, it looks like."

"What occupation has that kind of flexibility?"

"She's a writer- magazine articles mostly, but she's been working on a book for awhile."

"That's interesting."

"You'd be doing me a favor if you asked her out. She doesn't know anyone around here either and I know that I'm boring her to tears. She's rude. She'll tell me eventually. I'd rather head that off at the pass."

"Well..."

"She thinks you're hot. She said that when we saw you down at the beach."

"She did?"

"Yeah. I'll even babysit Mattie. Why don't you go tonight? Have some dinner?"

There was a knock at the front door. Gabe excused himself to answer it. I was perturbed that we were interrupted when I was on the crux of sealing the deal. He returned with Kate in tow.

"Look who's here," Gabe said fidgeting.

"How was your nap?"

"Uneventful. No crazy ex-husbands disturbing the peace."

Mattie ran in to the room and stood by Gabe.

"This is Mattie."

Kate knelt down, realizing that he wouldn't respond and hugged him tightly.

"Hi Mattie, I'm Kate. I live next door in that big white house. You must come and have tea with me sometime."

Mattie ran back to the living room and began lining up his trucks. She followed and sat down in front of him, mirroring his every move, car for car, until two lines were forming. I looked up at Gabe and smiled with that 'told you so' grin. Kate had just affirmed my earlier argument for dating. I motioned my head towards her, egging him on to be assertive. We walked over to join them. Gabe knelt down beside Mattie and looked up at Kate.

"Mattie has horse therapy at a nearby farm. We usually go for ice cream before he leaves with my mom for the weekend. Would you like to join us?"

Kate was trying to be calm, but she was visibly about to jump out of her skin.

"Love to go."

Her smile made my heart happy. Maybe her joy would be contagious. She paused and turned her head back toward me, concerned to leave me alone.

"Do we have plans? Do you want to come?"

Gabe realized that she was trying to be inclusive.

"Of course, you're welcome to come with us, Julia."

"No. I have thank you notes to write. The sooner I start them, the sooner I'll be done. Why doesn't Gabe join us for card night?"

"What's card night?" Gabe inquired.

"We try our hand at poker and blackjack; have some pizza and a few drinks. We're not that good, but we enjoy playing."

"That sounds like fun. Maybe once I get Mattie on his way."

"Good. It's settled. I'll see you both back at the house around seven o'clock? I'll order the pizzas."

I said my goodbyes to Mattie and left, relishing in my match making abilities. On my way back to the house, I stopped at the gate to the cemetery. I still couldn't go in, but I decided to sit awhile in the chapel and ponder Gabe's opinions on suffering, before heading home.

After fifty notes of thanks, I ordered the pizzas and hopped in the shower. Kate and Gabe arrived a little after seven o'clock. I could tell that they had hit it off. She was laughing like a schoolgirl and hanging on his every word. He was eating it up. He certainly wasn't used to the attention. He and I were very similar. We were both suffering from a failure to thrive.

No one had touched us in so long that we were wasting away. At least Gabe had a prospect. Good for him.

We finished eating and adjourned to the drawing room. Kate turned on music while Gabe shuffled the cards. I filled three baskets full of food. They would act as our poker chips. We took our seats. Let the games begin.

6

No one had noticed Henry walking through the front door. Gabe, Kate, and I were about to show our cards. We were playing the final hand. By this time, we were plastered. I had won Gabe's tie and was wearing it around my face like a headband with it hanging down my cheek. Kate had swindled him out of his hat an hour ago and took to wearing it backwards. Gabe had won my pink kiss the cook apron that he wore proudly with the accompanying chef's hat. Little did he know that we were strategically letting him win to give him a false sense of security. Kate and I were in our element. We were the Harvard card sharks. Many a monthly allotments from daddy had been lost to us during college.

I was sitting on a queen-nine. The pot was full of every delicacy stashed away by the caterers. I knew what I had to do. I was feeling lucky. I would bet my favorite Godiva chocolates against Kate's caviar and Gabe's Kobe steaks. They were going down.

The bets were placed and there was only one thing left to do. Kate knew she was beaten with sixteen. She graciously bowed out and threw her hand down in resigned defeat. -Gabe's turn. He dazzled us with his saucy smile and then tossed his queen-eight into the center of the table.

"How do you like that, you vixens?" He began taking stock of his winnings- his hands rummaging through the pot.

Kate was amused. "I don't know, Jewels, how do we like that?" She filled our shot glasses with tequila and slid one in front of me.

"I don't know Kate. Usually, we like to lick it, slam it, and suck it, don't we?" I slowly laid the queen down on the table as she dusted the side of our hands with salt. Gabe looked like a deer in the headlights.

I started to lay down my final card as Kate taunted him. "Wait for it… wait for it…" Gabe could barely contain his impatience.

The nine hit the table and our happy dance began. We made one full circle around the table hooting and hollering before stopping in front of our shots. We were a sight. In unison, we lifted the glasses and toasted our victory.

"God save the Queen," I announced, in my best British accent, complete with a proper curtsy.

"God bless America," Kate twanged in her best Southern belle impression.

We roared laughing as we licked the salt, slammed the drinks, and sucked the limes. Gabe looked oddly perplexed. I grabbed a beer off the table to chase the tequila.

"Don't be a sorry sport. You're just a loser." I couldn't contain my laughter, but quickly noticed that no one was joining in. Kate had that serious English look on her face like she was straining.

"What?" I inquired. Gabe cleared his throat and nodded his head toward the door- a clear signal that I was too drunk to pick up on.

"What's wrong with your head?"

A smooth male voice said, "He's trying to warn you." I couldn't register where it was coming from.

"Warn me about what Gabe?" I still couldn't see how the sound came out of his mouth without his lips moving.

"I need to be getting home," Gabe heralded, quickly standing and gathering his meager winnings, which included a bottle of Dom Perignon-early card shark sacrifice to reel him in. He skulked out the front door, awkwardly saying hello to Henry as he left.

"Tru," I gleefully announced. "Where have you been hiding?" I sauntered over to him with the tie still hanging down, partially covering my eye. I threw my arms around him.

"You're smashed." He released my hold and walked over to turn the music off.

Kate started to walk up the stairs. "And don't think you're off the hook. I gave you one job- one job! You had to keep Julia out of trouble for three days. Three days while I tried to get some things sorted. This is how I find you? You're both lit. Jackson called today, I'll have you know, threatening a lawsuit about his car. The sheriff came here?"

Kate was glad to speak in our defense. "The man in the pink apron was the sheriff."

"Be serious." Henry was irate.

"No. Really. The man in the apron...yeah, the sheriff," I added.

He stood shaking his head in disapproval.

"I don't feel so good," Kate said, sitting down and vomiting on the steps.

Henry looked me in the eyes and pointed to the chair. "You sit here while I take her upstairs." He walked over and took the bottle out of my hand, throwing it out the front door. Lifting Kate over his shoulders like a sack of potatoes, they disappeared.

Considering that I was in no mood to follow his silly rules, I confiscated the six pack of beer on the table, and opened another brew. Swaying back and forth to Ray Charles singing *Ev'ry Time We Say Goodbye*, I turned right into Henry's waiting arms. I hadn't won him over yet. His smile was still crooked.

"You're cross with me."

"Yes."

"Dance with me."

"You're impossible."

"Dance with me, come on. You want to. I can tell." He reluctantly moved to the music.

"Why would I want to?"

"Because, I'm irresistible." I gave him my best seductive grin.

"Well, there is that, but then again...I have a strict policy about..."

I kissed him mid sentence. Enough chatter. Full on, hands in the hair, where have you been all my life type of kiss. My legs lifted off the ground and wrapped around his waist.

"You taste like a distillery, Jewels. Honestly...off to bed."

I kissed his neck and lips as he carried me up the stairs and into my room, pulling him down on to me as he tried to lay me back on the bed.

"You won't sleep with your girlfriend?"

"Girlfriend?"

"Well, what am I?" This was unchartered territory.

Henry sat up and started to undress me, removing the tie off my forehead and then my pants.

"Now we're getting somewhere." I leaned forward and began trying to lift his shirt. He thwarted my attempt.

"Typically, when I have sex with a beautiful woman, I require some level of active participation...that she'll remember. No you don't." He quickly moved my hands off his trousers. "We've waited far too long for me to make love to you in this state of depravity. Sleep it off. You have a nasty mess to clean up tomorrow. -Night."

Henry flipped the light off and closed the door. My eyes were heavy. I could fall asleep, except for the washing machine in my stomach, turning and churning. I could feel the burn start moving up my throat. Quickly stumbling to the bathroom, I knocked over everything in my path. Throwing back the toilet seat in the knick of time, I vomited on the curls that had fallen forward. I aimlessly searched for a towel, but felt his leg instead. He stood over me, pulling my hair back while the alcohol and food had their revenge.

"Let's get you back to bed." He handed me a cool washcloth.

"No...stay here." I wouldn't budge. Movement of any kind made me queasy.

Henry sat down, leaning up against the bathroom wall, opposite the toilet. He pulled me back between his legs and my head rested on his chest. I fell asleep.

Loud noises crashed through my consciousness. *What was that damn noise?* I forced my eyelids partially open. The sun blazing through the uncovered windows immediately scalded them. The sound of metal clanging together was brutal and unnecessary. Kate pushed my door open bewildered.

"Bugger. What is it with you Americans in the morning? Why don't people use the expensive intercom system in this mansion?" There she stood in the same clothes she had worn the previous evening and her eyeshades pushed up on her forehead. Her hair was sticking out in several different directions. Dried vomit had made a visible line from her mouth to the bottom of her chin.

"Not American. It's a Brit...your brother, I imagine. Yes, I'll have to show him how to use the intercom system. Either that or duct tape his mouth and hands."

"I vote for duct tape."

"Let's go you tarts. The noise ends when you're sitting at the kitchen table." Henry persisted to torment us with his demands from below, banging the pots and pans until we essentially half-crawled and half-walked down the stairs, stopping for a rest mid-way.

He sat at the head of the kitchen table, behind his Wall Street Journal feeling awfully smug. The smell of eggs made Kate and me audibly gag. He had prepared breakfast with all the trimmings. We sat at his side, across from one another. My head found its rest on the table about the same time Kate began to laugh.

"Nice hair," she said, pointing at me.

I gave no reply. Instead, I slid the food off the silver tray and held it up to her like a mirror. "Who's laughing now, rooster?"

Henry was amused as he peeked over his newspaper. He neatly folded it and laid it down in front of him. He was all business now, sitting forward and preparing us for his plan.

"Eat if you like, then go upstairs and put some work clothes on. No arguments."

Kate's face visibly soured. "Work clothes?"

"Julia has felt sorry for herself long enough and you've proven yourself to be a wretched influence. Today, we move forward." I started to open my mouth. "No talking. Listening. While you hung-over degenerates slept the morning away, I rode to the nursery and purchased sod and flowers to repair Connor's grave from the storm. We're working in the cemetery today to make it a place that we can go and be with him. It is time to trim down those privacy hedges and work it out- together. So...go upstairs and get dressed. We don't honor the dead by getting drunk and going mad. We honor Connor by living."

"But I have plans with Gabe today..."

Henry shot Kate a look that clearly demanded compliance.

"...and I'll call him to push it back until this evening."

"Perfect. Daylight is burning. I have to leave this afternoon to take care of some business. Let's get a move on."

"You're leaving again." My face instantly formed a pathetic pout.

He leaned over, kissing me on the forehead and stroked my tangled web of hair.

"Cheer up. I'll be back tomorrow."

I wasn't cheery. I was tired of him leaving.

He stood and walked away from the table. We grumbled, but eventually changed clothes and made our way to the cemetery. I stopped in front of the gate, frozen, unable to go in. Kate saw me hesitate and grabbed my hand in a show of support as she swung it open. I jumped as it banged closed behind us.

Henry quickly placed a square of sod in my hand and instructed me on how to lay it out. He was cutting pieces to fit near the walkway. Kate drew a sponge from a bucket of soapy water and washed down Connor's headstone. When we completed the clean up, we moved over to my mom's grave. I hadn't visited the house since her birthday last year and the plants had become overgrown. We trimmed the trees and shrubs and fished leaves out of the fountain. Within a few hours, we had restored beauty to an ugly place.

Henry pulled out the hose to water down the sod. We felt compelled to pour our bucket of water over his unsuspecting head. A full on water fight ensued. It felt good to be able to laugh in the cemetery, with my son. I knew that this was a place for me- for my comfort. Tommy was right when he said that Connor only knew joy and peace. Funerals and headstones are for the living.

Henry began to eye his watch. I knew that our time together was coming to an end. I was getting used to the view of his back as he left me. He recoiled the hose and went on ahead to change, while Kate and I stayed back to gather the garden tools.

"What are your big plans with Gabe?"

"It's a surprise." She looked at her watch.

"What time are you meeting him?"

"Thirty minutes. I better run ahead and get a shower. Will you be okay? You can always come over."

"I'm a big girl. I do alone very well. I've had lots of practice."

"If you're sure?"

"I'm sure. No butter knives or razors. Don't worry. Go on. I'll get this stuff put up. I plan on taking a very long nap. I need one after last night's festivities. Give Gabe a kiss for me."

"Can't. I don't share well with others. Call if you need me."

"Go."

I sat down enjoying the peace and rest. I was feeling old- tired and worn out. I looked through the bag of food that Henry assembled to snack on during our work. I inhaled a ham sandwich and a bag of chips, sharing them with that same red cardinal.

Henry came out to say goodbye. The shower had done wonders. He looked amazing even though he was in jeans and a blue button down shirt. The color brought out his eyes. He sat down on the bench next to me.

"You smell good," I commented, sniffing his skin.

"You don't."

I gave him a well-deserved smack.

"Are you gone yet?"

"I'll be back tomorrow."

"I miss you already."

A quick kiss, but an even faster departure; Henry seemed in a hurry. I took my time walking back; stopping to cut some flowers with the shears I'd kept. The house was silent and I was exhausted. I found a vase for the blooms and then proceeded upstairs to take a long, hot shower.

I spent time shaving and pampering myself with the abundance of products left by Henry. Being a guy and not knowing what to buy me, he managed to get one of just about everything in the way of toiletries. With nothing better to do, I used the loofah, did a ten minute hair mask, and then exfoliated my face before the water ran cold.

Since I'd be sleeping alone, I decided to forego the seductive lingerie that was just begging to be worn. Instead, I chose a long white gown, with an empire waist. The lace dropped from under my breast, flowing down to the floor. I dried my hair and even put a coat of paint on my nails. A final dab of lip moisturizer and I was done. I admired my handiwork, even though there was no one around to appreciate it. I didn't care. I felt pretty. All of the primping had left me tired. Retreating to my bed, I rested my eyes.

Sounds of Henry talking to me seemed distant. He was in New York. I knew I must be dreaming and I didn't want to wake up. I missed him. I rolled over to look at the clock- nine. I'd slept for several hours. An odd light was coming from the wall. As I sat up and focused my eyes, I heard Henry's voice again. I finally realized that the light was coming from the intercom system. I pushed the talk button, curious.

"Hello."

I waited for a reply.

"You're awake."

"Tru?"

"Come and find me."

"I thought…you're not coming back till tomorrow."

"A necessary lie."

"For what?"

"For your surprise. Come find me."

"How am I supposed to do that?"

"Walk out onto the veranda. I'll see you soon."

The light went off and I practically flew out of bed. I pulled the drapes back and opened the doors. My yard was transformed into a fantasy. Walking out, I could see glass hurricanes with candles inside lighting the path for as far as the eye could see. Their light danced off the trees and made the moon feel jealous. I ran back in to brush my teeth and wash my face. A little perfume wouldn't hurt. I refreshed my curls with some water and took a calming deep breath. I was too excited to change into the racy lingerie hiding in my dresser. I had to find him

The walk was pure magic. Along the center of the path, Henry had left two wrapped boxes with attached instructions. The first was a silver antique box. A black ribbon, tied in a magnificent bow, kept it closed. I knelt down to discover its contents. Inside was an old Walker family bible. Names of his ancestors graced the first few pages and it made me feel anxious about touching the aged paper. Walking on, I came upon another silver wrapped present that contained a blue negligee. I considered changing into the lingerie, but felt too modest to change in the open; especially with the path so beautifully lit. Carrying them both with me, I wondered what was in store for this night.

When the path luminaries stopped and the boardwalk began, I could see the torches that lit the long peer, ending at the boat house. I couldn't see him yet. I was a little nervous. The light from the torches skipped across the water playfully. I felt Henry pulling me to him. Our connection seemed stronger than ever. Stepping onto the pier, I made my way slowly, trying to savor each step closer to my destiny. Life had dealt us some unfair blows, but we'd survived them together. After all these years, we would make love and celebrate the future.

The boathouse was closed on three sides, but open in the back, giving a view of the water. It used to hold John's racing boat, but now we just used it for fishing or swimming. We didn't even keep chairs down there, due to our infrequent visits.

I walked all the way to the end and stopped to cherish what was about to take place. When I turned back toward the boathouse, I saw him standing amidst a hundred lit candles. Large floor pillows were piled in the back as a makeshift bed. Music was softly serenading us and a single tear of joy fell from my eye. Every cell of my being was truly happy. My white gown flowed back and forth as the breeze touched my body. He held out his hand and I walked to him. Taking the boxes from me, he placed them on a candlelit table.

"You found me."

"When did you do all this?"

"Why do you think I worked you so hard today? I needed you to sleep."

"This is amazing."

He took me into the boathouse and kissed me gently on the lips.

"Dance with me," he said sweetly.

He pulled me close, placing my hands on his chest. We barely made it to the chorus before he unbuttoned my gown and watched it slide down my body to the floor. I stood there, almost naked, unbuttoning his shirt-my eyes never leaving his. As I pulled it down off his arms, he kissed me passionately, stopping once to memorize my curves. His hands traced my outline as I unbuttoned his pants and watched them fall. I kissed him like it was the first time, my legs cradled upward as he lifted me off the ground, carrying me over to the mountain of pillows he'd assembled. He paused to run his fingers across the scar that graced my lower abdomen. I felt a little self-conscious, but he ran his lips over the raised red line, showing me that he loved all of me- even the wounded parts.

"If I hurt you, you have to tell me. We need to be careful."

"We will be."

Our bodies moved in unison as we pleasured each other for hours, rediscovering territory from years spent apart. Exhausted, I relaxed back into his arms, sipping the last of the champagne we had uncorked during an earlier break from lovemaking. He walked out of the covers to the table, retrieving the two boxes I had opened.

"The bible is too much."

"It's a loaner."

"Oh," I replied with great curiosity.

"You have two more gifts to open."

He reached into the pocket of his jacket which hung off a hook above our heads, and pulled out two black velvet boxes.

"Open the larger one first."

When I unbuttoned the closure and looked inside, I saw a silver pendant with the monogram JWG. As the W initial started to sink in, Henry opened the last velvet box and placed it in my hands. A stunning diamond ring was sparkling- the light bouncing off the meticulously cut facets.

"Something old, something new, something borrowed, and something blue..."

I panicked, putting my finger to his mouth.

"We love each other. Isn't that enough?"

"Not anymore. Not for me."

"Be serious."

"I am serious Jewels. I want you to be my wife."

"What does that mean to you? How does marrying me change our relationship?"

"We would live together."

"-Doesn't require marriage."

"Financially, we'd be on more equal footing."

"Never gonna happen. I'll always have more money than you. You know it means nothing to me. Money doesn't matter."

"That is exactly the rubbish spouted by those who have it."

"Even still..."

"I want to start a family. We can adopt."

"That requires a good marriage."

"You didn't have one before," he argued.

"Not funny."

"It's important to me. I'm a traditional guy."

"Tell me why now?"

"-Because life is too short. We've lost so much time trying to make it without each other. We've never been very good at it. We leave mayhem and destruction in our path."

"Please don't take this the wrong way, but you're not exactly commitment material, Tru."

"Why do you say that?"

"You can't balance work and a personal life. I know that. I don't have the expectation that you can so the hurt is manageable when you leave. If I'm your wife, the expectations are different. If we have a family, the expectations are a whole lot different. A child deserves an involved father. I want the total package- marriage and family."

"I want the same things."

"Are you prepared to quit Spencer Industries? If my father finds out, he'll fire you."

"I'll handle your father."

"Even with his blessing, your job is not normal. You leave on a moment's notice all the time. If our child has a basketball game or dance recital, and you get a phone call, you'll leave. You know you will. Those disappearing acts get embedded in the memory of a child. I want to co-parent. I don't want to be a married single mom."

"I can give you what you're asking for, but you have to give me the opportunity to show you that. Don't just shoot me down based on speculation. Give me a chance."

"-A chance?"

"That's all I'm asking for."

"Okay...one chance. For the next week, and I mean seven whole days, you can not do any business. No phone calls. No emails. No quick trips. If you can make me a priority for one week, I'll give you an answer."

"No business for one week and you'll be my wife?"

"No business for one week and I'll give you my answer."

"Now, my condition. You have to wear the ring this week. You need a reminder."

"Agreed. Do you need a reminder?"

"No Jewels. I promise. No business."

Henry took the Tiffany set diamond out of the box and slid it on my left ring finger. I didn't want to admit it to him, but I was ecstatic. The man of my dreams just asked me to marry him. I didn't fold quickly. He would have to prove me wrong. God, how I hope he proved me wrong.

He kissed the ring and turned my hand over to kiss the inside of my palm. That always sent shivers down my spine. He moved up my forearm and to my shoulder, before pulling me on top of him. He pushed my hair back off my face and smiled.

"By the end of this week, you will be Mrs. Henry Truman Walker. Julia Grace Walker."

"It does sound good."

I stared down at the beautiful ring- a diamond that had symbolized eternity to his grandparents. They were happy. Why couldn't we share a similar fate?

"Believe in me Julia. I just need you to believe. I'll do the rest."

"I'll believe." *I'll do my best.* "We should go back to the main house."

"It's nice here," he said, exploring my neck.

"Yes- very, but we should blow out the candles on the path. I'm rather fond of my house."

We extinguished the candles as we made our way back home, walking hand in hand. The night had been perfect, even if he didn't get the immediate answer he was hoping for. He was correct. I was a bit too practical to always be romantic and carefree. I also wasn't one to ignore the lessons of the past. I had Henry back. I didn't feel the need to complicate our life with a marriage proposal, but I would give his proposal the consideration it deserved. At the end of the week, I would answer his question.

The house was quiet. There was no sign of Kate, which was good since I was carrying my dress instead of wearing it. His shirt just covered my assets and I wasn't in a state to entertain Gabe.

I hopped onto the kitchen counter and tossed my dress aside.

"I'm starving. Do you want something to eat?" he asked.

He began riffling through the fridge and pantry.

"Take your pick. I could run a grocery store out of this kitchen."

"That was your father. It was nice for him to think of that."

"It was nice for him to pay someone to think of that."

"You've got to give him a break, Jewels. You can't hate him forever."

"I don't hate- I dislike. I still love his black, cold heart."

"Ouch."

He halted his mission and walked to me, placing his body between my open knees. I felt his hands rest on my backside as he scooted me forward in his hold.

"Be sweet."

I gave him that grin- the one that gets me out of trouble and he relented, kissing me. I pulled back.

"I'm weak as dishwater. How about an early breakfast? Pancakes?"

"Bacon?" he added.

His hands unbuttoned the shirt I was wearing and I started to giggle.

"What if Kate comes back? Seeing her brother's naked body would scar her for life."

"Danishes instead? Breakfast in bed?" he offered.

"Race you."

8

I woke up in his arms and all was right with the world, for this day. I didn't want to wake him. Knowing that he was mine, and hoping for the promise to bring about a happy future, made me feel that elusive sense of peace that always seemed out of reach. He had promised one week of no interruptions. No business calls or business trips was his pledge. It was going to be Jewels all day, all night, and all the time for seven glorious days. I was so excited over the prospect. My hands moved to feel the smile on my face. He hadn't agreed to quit his job, yet; baby steps. His promise of one week was enough for now.

I ran my hands over his sculpted chest. I couldn't help myself. He began to open his eyes as I rolled on top of him.

"Hi gorgeous," he said as he brushed my hair off my face.

I began to kiss his neck with those dainty little butterfly kisses he loved so much. As I moved to his chest, he distracted me with conversation.

"What's on tap for today?" he asked.

My hand moved below the sheets to answer his question. He smiled and breathed deeply.

"You're a naughty girl. I do need to eat, you know. You have to be hungry after last night."

"Not for food."

He pulled me up to his face.

"I love you, Jewels. You know that, right?"

"Yes," I replied inquisitively.

"Then why won't you answer me? Tell me you'll be my wife."

"Whoa- a deals a deal. One week. You promised. No pressure. One week of all Jewels all the time- no business. Keep your end of the bargain and you'll have your answer."

"One week." He smiled that devastating smile that would have weakened my resolve if I didn't have history to remind me that I usually finished last.

"One week," I reiterated.

"I have no choice." He started to sit up.

"Where do you think you're going?" I locked my arms around his waist from behind which he squeezed tightly before getting up. His naked body was amazing. I felt no embarrassment in staring, pinching my arm, and mouthing the words *'He's mine'* to myself. He turned back and laughed, obviously invading my thoughts.

"I need a hot shower. Care to join me? Round five?"

"Six. I'll be right there."

I lay in bed, relishing the memories of the past evening, wishing we lived in a bubble, insulated from the rest of the world. The steam was billowing out from the bathroom when his cell rang. My heart sank. I picked it up off the nightstand and looked at the number. His office was calling. I panicked, hitting ignore. *What am I doing?* I couldn't leave the bed once I heard the message alert sound. I had to figure out what to do before the water eventually stopped. I could hear the shower door open and Henry questioning my whereabouts.

"I thought you were going to shower with me," he called out.

I shoved his phone under the covers as he appeared, dressed in shorts, pulling a t-shirt over his head. He sat down next to me.

"Good morning, Mrs. Walker." He smirked, grabbing my ring finger, admiring his grandmother's diamond.

"Mr. Walker isn't supposed to pressure Ms. Spencer."

"True. What would you like for breakfast?"

I needed to get him out of the house to regroup and formulate a plan.

"-Chocolate croissants from my favorite bakery?"

"I'll be back. Think about what you want to do today."

I nodded. He searched for his wallet and keys. I prayed that he wouldn't look for his cell phone. It was time for a distraction. I'd have to throw Kate under the bus.

"Did Kate come home last night?"

He stopped in his tracks, turning away from the dresser.

"I don't think she did. I'll stop by her room and see if she wants anything from the bakery."

"Good idea. She'll probably want a vanilla latte."

"Do you?"

"No. I'll just take the croissants."

He kissed me.

"Love you."

"What's not to love?" I replied.

As he left laughing, I answered my own question out loud. *What's not to love? That I have no faith in you. That I'm sabotaging your phone because I know you'll screw this up.* I rolled over and looked at our framed picture on the nightstand, talking to him; *don't screw this up, Tru.*

I looked at that phone for a long time trying to decipher right from wrong. If I trusted him, there was no need to tamper with the phone, but the ringing of it halted my quandary. Once again, Spencer Industries was calling. They weren't going to play nice. Neither was I. Flipping over the phone, I removed the battery and placed it on the floor next to the dresser. He'll just think it slipped out of his pocket last night.

I spent my time in the shower arguing with myself. I got nowhere. I considered replacing the battery, but I couldn't work out a better solution. No one knew he was with me. That information was highly classified so my father wouldn't feel betrayed. The cell phone was his link to the outside world. He promised one week.

I dressed and stopped by Kate's room. Her bed wasn't slept in and it made me snicker. Good for them. Gabe seemed like a man in desperate need of a good time. Kate was just the person to give it to him- all night.

I made a pot of tea and some coffee for Tru. The kitchen door creaked open and Kate skulked half way across the room before I called her out.

"Is this the walk of shame?"

"There is no shame in what we did last night." Laughing at her conquest, she searched around the room. "Where's my brother?"

"He went to the bakery. You're safe. Just tell him you got up early to go for a walk–explains the made up bed."

"I never knew you had such a devious side."

I just shook my head in agreement, knowing Henry's phone battery was in the pocket of my shorts.

"You won't tell him?" she wondered aloud.

"Secrets to the grave, remember?"

"Can I have a cup?" she asked.

"Henry is bringing you a latte."

"Great." She plopped down on the barstool.

"Spill. What's the 4-1-1 on Gabe?" I inquired.

"There's nothing to tell. We played scrabble all night."

"And I'm the Queen of England."

She smiled a very satisfied smile.

"And how was your night?" she asked with a wink and nudge.

"It's kind of weird to talk to you about sex with your brother."

She covered her ears and began singing, "La, la, la, la, la. Good point. That's gross. How can you do it? I mean, he's Henry."

Over Kate's shoulder, I saw his rental car coming down the long drive.

"You better go change your clothes. He's coming down the driveway. We'll leave your latte and a croissant on the counter."

"You're the best. What are you doing today?"

"We're taking the boat out. Do you want to join us?"

"I'd have to say definitely no. You have that freshly shagged glow about you and a lot of time to make up for. Have your fun. Gabe and I are taking Mattie to the beach."

"You should pack a basket of food."

"I suggested that but Gabe pointed out that kids don't eat caviar. We really need some normal food around here."

"We'll get groceries on our way home from the marina. Hurry, he's walking up."

"Have fun."

Kate flew up the stairs just as Henry opened the door.

"Was that Kate?"

"Yes. She got up early and went for a walk."

"Oh."

He unloaded his bag and cardboard drink holder.

"I made you coffee."

"That's why I bought this."

"Not nice," I scolded.

"Hello again." He held me, kissing my lips.

"I thought we could go down to the marina and take the boat out," I suggested.

"That'll be fun. I just need to get my togs."

"I already packed them and some food. We're ready to go."

"What about breakfast?"

"I'll eat on the way."

"Are we rushing for a reason? Why don't we change into our suits?"

"I already packed them, silly. I want to beat the Sunday cruising crowd. The crew is expecting us. We can change on the boat."

"Okay. Let's hurry, Jewels. I'm tired of waiting on you. Go, go, go."

Henry shooed me out the door making fun of my haste. Half way to the marina, he realized that he didn't have his phone. He inquired whether I brought mine, but I alleviated his concern by mentioning that the ship had a radio in case we needed to communicate with the outside world.

The day was spent on my father's yacht. With only the captain and a crew of two, we felt very alone. We laid on the deck, side by side, enjoying the sun and making plans for our future. The water was barely warm when we anchored for a swim. Henry talked me in to riding the Jet Ski which was an adventure. I felt a little sea sick after enduring the bumpiness of the waves created by his hairpin turns. Three hours had come and gone when the captain asked us about returning. Henry tried to talk me into anchoring and sleeping on the boat, but I felt the need to go home. Connor was there, without me.

We stopped briefly for groceries. Kate would be happy. I bought some beautiful hydrangea blossoms from a roadside market to put on Connor's grave. We rode in comfortable silence listening to music and taking in the scenery.

Kate was waiting for us in the kitchen when we returned. She looked perplexed, but Henry didn't notice. He just announced that he was going to take a shower and went upstairs.

"What's the matter?"

She handed me a note pad full of scribbled writing- messages for Henry from the office.

"This is just the first page. Why isn't he answering his phone? That's not like him."

"I removed the battery."

"You did what?"

"He promised me no business. I'm helping him keep his promise."

"He's not going to see it that way, Jewels."

I took the pages from her hand and crumpled them before tossing them in the trash bin.

"We'll see. Don't worry. I'm going to take these flowers to Connor. Do you want to come?"

She hesitated, still worried, but finally shook her head in agreement. I opened the kitchen door and she followed me out. Our walk to the cemetery was filled with sailor talk about her night with Gabe. I took the opportunity to tease her about her heart being stolen, as I had predicted earlier. She brushed off the observation, but I could tell that she was head over heels in love- or lust, at least. Love would follow. Gabe seemed like an awfully good man. They were in short supply these days.

Kate left me to walk over to the cottage. Gabe was making hamburgers with Kraft macaroni and cheese for her and Mattie- his favorite. She mentioned that she might stay over again under the guise of giving us our privacy. I sat awhile longer, listening to the birds chirp and the calming sounds coming from the fountain. The sod Henry bought for the grave was a magnificent green. The blooms on the crepe myrtles were snow white. I touched my belly, remembering a time when he was thriving and kicking inside me.

I figured Henry would come looking for me, but he never did. After an hour, I made my way back to the house. His car trunk was open and the kitchen door was slightly ajar. His briefcase and papers were spread out over the table. He quickly shuffled them into a pile as I made my entrance, but he never acknowledged my presence. He was on the landline, conversing with someone, wearing a suit and tie- not proper attire for a casual evening at home with me. My heart sank. He screwed it up- again.

I sat down at the kitchen table while he closed his briefcase and walked outside. I heard the trunk close. I slid the diamond ring off my finger and laid it by his keys. He walked back in and sat down next to me, picking up the ring.

"What's this?"

"The answer I promised you."

"There's a crisis at work. One of the lawyers I left in charge screwed up the land contracts for a big deal we've been working on for months. I'm the only one who can fix this. By the way, I got an ear full from your dad about not being able to get in touch with me. Would you know anything about that?"

The jig was up. I slid my hand into my pocket and pulled out the battery, depositing it next to his grandmother's ring. I stood up and walked to the island, leaning against it for support. I knew that this was a possibility. The odds were 50/50 at best, but I had hoped for a better outcome.

"That's just perfect." He took his keys and the battery, placing them in his pants pocket, purposefully leaving the ring.

"What do you want me to say? Sorry? I'm not sorry."

"You have very little faith in me, Julia."

"Well, you lived up to my usual expectations."

Henry stood and walked over. He was geared up for a fight. He wanted an excuse to leave- just like before.

"You don't trust me. You don't trust that I can do both things well."

"Trust is earned. I've been here before, remember- déjà vu."

"Yes, I recall. Now we just need a bloke to stand in for Jackson. Gabe will do, I suppose."

"You should go. You should go before you say something else stupid."

"Why did you do it? Why did you sabotage me and put my job in jeopardy?"

"I knew you'd make the wrong choice. You couldn't possibly put me above business. It was mean for you to get my hopes up this time- especially now."

"You know a little bit about mean, don't you sweetheart? That's like the kettle calling the pot black. So now it will be another Jackson, huh? He'll probably be here before the end of the night. My side of the bed won't even be cold. I'll always be the get over guy to you; the one to call in a pinch, when you're in some major meltdown and need a safety net."

"First of all, it's the pot calling the kettle black," I said light-heartedly. "Second, you can't possibly think that's what you are to me? You're being ridiculous."

"Pot-kettle- whatever. You know what I'm saying. I don't want to always be that guy, Jewels. I want to be the chosen one- not the winner by default."

He turned away and walked to the end of the kitchen island, where he seemed to pause and contemplate his next words.

"Haven't you always known?" I cautiously took a step forward.

"Known what?" Henry replied exasperated, refusing to face me.

"It's you...always has been." I took a few more steps forward until stopping directly behind him. "Jackson was the get over guy...the guy to get over you."

Minutes passed with no reply. I began to feel embarrassed for cracking the only wall I'd managed to keep intact. I slowly started to retreat, backing up, watching for any sign of movement on his part, but it never came. He couldn't even stand to look at me now. I was hurt. Henry had been the one bright spot in a storm of very bad days. I felt truly alone for the first time since losing Conner.

"Silence wasn't really the reaction I was going for." I tried to sound sincere, but in an oddly humorous sort of way. I turned and walked toward the back door. Sensing movement, I quickly looked back, but he had barely changed positions. "I'm going to go now. You should go... Go home, Tru."

Henry finally turned towards me. His face looked like a blank piece of paper. I couldn't read our history in his eyes. In that moment of nothingness, I couldn't envision a future.

"What is the proper response?" He took a step forward, but remained guarded, arms folded across his chest.

"I should have never walked out that door. I should have chosen you over your father. Love is more valuable than a job..."

He cut me off. "You're being unreasonable. Your demands required patience and you weren't willing to wait. Where's my apology?" He tried to restrain his anger, but he was mad as hell. "You make an ultimatum, become dissatisfied with the speed in which it is being carried out, and decide to punish me with that idiot Jackson. -Sleeping with someone else kind of made using the door a necessity, love."

"You were gone long before the door, Tru. —Long before Jackson. He was a convenient excuse to walk away and have us both- me and your precious job."

We were in each other's face now.

"What does that mean?"

"You knew my love belonged to you- you alone. Jackson's entrance just insured that you could work for my father and still have me in the corner pining away. You're selfish. I see that now."

"And you're so perfect…the girl dropping her dress for the next best thing?"

"You have no idea what you're talking about."

"Don't I?"

"I didn't drop my dress for Jackson that night. We were drunk. He was so plastered that he couldn't perform a sex act on a blow up doll. He walked me home and passed out on the sofa, waiting for the car I called to take him downtown. Who is lacking the faith now, love?"

"You never told me." He had a look of confusion on this face. The incident he'd used to solidify his cowardice had evaporated.

"You never asked. It wasn't important enough to you. I wasn't important enough to you. Just go home. Go back to New York where you're loved and adored."

"So you don't love me now? You're giving me back the ring. That's your answer."

"I don't love being alone. I don't love coming in second place. I don't love attention followed by desertion. I deserve better than that. I deserve better than you."

He was quiet now and thoughtful. My words, though honest, had injured him. He put his hand on my arm and stared deep inside me.

"You're not alone. I'm here."

"You're here and I've never felt more alone. My life has been complicated and not all together devoid of drama, but it's been a truthful journey. Our relationship is smoke and mirrors. I can't count on you. I used to think that I was the one that needed to be rescued, but I see that's just not the case anymore. I'm strong. My sadness doesn't alter my strength. I have flaws, but they make me a fine mess. Someone once told me that. We used to laugh at those flaws."

"We still can. Don't make a rash decision. Not this time. Take the week. Take some time to think things through, for Christ's sake. You're being irrational, like always."

"Tru, you're the love of my life, but I can live without you, even if I don't want to. Walk. Bask in the glow of your professional success. Gain power. Make your fortune. I may still be alone twenty years from now, but I'll have lived an authentic life. I wouldn't have spent precious years chasing an illusion. Just go away. We're through. You've never been more unattractive to me then right now. Fear doesn't become you."

My dismissal of him made Henry visibly angry. I started to walk away, but he grabbed me and pulled me back harshly, taking my breath from me. The desperate aggressiveness in his actions and tone really annoyed me. I brought my arms up through the center and turned them outward, breaking his hold on me. He pointed his finger in my face and began yelling at me.

"You could use a healthy dose of fear. Flying by the seat of your pants without considering the consequences has caused you to lose a great deal, don't you think?"

"You're an ass."

He answered under his breath, though still audible. "You're the pain in my ass."

I understood what he was implying and it made me sad that he would drag Connor into our argument. If he wanted to play the blame game, he was about to get a heaping dose.

"Well, I've been waiting for that- for someone to affirm that I killed my own baby. I just never thought it would come from you. Don't you think that I blame myself every day for Connor's death? Don't you think I wonder, every day, every second of every minute, what would have happened if I didn't flee from my life with Jackson and I had stayed in New York? It haunts me. I should be the one in the ground- not him. Not him."

The tears began to flow now. He just stared at me like he was watching a building implode in front of his eyes. I had no sense that he wished he could take the words back that brought me to this sad place, again. I shook my head in disappointment and then wiped the tears from my face. Now I was mad. There was nothing left buried, deep down; those redeeming qualities of his that made me feel even a small amount of love for him.

"Where's your sin in all of this- your responsibility? Have you ever stopped to consider how our lives might be right now if you'd stepped up...offered me a future when I told you about Jackson's affair? I would never have gotten on that damn plane. My child would be alive. You ask me to marry you now...now, after I've already lost my baby? Your timing sucks. You're just as much responsible as me."

"You won't lie that at my door, sweetheart. You got on that plane. You have to live with that decision. I can't always rescue you from yourself."

"No one is more in need of rescuing than you. One day, you'll come to me. You'll ask me to rescue you. Maybe I'll have moved on."

"So this is it then? You're telling me that you don't love me?"

"No. Unfortunately, it's a split decision between my mind and my heart. You may have my love, but that emotion is something I can control. I'm not weak. I think I can keep my dress on when you're around. The problem for you is that I don't like you anymore. That's a head thing."

He took my face in his hands and caressed my cheeks. I closed my eyes. I couldn't look at him and remain composed. He kissed my lips, but I didn't return his affection. I pulled his hands together and dropped them down between us.

"If you love me, you'll let me go."

"You don't get to determine who I love."

"If you don't go now, we won't have a friendship left to salvage."

"You demand everything from people."

"I give everything."

"Damn it Jewels, we can make this work."

"No, we can't. You can't dangle a life in front of me that you're not prepared to give. It's not fair. No matter how much progress we make, finding our way back to one another, we always end up here- in this place. Just go and stay gone this time."

"Well, I'm not going to beg you to stay with me. I'll leave while I have a bit of my pride left intact." He stood before me broken- it was like looking in the mirror- both our eyes full of tears and rage; neither of us knew how to let go completely.

"Good" I said uncaring and dismissive.

"I love you," he pleaded.

"You love yourself first and best- always have."

"You don't know what you're saying."

"But I do. I choose me."

"I choose you too," he insisted, "I love you."

"You can't love me."

"That's like telling my heart not to beat."

I turned and walked out the kitchen door. He followed me, stopping just inside the doorframe.

"Don't leave again Jewels. You have to stop running."

I walked back inside the kitchen and pushed him back until he cleared the door.

"You're right. This is my house. You leave." With that, I slammed the door in his face and locked it. Walking by the ring that he left on the kitchen table, I made my way upstairs. Parting the drapes, I watched him abide by my wishes. He left me, as requested.

No overture was made on his part- no beating on the door and yelling to me on the veranda above. He simply got into his rental car and drove away. I had undergone a great transformation of self. I made the hard choice- the kind of choice that hurt now, but would be better later- or at least I kept telling myself that.

My choice had become a poison, killing me slowly from the inside out. I talked a big game with Henry, but whom was I kidding? I didn't want to live without him, but I had my pride too. He broke his promise. If I didn't take a stand now, I would be the fool who realized, after twenty years, that our life was built on broken pledges and small little deceptions that just seemed harmless at the time.

As much as I didn't like the things he said to me, there was some truth in his assessments. He was always the person I turned to when times got tough. This wasn't out of some necessity on my part. I was a strong and capable woman. I could solve my own problems; but sharing them with someone I loved made the difficulties seem more bearable. Falling into his arms and having the ability to let my guard down, and just relax through the stress, made finding a way out of the darkness easier.

I'd never given much thought to being destroyed by the one person I loved most in the world. Then again, I never let anyone besides Henry close enough to hurt me. Since my mom's death, I had become a master at internalizing every sorrow, every bitter disappointment, and every lonely moment. They were my burdens. I categorized them by affliction and moved on. The problem with hiding my emotions was that, eventually, I lost myself altogether. I'd forgotten that the sorrows and disappointments made me strong- that my mistakes and failures provided an opportunity for me to learn. When I chose not to feel my way through life, I had nothing to give others. That fact had become painfully evident with his departure.

Henry was the first man to ever cast light into those dark areas. His first sweet smile stopped me in my tracks. After dropping my books outside of the library, he came to my aide. His hand fell on top of mine as we both reached for the fallen books. He didn't apologize for our touching. Instead, his hand lingered. It made me feel uncomfortable- like unchartered territory. Then, he spoke. *Here's your book* never sounded so sexy in his British accent. He effortlessly grabbed my arms and pulled me to my feet. After insisting that he walk me back to my car, I was informed that I was required to take him to dinner as a thank you- repayment for services rendered. Henry was disastrously charming. I never stood a chance.

We sat in that restaurant for hours, listening and talking with one another, until the wine made me brave enough to kiss him. It was the most delicious and sensual kiss I had ever experienced; slow and intense. That one kiss ruined me for every other man I would ever meet. He was my *Tru* North- an internal compass- my way out of the fear that had handicapped me since the day I let my mom go. The kiss released a confidence in me that made me shine. I was audacious again. I was his Jewel.

Our life together was exciting. He was always full of surprises. When friends were complaining about their boyfriends being disinterested, I couldn't empathize. Tru was the boyfriend that would scout out a place in the park to hide champagne and strawberries ahead of our date. We didn't lie around letting life pass us by: we explored the city; we traveled to Savannah; and we spent breaks in London with his mom. He wasn't afraid to let me in. I had an all access pass to his life and I was slowly learning to let my guard down.

Our physical relationship came on quickly; partly because we were so taken with one another. I was worried that we were rushing intimacy, before a strong foundation could be built, but we were so easy in the other's company. Our undeniable chemistry was backed up by a hefty dose of respect and trust. We weren't the couple making love in the dark- the more lights the better. It was important to both of us to connect not just through touch, but with our eyes. I wanted to see his mouth when he spoke the words that melted my heart. We conveyed an acceptance of the other person's body just as it was, regardless of our own personal warped sight.

We spent long afternoons, naked, wrapped in sheets, discussing our future. We talked about children and splitting our time between New York and Savannah. I would do pro-bono work and he would start his own law firm. We passed the Georgia bar and started to look for suitable office space in Savannah. Our dreams were becoming a reality. But dreams change.

I'm not sure at what point money became an equal object of his desire, but we suffered due to his relentless pursuit for power. To this day, I'm certain that my father enticed him, like the devil, offering water to a man burning in hell. He probably made Henry feel that he wouldn't be worthy of me until he had made something of himself. I've never understood why Henry couldn't see himself through my eyes.

Now, sitting on the upper veranda, having watched his car drive away- my heart was heavy. My eyes were full of tears. I could lie to Henry, but not to myself. I knew in losing him, I lost the best part of me. He brought that out. Sure, I could wake up and move through each day unscathed, but moving forward meant learning who I was without him. I knew that I would have to become my biggest fan again- to fall in love with my own singular qualities.

I had the night alone to dwell on his departure. Kate returned in the morning. She wanted to know what happened, word for word, but I felt it best to honor Henry by not assigning blame. She assured me that our split was temporary and that cooler heads would prevail, but I had my doubts. She didn't hear the things that we said to one another. Words tend to take on a life of their own. I couldn't forgive him for implying I facilitated Connor's death and I'm certain my finger pointing made him less apt to apologize. We were at an impasse.

I urged Kate to stay out of our fight and she reluctantly agreed. I didn't want to lose a lover and a best friend in one week. As much as she loved me, Henry was her brother- her blood. The less I shared with her the better.

10

⊸⊶

Three weeks had passed with no communication. I'd kept my sadness under wraps fairly well, putting on a cheery face when others were around. If Kate was speaking to Henry, she wasn't letting me in on it. Maybe this was at his request or maybe she was being merciful to me. Either way, there was a hole in my heart that I couldn't seem to fill with shopping or redecorating.

I tried to keep busy in an effort to distract myself from the overwhelming sense of loss I was feeling. I took on the task of cleaning the house from top to bottom, scrubbing the old hardwood floors on my hands and knees, while continuously replaying our argument over and over again in my mind as I scrubbed. The *What ifs* began to creep into my thoughts: *What if I didn't say this or that?; What if I said I love you back and left it at that?; and What if I didn't place blame at his feet- the man that always stood by me?* When I was alone, my game face disappeared. I discovered that the hurt was hiding just under the surface, available to me at a moment's notice.

I finally halted my assault on the wood, long enough to have a good cry and a loud scream. One scream turned into another and I found myself at my bedside table looking at the man in charge of my misery. Before I had time to make a better decision, the frame flew out of my hand and hit the dresser mirror. I pulled the picture out from under the broken glass and tried to tear it, but something within me couldn't do it. Hope was still lurking around. I hate hope.

Kate had been spending every other weekend with Gabe, when Mattie was away at his mom's house. My home was feeling more like a bed and breakfast, but I didn't mind. Sure, I was a tiny bit jealous. They were happy. Their conversations were precious. They had chemistry. I had sour grapes. I was working on my attitude.

Four weeks passed and no cards or calls. I started calling Henry's home phone when I knew that he'd be at work, just to hear his voice. I never left a message and hoped that he wasn't checking his caller ID. We were playing chicken. I wouldn't be the first to surrender. This was all a test.

Kate was undergoing a test of her own. Gabe's mom had come down to spend the month with him and Mattie. She was worried about making a good impression, but I knew that Kate was a hard person not to like. As it turned out, she could have been on the FBI most wanted list and Momma Martin would have still adored her. Gabe had moped around for so long that his showing interest in any woman made Ms. Martin the happiest mother in America. Seeing Kate with Mattie sealed the deal for her. She and Kate had become fast friends, which in turn made Gabe happy. Everyone was happy, but me. I was starting to get on my own nerves.

Kate had been under the weather for several days. In caring for her, I'd become sick as well. I was surprised that Gabe wasn't coming down with it, considering all their kissing- in front of me- like teenagers. We quarantined ourselves in my room, away from Mattie. Ms. Martin made us some delicious chicken soup to cure what ailed us. We were a sight. Luckily, our fevers cycled together. We threw the covers off and replaced them at precisely the same time. We were the cleanest sick women in the history of the world. Since we couldn't breathe, we'd spend most of the day and night in my steam shower, wearing our bathing suits and drinking Gatorade. I was selfishly enjoying being sick with her since we rarely saw each other anymore. We reminisced about college life and had many healing laughs. She began to improve and left me. That was becoming a recurring theme.

I was starting to get over my head and chest cold, but my stomach had other dastardly plans. Most everything I ate came back up looking exactly the same as when I ate it. I was withering away and felt weak. Kate wanted to call Henry and tell him, but that was ridiculous. I obviously needed to reign in my need to be rescued. She did the next best thing- she called Tommy. He threatened to come for a week if I didn't go to the doctor. Considering my options, I agreed.

Gabe called and made an appointment with a physician he knew in town. I didn't have much choice about accepting his charitable act, but I wasn't about to let them accompany me as they had hoped. I called back and changed my appointment to an earlier time.

I took a shower before leaving for the doctor. I considered drying my hair and applying makeup, but I just couldn't bring myself to put forth the effort. I threw on a pair of sweats, my flip-flops, and was out the door. My head was pounding. My stomach was killing me. This virus should have already run its course.

I followed Gabe's directions and managed not to get lost. After parking, I sat in my car deciding whether or not I really needed to go in. The only thing that made me get out of the car was the fact that Gabe would check up on me. Plus, Kate had made herself in charge of filling my prescriptions. She probably wouldn't buy that he didn't write for any medicine, with how I looked.

The office was crowded. People were coughing. I could just picture their germ droplets landing on my face, which made me queasy. The chairs were made of fake tan leather slings and were extremely uncomfortable. I signed in and took the only seat left. I was sandwiched between two men. One was wearing a bottle of cologne and the other kept sneezing. I quickly filled out the three pages of paperwork, hoping that it would expedite my exodus into the promised land of the back office. The doctor now knew everything about me that I did. I returned the clipboard and was about to collapse in the chair when the nurse called my name.

She led me to a room and instructed me to put on a gown and get on the examining table. I didn't. I couldn't see the point of removing my clothes when I was already freezing. I laid it back on the table and sat in the chair against the wall. She returned to take my vital signs and gave me that look. I had joined the ranks of the other sick and uncooperative patients making her job a nightmare. After jamming a long cotton ball on a stick down my throat, she regurgitated the answers I had written down on the questionnaire. She gave me a cup for a urine sample, instructed me where to leave it, showed me to the restroom, and told me to go back to the exam room when the task was completed. It was a lot of information to remember, but I complied, hoping to make it on the good patients' list in case she had to give me an injection.

The doctor came in, and thankfully, was not handsome in any way. No one needs a hot doctor seeing their bodies, especially when they're sick. All doctors should be ugly. He was nice. After the exam, he left the room to get my strep test results. He came back in with a smile on his face that made me feel more at ease. He could write me a script and I would be on my way.

"Ms. Spencer, when was your last menstrual period?"

"I'm not sure. I just lost my son in June."

"You haven't had a period since then?"

Whoa. Wait one minute. It was the end of August. Holy shit.

"Holy shit. Sorry. Sorry. I've had a lot going on. I haven't really thought about periods."

He flipped through the forms I had filled out earlier while I took the opportunity to have a private mini-panic attack.

"Since the beginning of June, you haven't had one…from what you wrote in the medical questionnaire?"

"Yes. Why?"

"We need to take some blood. When it comes back, we'll have a quantitative result that will give me a better idea of how far along you are, but the urine test is positive. You're definitely pregnant."

"No, I'm not."

"Have you had physical relations with a man since early June?"

"That's not the point. There must be some mistake…with the test. You should run it again," I demanded, motioning towards the door. "The doctor in Peru said that this kind of thing wouldn't be easy. Maybe the test got switched."

"There's no mistake. You're pregnant."

"No."

"Yes."

"No."

"Yes."

"So, the throwing up…"

"…is pregnancy related. Do you have an obstetrician in mind?"

"Do you have a shrink in mind?"

He started laughing.

"I'm not kidding," I said most sincerely.

"This is a lot for you to take in right now- it's understandable. Do you have someone I can call for you?"

"No. No one can know about this."

"With your history, you'll need to be monitored very closely. You'll be considered high risk. "

The Battered Heiress Blues

"Which means what exactly?"

"You'll be seeing a lot of your obstetrician over the next eight months."

I just shook my head. This was all a little much. I never thought that I would conceive again, especially this close to having lost Connor.

"I'm going to write a prescription for some vitamins that you should start taking immediately. We'll run some hormone levels and forward the results to Dr. Brandon. He's very nice and deals exclusively with high-risk patients like you. Manage your stress level, eat healthy, and get lots of sleep. I'll have my office call you this afternoon with an appointment time for Dr. Brandon. His office is in this building on the 4th floor."

"Your staff can't call my home." I pointed to my chart. "Write that down. I have a lot of visitors these days and I'm not ready to share this information. Please scratch out my home phone and circle my cell phone for the contact number."

"Relax, Julia. We're not allowed to release your information to anyone without your permission. It's a HIPAA violation."

"Yeah…and I'm a lawyer so be sure your staff understands that."

"Okay. I'll do that. Someone will be coming in to draw your blood."

"Great."

I paid for the visit and somehow made it out to my car. After turning on the ignition, I started the air conditioner and just sat there, in shock. Henry and I always wanted to have children, but not now, with how things were between us. I couldn't call him. What would I say? *I hate you and guess what…I'm having your baby?* Never.

Finally concluding that sitting in the parking lot wasn't going to solve anything; I drove on to the pharmacy and purchased the vitamins. Discarding the bag when I cleared the store, I buried them deep in the bottom of my purse, away from prying eyes. When I returned to the car, I pulled out my cell and stared at it for a long time. *Who should I call? Tommy.* I phoned and got his voice mail to which I left a 9-1-1 message about getting to Savannah with great speed. He was a worrier. I knew the message would get him to me quickly. I just couldn't break the news to him over the phone.

No one was home when I returned. Kate had left a note on the kitchen table that she had gone to horse therapy with Gabe and Mattie. I was thankful. I couldn't play twenty questions when I didn't have any of the answers.

Today was a hot Savannah day. I took the pitcher of iced tea and cut lemons from the fridge. Once poured, I realized, as I raised the glass to my

93

lips that it was caffeinated. Pouring it down the drain, I found a bottle of cold water and walked out the door for some solace in the chapel.

The inside was plain again. All the ridiculous candelabras and white roses were gone. The stain glass radiated beautiful colors as the sun shone through them. I sat in the same first pew and put my water at my feet. My hands found my belly and I rubbed it, remembering the last time life grew within me. I should have been happy, but I was stuck. I wanted to rejoice that God blessed me again, but all I could say, with tears running down my tired face was, "Just give me my Connor back."

Gabe's truck was parked in front of the house when I returned. I had to mask my emotions; which weren't hard to do, considering that I couldn't possibly identify what any of them were yet. They were hanging out in the family room, off the kitchen, watching cartoons with Mattie. Kate was relieved to see me.

"Where have you been? What did the doctor say?"

"-At the chapel. -Virus. I'll be fine."

"Medicine?"

"No medicine. It's not bacterial. You just have to suffer with viruses." I put my arms out like Jesus on the cross and Kate threw a pillow at me.

"You're so dramatic."

"There will be suffering. There will be a lot more throwing up, I can assure you."

"How long?"

"A few more weeks at least- until my stomach warms up to the notion of food again."

"Tommy called. He was freaking out about some message you left him saying something was the matter. Why did you do that? You know he's a ninny."

"-Weak moment. I just really needed someone to talk to."

"Hello. I'm here."

"I know. It's nothing. Really. It's spiritual junk- more Tommy's thing."

"Sure?"

I nodded my head and opened my eyes wide so she'd know I was annoyed with the interrogation. I sat down next to Mattie and squeezed him tightly. The therapist working with him on sensory integration told us to increase the intensity with which we hugged him.

"Hi Little Man. How are you? How was the horse riding?" I wanted to get Kate out of the house so I had time to digest my news. "Why don't you and Gabe get lost for a couple of hours and leave us be?"

"Yeah?" Gabe hadn't had adult time with Kate in a few days, since her recovery.

"Who needs yah? Hit the road. Mattie and I have plans."

They looked at each other and smiled. Kate excused herself to freshen up which left me to fend off Gabe's inquiry.

"What's the matter Julia? You're acting weird."

"I'm always weird." My eyes didn't break from viewing the television.

"-Can't argue with that, but you're a little weirder than usual."

I looked at him with the cat that ate the canary type of grin.

"Alright copper...you've got me...I'm hiding something."

"I knew it. That's why I'm the cop."

I leaned toward him and hushed my voice as if I was about to divulge a bit of juicy news.

"Do you want to know what it is?" I whispered.

He nodded, leaning in.

"Kate's in love with you."

He shook his head and rolled his eyes as Kate walked back into the room.

"Am I interrupting something?"

"No. Gabe was just telling me that he loves..."

"Let's go Kate."

He gave me an irritated look, kissed Mattie, and they abruptly left. Me, and Mattie, and baby Henry were alone at last. Mattie and I lined up a bucket of cars and then tore into the band in a box I had bought him at the toy store. I wasn't sure if the noise would upset him, but he genuinely seemed to like the wooden instrument with the mallet. He had rhythm. I danced around the room to his beat and he took to following me after awhile. We were the soul train. Later, I put on some blues and we relaxed on the couch. My fatigue was kicking in and we fell asleep together.

Gabe woke me when he moved my arm out from around Mattie. He whispered that he was taking him home and thanked me. Kate entered as he left, with a bowl of homemade chicken soup, left by Momma Martin. She was on her way home to Tybee Island and sent me well wishes for a speedy recovery. -If she only knew. I had eight long months to go. Kate picked up where she left off with the Spanish Inquisition.

"Tommy called and left a message on the machine saying that he was on his way. Why is he coming? What's going on? You're acting weird."

My cell phone rang, interrupting her quizzical tone. I motioned for her to stop talking while I answered the call.

"I better get this."

"Yeah, yeah, go ahead."

The doctor's office was calling to apprise me of my OBGYN appointment. All I could do was be as nonchalant about the information being given to me as possible.

"Who was that?"

"The doctor's office lost my blood sample. They asked me to come back in tomorrow."

"I thought it was a virus- you were fine?"

"It is. I am. They just want to make sure it's viral and not bacterial."

"Oh. Okay. Do you want me to go?"

"No. Tommy will be here. You know how he is."

"Over protective?"

"Yes. He'll want to go with me. I couldn't handle both of your neurotic behaviors at the same time."

"You are feeling better- back to being sassy."

She plopped down next to me and I felt too exhausted to endure anymore deep conversation about how I was or why I was acting so weird.

"Did you and Gabe...ya know?"

"Why?"

"Have you showered?"

"Not yet. I will. I'm going to."

"I don't want all that on my furniture."

"You're so crass."

"I'm honest. Go shower."

Kate left and I felt relieved. I hated not wanting her around, but I hated lying to her more. I inhaled the chicken soup and crackers and should have stopped there. Gabe's mom had also sent a piece of chocolate cake, which was irresistible. I instantly regretted the decision to indulge. Within ten minutes, I was running to the guest bath to vomit. Bye-bye dinner. Hello bland food.

11

⊶

Tommy arrived in the evening. We were all gathered outside throwing horseshoes when his rental car stopped by the side of the house. I met him at his door and opened it. He let me have it straight away as he got out.

"What's going on? You're acting weird? What's with the message you left?"

"Could I have a new word, please? -Anything besides weird?" Everyone laughed.

"Hi Kate. It's great to see you." Tommy embraced her which left Gabe standing all by himself.

"Kate's rude. Sorry. Tommy, this is our new friend Gabe. He's renting the cottage."

Tommy walked to him and extended his hand.

"Good to meet you Gabe. Has my sister been a good landlord?"

I interrupted. "Landlord-matchmaker..."

"Yes. She's been a doll."

"I hate to steal my brother away so soon after his arrival, but I really need to speak with him."

Kate knew something was up, but couldn't quite put her finger on it. Tommy wouldn't have come all this way and have the burden of finding another priest to say his Masses unless something big was happening.

"We'll catch up with you guys later," Kate said.

"Nice to meet you, Tommy."

"You too, Gabe."

They walked back into the house which left my brother and me alone, standing face to face. He took me by the hand.

"What's going on?"

"Let's take a walk. Do you mind?"

"No. -Of course not. Is this about Connor or Henry?"

"-In due time. Let's walk."

We started toward the chapel.

"I called him after your odd message."

"Him who?"

"Henry."

That piece of information stopped me in my tracks and solicited a punch in the arm for my brother.

"No. Why did you call him?"

"Julia, you have to admit, your message was strange. I was worried and you wouldn't answer your phone. I figured Henry would know what was going on, but all he said was that you had the fight to end all fights."

We continued our walk to the chapel, the overhanging trees shading our journey.

"We did. It's over."

"You've said that before," he replied in disbelief.

"I mean it this time."

"Sure."

I couldn't pass on the opportunity to know how Henry was doing. I wanted all the news that Kate was keeping from me. Tommy's allegiance was to me.

"How was he?"

"-A mess. A lot like you."

We approached the cemetery gate and I pushed it open, holding it for him. He looked puzzled at my new ease with this sacred space.

"I come here now to think and be with Connor."

"That's good. -Enough procrastinating. What is all this about?"

We sat down on the bench that faced Connor's grave.

"I have something that I wanted to tell you in person, but I have to tell you under the seal of the confessional."

"Julia, you don't have to go to those lengths. I can keep a promise."

"Yes, but you're not bound by that promise."

"To you, I am. I will keep whatever you tell me in confidence. You have my word. I'm your brother, first."

I paused to try and think of a way to tell him the news without having to endure his disappointment. He was my brother, but he was still a priest.

"I wanted to tell you this news with the whole family together- all five of us."

"Four of us." He loved to correct me.

"No, five of us."

"Wait. What are you saying?"

"I can't believe I'm saying it."

"Julia?"

"God has blessed me with another child."

"Henry?"

"Yes. I'm not a complete harlot- Henry- who else, you big jerk?"

He sat there quiet, looking straight ahead for a few minutes.

"Say something."

"I don't want to say the wrong thing. I'm trying to separate the priest from the brother, which is awfully hard to do. How did this happen?"

"Well... Henry and I...we...kind of...ya know..."

"I don't mean that, Julia. I'm very well aware of how it physically happened. I mean, how did you let this happen?"

"Honestly Tommy, I didn't think that this could happen- so soon after Connor. The doctor in Lima said that it would be very difficult for me to get pregnant again. I wasn't thinking."

"Obviously."

"You're telling me."

He paused again and I was left staring at his face while he stared at Connor's headstone. I couldn't take it anymore. He could yell if he wanted to, but he had to say something and put me out of my misery. Tommy's opinion was the most important to me. I loved Henry, but Tommy had my best interest at heart- always. There was never an ulterior motive. Tommy had no angle. He was just my little brother. When I was finally about to open my mouth, he responded, grabbing my hand in a show of support.

"What's done is done. A child is a blessing. Have you told Henry?"

"No. I'm not going to either."

"Yes you are."

"No. I'm not."

"He's the father. He has a right to know."

"You promised."

"I won't tell him. He won't hear it from me, but you should do the right thing."

"Did he tell you what our fight was about?"

"No."

"He asked me to marry him."

"That's wonderful. Isn't it wonderful?"

"No. It's not wonderful. He promised to make me a priority, but at the first fork in the road, he left me behind again to go solve one of John's problems. I can't have a marriage with Henry and our father. I can't live like that."

"I understand."

"Do you really?"

"I really do. Remember, I lived with the invisible dad- still do. I'll keep your secret, but at some point, I know you'll do what is necessary and prudent."

Tommy hugged me and we sat in silence as I cried.

"Why the tears? This is happy news, right?"

"I feel guilty loving this child. Connor still occupies my heart."

"Give it time, Julia. Connor wouldn't want you to be distant from this experience. This is his sibling. He's still the big brother, even if he's not physically present. He saved your life, you know. The doctor told Henry that you'd probably be dead if it wasn't for your pregnancy- the knife would have hit a major organ. Honor that fact. Love the child you have now. It's not an either/or...don't put conditions on a gift."

"You're right. I know you're right. Maybe once this sinks in, I'll feel the attachment."

"You've been to the doctor?"

"I go for my first obstetrician appointment tomorrow."

"I'm coming."

"Thanks. I could use the company. I'm nervous."

"Kate doesn't know?"

"Be serious. I'd expect her to pick the phone up and call Henry within seconds of hearing the news."

"She would."

"I know. -Hence the cloak and dagger routine. She thinks that the doctor's office lost my blood sample and I'm returning tomorrow to be stuck again."

"I'll keep your secret, Julia, but I won't directly lie for you."

"Agreed."

"I'm starving. Let's drive into town and eat some seafood- just the two of us. I have a lot more questions about the Henry situation."

We had a pleasant dinner together even though I was required to answer question after question about Henry. He made me promise to consider telling him and I told him that I would. I was thrilled to talk about the happenings at his church on the drive home. I was anxious to hear any news that did not involve me.

We returned to a dark house. Kate must have been with Gabe. She had no embarrassment about staying over, despite Tommy being a priest. She'd be the recipient of the moral virtue lecture in the morning. This wasn't scoring any points for Gabe.

I said my goodnight and decided to take a shower. Memories of Henry's naked body against mine made me miss him. There wasn't a place in this house that alienated me from those kinds of thoughts. We had loved each other in almost every room. Tomorrow, I would see my baby- a memory in the flesh- a reminder of that love.

I was still tired when Tommy's shuffling through the house woke me. Showering, again, I brushed my teeth, and dressed in preparation for the early morning appointment. Tommy made bacon which surprisingly smelled good to me. I had warned everyone that eggs could no longer be cooked in my house, until further notice. Thankfully, I made it through an entire bacon sandwich without gagging. We grabbed some water and headed out the door.

I wasn't as nervous this time since Tommy was accompanying me. I'm sure we looked like a pair. He always wore his priestly attire. I felt the need to tell perfect strangers that he was my brother. A person usually doesn't bring a priest to the obstetrician's office. He was the object of much staring.

After filling out more paperwork, we were escorted back to Dr. Brandon's office. I introduced Tommy and gave a limited, technical account of how I lost Connor. He explained the need to monitor me closely and watch for signs of uterine weakness and cervical incompetence. He was also concerned about keeping an eye on my blood pressure. He explained that there may be a need to supplement my own hormone production, but he wouldn't know for sure until the blood tests came back.

Tommy asked a few brotherly questions about safeguarding my health during the pregnancy. Dr. Brandon and I were anxiously awaiting him to come up for air. He wouldn't cut off a priest, but I had no problem shutting him down. I dismissed him to the waiting area and the nurse led me to an exam room. I'd have to be cold and uncomfortable this time.

After the internal exam, he performed an ultrasound. I was nine weeks and three days pregnant. The baby resembled Mr. Peanut, but it was the cutest thing I'd seen in a long time. The little heart flickering made my own skip a beat. In that moment, my heart grew in size, making me realize that there was more than ample room to love two children. I wouldn't lose Connor. They were equally important to me.

Dr. Brandon didn't seem to be vexed about anything he saw. I was warned about stress and taking care of myself. He wanted me to take my blood pressure at home every day and record the results in a book. I was told to return in two weeks for a quick check. Due to my age, he wanted to know how I felt about an amniocentesis. I didn't really see the point. Regardless of what was in store for me, I knew that this baby was a miracle and no illness or syndrome would change the course of seeing this pregnancy to its fruition. The baby was a testament to mine and Henry's love. That made him or her perfect.

Before leaving, the ultrasound tech gave me a few pictures of the baby. I'm glad I was paying attention when she described what we were seeing or the images would have looked like an alien encounter. Tommy was excited to see his new niece or nephew. He was truly happy for me. In one morning, everything had been made real to me. I couldn't wait to call Henry and share the good news.

12

---ᘓᘓᘓ---

I took advantage of the house being empty to coax my nerves into calling him. Tommy had gone to say afternoon Mass at the Catholic Church downtown and then was off to the airport to return to New York. Kate was inevitably at the cottage with Gabe and Mattie. I grabbed some ginger ale and crackers and bedded down in my room to do the deed.

I stared at the phone for a long time deciding whether I would be a coward and leave a message on his home phone or have some guts and call his cell. I opted to be a coward, but then couldn't think of what to say on the message. I rehearsed a few lines, but nothing quite fit the occasion. Telling him to prepare for fatherhood on voice mail just seemed distant and rude. Shoot. I'd have to call him directly.

I picked up the phone and started to dial his cell. Three digits in and I hung up. I walked around the room getting pumped up, telling myself that this was a small thing. I should just wait for him to answer, blurt out the news, and disconnect. I didn't even feel the need to wait for his response. I'd give him the news quick and dirty.

After pulling out the picture of our tiny peanut, I rubbed my belly, and dialed the number. Ring. Ring. Ring. *Answer the phone already*. When he did, I heard a woman laughing. I panicked. For once, I was speechless. Her voice was smooth as silk. She had one of those voices that gave me the mental image that I was talking to a supermodel. I hated her already. She was probably skinny; the kind of woman that magically disappears when she turns sideways. I was pale and getting plumper by the day.

"Hello. Henry's phone." She laughed over and over again, exaggerating every syllable, like she was on her first date and Tru had just said something hysterical. I could hear his voice too. He echoed her laugh and it made me sick. That wasn't his real laugh. That's not the laugh he gives me when I wake up in the morning and my hair is the size of Texas. That's not the laugh he gives me when I fall off a curb or walk into a door. That's not his laugh. Who is she and what has she done with my Henry? I absolutely hated her. I didn't care who she was.

"I said hello. Heeellloooo. I think we have a breather, Henry," the wench shrilled.

"Give me the phone, Tricia."

Who the hell was Tricia?

"Hello. This is Henry Truman Walker. Can I help you?"

I covered the mouthpiece with my hand and answered him.

"It's me. I have great news, Tru."

"Hello? Who was there, Tricia?"

"We're having a baby."

"Hello? Is anyone there?"

"You're going to be a father."

"Give me the phone, Henry."

"I love you. Come home. I'm sorry."

"Tricia, no"

The line went dead. I slowly placed the phone back in its cradle. I wasn't prepared for Tricia. I didn't see it coming. I guess a month is plenty of time for some people to move on. I sat back against my pillows and had a little cry.

The pity party lasted only a brief time. Truly, that type of party loses its appeal when no one else is in attendance. Who was around to care that my eyes were swelling and my cheeks were flushed with anger and rage? Nobody. I just needed a distraction. Maybe the television would provide a voyeuristic view into the life of someone more pathetic than me. Oprah had something smart on. She wouldn't do. I'd have to hit the hard stuff. There must be some poor loser on television asking themselves that all-important question of *"Who is my baby's daddy?"*. I just needed a cable programming fix as a quick pick me up. I wasn't a loser. I was alone, but not lonely. I'd keep telling myself that until I believed it.

The phone ringing startled me. I hit the mute button on the remote as I reached for the phone. I had the intention of answering it, but Henry's cell phone number was lighting up the caller ID display. Realizing that he would check his phone for the caller's number, I should have known he'd ring me back. Our chicken game had ended and he'd won. I called first.

I wasn't about to answer the phone with Tricia in earshot, laughing her fake, movie star laugh. He had obviously expedited his get over Jewels plan. He was on a new chapter. I was stuck in the table of contents. If he could move past life with me, then I would do the same. Ring until the ringer can't ring no more, I thought. For all he knew, Kate had placed the call. Done and done.

I was fighting the urge to retreat within myself again, but I had a pregnancy to nurture. I was a mom. People lose lovers all the time. They get over it. I would too. I flipped the television off, and turning on some soft music, I closed my eyes. A nap was just what the baby and I needed to vanquish the events of the last thirty minutes. I would awake with a better perspective.

"Jewels, wake up?"

I felt a nudge at my arm. I rolled over ignoring the interruption.

"Jewels."

I rolled back and opened my eyes. Kate was sitting next to me.

"What?"

"Henry said that I called him today, but we both know that's impossible because I didn't call him, you called him."

"No."

"I didn't call him so that leaves you. Why didn't you say anything?"

"I didn't call."

"Well, if I didn't call and you didn't call, and the call came from this house, then who called?"

"I'm too tired for riddles. Maybe, Tommy. I don't know. I didn't call, Kate."

"You really didn't call?"

"No matter how many times you ask me, the answer will remain the same. I didn't call. Is that what you woke me for?"

"-Partially, but not totally. Henry has asked me to fly to New York. I'm leaving tonight… in a few minutes actually."

"Does Gabe know?"

"Yes."

"What did he say about you leaving?"

"He didn't say anything. He didn't ask me not to go. He didn't ask me to stay."

"His saying nothing was saying something. Don't you get that?"

"- You Americans and your bloody games."

I ignored the dig and rolled onto my side, facing her, so she could see my disdain.

"Why don't you invite him to go with you?"

"What about Mattie?"

"Take Mattie with you. He'd love New York. You could do the tourist stuff. I bet he'd get a kick out of the Empire State Building."

She didn't answer. Kate measured her words carefully before speaking, while folding the quilt at the end of the bed.

"I'm not ready for Mattie, out in public..."

"What?" She pushed the protective mom button inside me. Mattie wasn't even my child, but the alarms were going off nonetheless. I knew the emotional toll that befell Gabe when his wife left. He'd finally gambled on love, at my insistence, and Kate was going to level him in one fail swoop.

"I know that makes me awful, but I'm not ready for the stares and comments. I can't ask Gabe to go without offering for Mattie to go too."

"Kathryn Emma Walker. I can't believe you're saying this."

"Anyways, Henry needs me right now, thanks to you, so I wouldn't have time to socially direct activities for Gabe and Mattie."

"Don't put this off on me, Kate."

"Henry is broken-hearted. Who did that?"

"He did."

"Whatever. I still have to go pick up the pieces, it would seem."

"Henry's doing just fine, believe me."

"How would you know?"

"I wouldn't know because I haven't spoken to him, but I imagine he's moved on to the next best thing."

"Yes. He's a lot like you."

"Oh...he's fine. Trust me."

"He will be fine, Julia."

"Oh, I know."

Under her breath, Kate responded, "No thanks to you."

"No thanks to me?"

She got up and walked to the door, grabbing a few final toiletries off the dresser, and shoving them into her carry on bag.

"Okay, so I'll be back in a week or two."

"Take your time. In fact, feel free to linger in New York for several months. Don't rush back."

"I won't," she said angrily.

"Good," I responded, not to be outdone.

"Good," she replied as she made her way to the door.

"Goodbye," I screamed in the harshest tone I could muster.

"Goodbye. And by the way, I'm taking my grandmother's ring from the kitchen table; seeing as you don't care to wear it."

Kate stomped her way down the steps, mad. Her embarrassment of Mattie really ticked me off. She didn't deserve either of them. They were a package deal. I yelled after her, hoping she would hear.

"Jerk."

She heard.

"Crazy," she hollered back.

Kate had the last word. With that, the front door slammed shut. The bed and breakfast was officially closed. I expected to get an immediate call from Gabe, but he never phoned. He must have been off licking his wounds.

The next couple of weeks were productive. I had made some connections at the legal aid clinic downtown and introduced myself to some local charities. Nothing says welcome like money and people seemed to want mine.

Before I knew it, I was in my eighteenth week of pregnancy. Tommy had called almost daily to do his phone check-up. He still prodded me about calling Henry, despite knowing about his involvement with Tricia, but I had made peace with raising the baby on my own. I also knew that Henry was Henry. As much as I wanted to never see him again, he would insist on being a part of the baby's life. He was destined to make a lousy husband, but maybe a better father. I would have to warm up to the idea of seeing him without seeing him. That would take time.

Weeks had passed and Gabe orchestrated his movements to avoid me altogether. I couldn't take the silent treatment from him anymore. I missed

Mattie too much to let Kate ruin our new friendship. Seeing them from my windows, pile in and out of the car, without conversing, was becoming ridiculous.

I knew that we had a hard conversation ahead of us. Our words would undoubtedly turn to analyzing Kate's motives. What he didn't realize was that I would be as equally disadvantaged as him. Speaking as someone with a track record for being spontaneous and irrational, Kate was even more over the top than me. Her likes and dislikes had the potential to change daily. I'm only surprised that she had invested so much time into Gabe and his family if leaving was going to be her final act.

I started becoming a stalker, watching for an opportunity to initiate a truce with him. I saw them heading down to the beach with Mattie's kite and decided to follow. I had purchased a beach play kit for Mattie and brought it along to surprise him. Nervousness overtook me on the walk. I became afraid that he would blame me for introducing him to Kate. My opinions on the matter had softened over the last couple of weeks. I'd come to realize that not everyone has the coping mechanism to deal with life's big curve balls. Not too long ago, I was counting bathroom tiles and walking laps throughout the house. Perhaps, that is why God entrusted Mattie to someone like Gabe and not to someone like Kate. Not everyone has the patience and understanding to realize Mattie's greatness.

Why do people want the world to be filled with only vanilla, when chocolate, strawberry and mango are so much more interesting? Who wants an army of sedate kids that aren't in any way interesting? I love mango. Mattie was mango.

When I turned down the path to the beach, I could see their kite soaring against the blue sky. Gabe noticed me approaching and didn't offer a friendly wave. He simply turned back towards the ocean. Unsure of what to do, I decided that I'd obligated myself to continue since he'd already seen me. Moving slowly, I tried to decide the best course of action. Our meeting would be hard no matter when it took place. Leaving would just delay the inevitable. Getting the strained conversation out of the way would be a relief.

I walked up next to Mattie and dropped the beach toys in the sand, kneeling down to hug his neck. He began lining them up, as if doing his usual inventory. I looked back at Gabe and gave him a guarded smile.

"Where have you been hiding?" I cautiously inquired, testing the waters.

He motioned for me to step a few feet from Mattie. I was afraid of what was coming next, especially considering that his words weren't suitable for Mattie's ears. I was hoping that he wouldn't ask me to leave, realizing that I needed all the friends I could get lately. Kate leaving for New York made me keenly aware that I was all alone.

"What's going on with Kate?"

"Well…straight to it then. I wasn't expecting the direct approach."

"She started acting aloof when her brother left. She was different-distant."

"Kate is different, Gabe."

"That's not going to pass for an answer."

"What are you asking then?"

"What did I do?"

"This may not be so much about you. I think this has a lot more to do with me. Henry and I had a terrible fight."

"She mentioned that, but what does that have to do with me and her?"

"Henry and Kate are very close. They always have been. She's upset with me. Her desire wasn't to get away from you. She just wanted to get as far away from me as possible. You're simply a victim of location. Knowing Henry, he probably demanded that she go to New York and show some allegiance to him. I don't know, but make no mistake, Gabe; she'd fall on her sword for Henry every day of the week and twice on Sunday. She may be smitten with you, but she loves her brother more. I don't mean to be hurtful, and maybe she'll return in a week and make amends, but it is very hard to tell with Kate. Her free spirit is one of her greatest strengths while at the same time being her most challenging flaw."

"If I ask you a question, will you answer me honestly?"

"I'll try."

Gabe looked serious and sad as if he truly didn't want the answer.

"Did this have anything, at all, to do with Mattie?"

"Why would you think that?"

Both of our heads turned to watch him as he continued to play. Our eyes locked again, making me uneasy, as he continued with his inquisition. He was irritated with my evasiveness.

"Why are you answering a question with a question?"

"What would you like to hear?"

"The truth would be refreshing."

"No one wants to hear the truth, Gabe," I replied, shaking my head.

"Maybe not, but I need to know what I did or didn't do to warrant her leaving. I'm not at ease around women anymore. I must have done something. I just don't understand. Things were going so well. I just need to know. I don't want to continue to repeat the same mistakes."

I ran my fingers through my hair and gave the ends a yank. I didn't see the point in relating what Kate had told me. Grown-ups can be a lot like babies who are started on mushy food until they can stomach the real stuff. Kate was eating Hawaiian delight, but someday she'd be ready for steak. She needed time. At certain points in life, our mental facilities need time to catch up to the world's ideals of what we should be equipped to handle. Telling Gabe would end any chance she'd have to get him back, when she finally came to her senses. I loved Kate. I wouldn't cut her off at the knees.

"I'm not good at these kinds of talks and I'm absolutely devoid of grace and tact, despite my middle name. Okay. Here it is- the ugly truth. Prepare yourself. I'm not good at bullshit. The quick and painful answer is that Kate cares about you. She cares about Mattie. She just doesn't care enough. You don't have enough time in the relationship to warrant the fight. You have one month together challenging a lifetime with her brother. Henry called, and because your relationship is so new, she's able to cut her losses and move on. You didn't do anything. Mattie is perfect just as he is. She adored him. This has everything to do with external pressures- one person- namely Henry."

"Well then he's not my favorite person anymore."

"We should form a club," I smiled.

"This really isn't about Mattie being different?"

"-Absolutely not."

"Well, that makes a difference to me. It doesn't hurt any less, but it makes a difference. Thanks for being honest."

"I'm sure Kate will come to her senses and be back by Christmas. Just promise me that you won't let time stand still waiting. You need to have a back up plan just in case she flakes out and returns to London."

"So do you."

"That train has already left the station, I assure you. I've moved on."

"You say that like you almost mean it."

"I do."

"I'm happy for you and a bit envious."

"Time heals all things," I said, encouragingly.

"Not really. The pain just dulls, somewhat."

I started to walk back toward Mattie, hoping movement would change the subject. I couldn't continue to be Kate's cheerleader when I was so upset with her. Gabe was sharp. Eventually, he would crack the façade if I wasn't on my toes and Kate's true feelings would spew like vomit from my mouth.

"What would you say about me taking Mattie to his therapy appointments? I mean, if that's agreeable to you. I've missed spending time with him...you too. That big house can get lonely- it needs a kid like Mattie to fill it with the exuberance of youth."

"That would be fine. He'd love it actually, but sometimes I have to work late or pull a night shift, and I couldn't be back at a decent hour to pick him up. The church volunteers usually take him home and I get him in the morning. I wouldn't want to inconvenience you."

"Don't be silly. I have ample rooms for guests. Mattie can stay over. You can get him when you get off or just come by in the morning."

"Are you sure?"

"Yes, of course. You can even stay at my house with Mattie instead of waking him up, if you'd like."

"Really?"

"Yes."

"When do you want to start taking him?"

"Is tomorrow too soon?"

"No. He goes to horse therapy from 3:00-4:00 PM on Monday, Wednesday, and Friday. Sensory therapy is Tuesday and Thursday. That seems like a lot for one person to volunteer for."

"We'll play it by ear. You can take him on your off days. I'll share your son with you."

Gabe laughed. I responded with a chuckle.

"What's going on with you, Julia? Something is different, but I can't quite put my finger on it?"

"Can you stop being Sherlock Holmes for even a second? You have an overactive imagination."

"I don't think so."

Thank God I'd brought some old bread for the birds. I reached in my knap sack and pulled out a couple of loaves that had been put in the freezer by the caterers during Connor's funeral. The birds scurrying around for the tossed bread captured Mattie's attention. He even looked like he smiled. My makeshift family was pieced back together.

13

Mattie and I spent our days romping through the big house, finding new ways to play with old objects that belonged to my mom. He loved to take things apart. We spent several days dismantling an old type-writer. Then, we broke down a beat up radio that no longer worked. He was very good with screwdrivers. As each piece was removed, he laid it out to the side in some order that I didn't understand. His typical inventory was left undisturbed. We simply stepped over the pieces as we moved through the rooms. This mechanical work usually occupied our mornings.

After lunch, we would take a walk to the chapel. I would try to orga-nize my thoughts and pray as he ran through each pew. I prayed for that little boy with so much heart and conviction that I was almost brought to tears on occasions. Sometimes, after my prayers, we'd go in to the cemetery to sit with Connor and my mom. While I held down the bench, with my ever growing girth, Mattie would step into the fountain and walk in cir-cles around the statue of Jesus. The fountain had become almost coin-free thanks to him. He didn't like them cluttering up the bottom. I thought about getting some fish, but I wasn't sure if the change would go over well.

Therapy consumed our afternoons. The evenings that he stayed over were special to me. We'd pop popcorn and I'd watch old movies while he colored in his sketchpad. Before mid way though the flick, he'd be sound asleep on a mountain of crayons in my bed. I lay next to him, watching his chest rise and fall, envisioning a life full of adventure and love for us all. Gabe had placed his happiness in the palms of this little boy's hands. Apart from Mattie, he would have no joy. His contentment with Mattie's current level of functioning made me admire him all the more. The same big dreams that I held for Connor, I now held for Mattie.

I was still unclear as to why a good God would inflict such a mystery on an innocent child. Gabe was in a better place of acceptance than me. I was struggling to find peace with losing Connor. I was still sad and depressed, but I was fighting the good fight, and getting on with life for the sake of the baby. Gabe trudged through difficulties every day. Nothing was ever easy with Mattie, but Gabe continued to remain strong and assured of better days ahead. I was starting to believe that Mattie would come back to us. I prayed night after night for God to unlock his world. Was he hearing me? Would he see him amongst all the other hurts and sorrows of the world and heal this one particular boy? I was betting on a miracle.

Horse therapy was interesting. I had been taking Mattie for several weeks. The horse trainer was wonderful with the kids, but I didn't love the therapist. I voiced my concerns to Gabe, but he brushed me off, telling me that he'd investigated her credentials and equine therapy was proven to be helpful for autistic children. I was very much a skeptic, based on her disposition.

There were about ten kids in his therapy class with varying degrees of autism. From first impressions, I would say that Mattie's struggle fell somewhere in the middle. Two of them could verbally communicate with others while another two, on the other end of the spectrum only had the capability of non-verbal communication.

Mattie was able to meaningfully engage in play, although it was usually by himself. He seemed to find his own environment interesting even if he chose not to interact with the outside world. He was able to communicate his needs by banging his cup on the kitchen counter or by standing in front of a cabinet that held an object he desired. If he didn't want to participate in an activity, he disconnected from the situation and went inside himself.

Mattie was in there somewhere. This was never more evident to me than when we fed the birds. I could never give him the bread fast enough. He would toss piece after piece and stand still until the birds landed on the sand. Once they drew close, he would chase them up and down the beach, delighting in their flight. I knew he was smiling on the inside. Perhaps with his therapy, he'd be able to tell us someday.

After four weeks of smooth sailing in the horse arena, Friday's therapy did not go as planned. Mattie had decided, before we even left the house, that he had no interest in going. He gave Gabe trouble when he tried to dress him and he hit his hand against the car window as we passed the ice cream parlor. I didn't know whether to pull over or just try to make it to the farm as quickly as I could. I tried to appease him by promising to take him for ice cream after his ride. The overture did little to detour his actions.

When we finally arrived, he refused to get out of the car. The therapist walked over, trying to discover why we were holding up her class. She tried to coax him out, but he wouldn't cooperate. I was severely out of my element. Never having known a child with autism, I had little experience in knowing how to motivate him to achieve a positive outcome. I had even less experience and success with behavior modification techniques. Getting people, like Henry, to do what I wanted wasn't really my strong suit. I had a poor track record.

Bribing him again with a trip to the ice cream store didn't do the trick. I honestly felt bad for sinking to those depths. I could easily remember times, even still as an adult, when I didn't want to do things either. Bribery never moved me to act as others expected, if I truly believed in my opposition to the task. Why was it not possible that Mattie just didn't feel like riding this particular day? His feelings seemed reasonable. He had participated in all the other therapy sessions; he wasn't just being obstinate. On this day, he wasn't up to it and I could feel his pain. Wasn't the boy entitled to one day off?

The therapist became impatient with both of us. Legally, she explained that she wasn't allowed to physically pull him out of my car. She informed me that physical correction was the sole responsibility of the parent. She instructed me to pull him out and then she and her staff would take it from there. I didn't like how that sounded.

I noticed one of the other moms dragging her son, kicking and screaming, across the parking lot. The sight of their interaction bothered me greatly. The mom probably didn't feel like she had a choice with the therapist touting her opinions so freely. Using intimidation and the need for conformity, the therapist had every parent falling in line with her way of thinking; everyone, but me, of course.

Unfortunately for her, I didn't have the years of sorrow that were wrapped up in both heartache and hope. I'm sure that everyone wanted Mattie to reach his full potential. I think we differed on the most advantageous way to go about that. Even with him refusing to cooperate and clutching the door handle, as if his life depended on remaining in my car, I loved him. The therapist was letting her expectations get in the way of unconditional love. If Mattie could solve this, he would.

Whatever happened to meeting people on their level? We make decisions for our lives based on the goods that we have stored in our soul. If the goods are pure, we positively enrich the lives of those around us. If the goods are tainted, we bring misery to the world. Mattie was pure. He enriched Gabe's life. He enriched my life. Understanding his level of functioning only made his gift that much more precious. Then there are the tainters- people like Jackson. He made crappy choices intentionally because he was a crappy person. His goods were directed to better his own existence, regardless of the personal cost to the world around him. There are good people and there are Jackson people. Mattie was good- a real treasure. Jackson was a tainted scumbag. My condemnation of him probably meant that I fell somewhere in between.

The therapist began to get visibly upset. Her face became strained. She gritted her teeth and balled her fists as they rested at her sides. We were standing next to one another, a few feet from the car, giving Mattie the space he needed to avoid feeling threatened.

"You need to pull him out of the car," she demanded angrily as she stepped toward the open door.

"You need to step back," I said as I wedged myself between her and Mattie.

"He needs to know that he doesn't have a choice about participating in therapy."

"But he does have a choice," I protested.

"No he doesn't. He's a child."

"He's a child with a choice," I corrected.

She lunged past me and began trying to peel his fingers from the door handle. Mattie became agitated and started rocking and turning his head from side to side.

"Take your hands off him...now," I demanded.

"All you're doing is setting low expectations for him."

"Lady, you've already met my low expectations quota for the day. Remove your hands from his fingers if you'd like to keep them."

"I can't hold off this lesson any longer. The other parents have their children ready."

"Don't let us keep you."

"I'm calling Sheriff Martin."

"Do you need the number?"

"You're only hurting him by allowing this. I hope you know what you're doing."

"The only thing I know for sure is that you won't be hurting him today. As far as knowing what I'm doing; I can assure you that I have no idea, but love covers a multitude of sins."

She stormed off and disappeared into the indoor arena. Mattie was still rocking as I knelt down and stroked his cheek.

"How would you feel about bird therapy today, Little Man? Would you like to go to the beach and feed the birds with me?"

After a silent stand off, Mattie let go of the door handle and sat back, grabbing a hold of his seat belt strap. I closed the door and walked around to the driver's side wondering if I needed to call Gabe myself, before the mean and nasty therapist beat me to the punch. Regardless, I had no intention of forcing Mattie to participate in horse therapy or any other kind of therapy- not on my watch. Even if Gabe asked, I wouldn't pull him out of the car and drag him across the lot, kicking and screaming. There was something inhumane in that option.

Mattie eagerly got out of the car at the beach. I sat at the water's edge allowing the waves to crash against my feet. I was starting to gain weight and the loose dresses I wore weren't going to hide my belly for much longer. After thirty minutes of chasing the birds, we decided to tackle some ice cream. I was starving- a common, daily complaint for me.

The ice cream parlor was crowded. There wasn't an available parking space in the lot. We parked at the business next door and walked over. As I opened the parlor door to allow Mattie to enter, he ran past all the people waiting in line to view the various flavors offered for the day. He pushed himself between two women and started banging on the display case. The woman's face soured and she started to scold him. I interceded quickly but Mattie wouldn't budge from his spot. She looked back at me as I walked up behind him.

"Your kid could use some manners."

"He's a child. What's your excuse?"

"You're just as rude as he is."

Another day, at another time, I would have pounced on this woman with every catty word in my repertoire, but not in front of Mattie. A lady, standing further down the line, but still in front of the case, motioned for us to move in front of her. Mattie still wouldn't move. As it became time for the line to move forward, I waved people ahead of us until the nice lady was behind us.

"I'm sorry. Thank you for being so nice. Mattie has autism. He doesn't quite get the concept of waiting yet. It's something we need to work on."

"No problem. Don't worry about it."

People didn't usually surprise me. Maybe I'm not as much of an optimist as I should be. I expected the cranky customer to rear her ugly head and try to steal our joy, but the nice lady full of compassion made me take pause. God seemed to send me those small glimmers of hope for encouragement.

Finally, it was our turn to order. Gabe had instructed me to stick to buying Mattie vanilla cones, but what is vanilla? How would he ever learn about the world eating only vanilla? I started buying a new flavor each trip. He didn't care for pistachio, but that was good to know. He loved blue cotton candy. Who would have thought? Today we would try another new flavor. The man approached and asked for our order.

"I'll have a chocolate turtle milkshake and this young man would like a scoop of mint chocolate chip in a waffle cone."

As soon as I placed the order, Mattie became agitated. He started to bang on the display case and shook his head no. I felt the stares of everyone in the long line, mentally willing us to wrap it up and move forward to pay. Again, Mattie wouldn't budge. The man asked again if I wanted to order something different. How did I know? I knelt down to Mattie and asked if he wanted some other flavor. He continued to tap his finger on the case.

"Just tell me what you want Mattie and we'll get it. I don't understand."

The man's head turned to take in the anxious looks of the waiting customers. I was beginning to feel a little self-conscience myself.

"Just go ahead and give us the mint chocolate chip, please."

When the man turned to grab the cone, Mattie tugged my arm. As I turned, he opened his mouth to speak his first words.

"Blue. Blue. Blue."

"What did you say?" I stared into his face and felt tears pooling in my eyes.

"Blue. Blue. Blue," he said as he pointed to the display case.

I threw my arms around him and squeezed him so hard. He didn't hug me back. He just pushed me off of him and continued to say the word blue. No one understood my pure happiness over hearing that one glorious word.

118

I was privileged to be the first to hear his beautiful voice. I stood up and addressed the employee.

"Give him a scoop of blue cotton candy in a cone, please."

I wiped away the tears that rolled down my cheek as I pulled out my phone to text Gabe. I wasn't sure what to write. What if he got to the parlor and Mattie said nothing. I typed *9-1-1 ice cream store*. After the man handed me my milkshake and we paid, I sat to wait for Gabe's arrival. Mattie wouldn't leave the display case. He stood there eating his ice cream cone as patrons passed him in line.

I heard the sounds of sirens approaching and thought that it might not have been the best idea to text him that message. His sport utility came to a screeching halt and he flew through the front door, as I stood to greet him. He looked harried and upset.

"What's the matter?"

"Nothing is the matter."

"You texted me 9-1-1, Jewels."

He looked mad as he scanned the room for his son.

"Mattie is fine, but something has happened...something wonderful. That's why I texted you 9-1-1."

"What? Have you been crying?"

"Never mind me. Come here."

I pulled him over to Mattie who had just finished his cone and was banging on the display case for more.

"Tell Mattie that you're going to order him a mint chocolate chip ice cream cone."

"What? Why?"

"Trust me. Just do it."

Gabe looked at the next person in line and asked politely if he could cut in line. The man shook his head yes.

"Can I get my son a mint chocolate chip single scoop cone, please?" He looked to me, standing beside him, as he ordered, wondering why he was humoring me with this ridiculous request.

Mattie became agitated again. "Blue. Blue. Blue," he shouted as he tapped the display case. Turning to face Gabe, with no particular attachment, he said, "Dad."

Gabe looked at me in shock, his mouth hanging open, unable to speak. All I could do was shake my head and hold my arms up in front of me, mirroring his same disbelief. He pulled me to him, hugging me tightly as we laughed and cried. When I broke his hold and pulled us apart, he kissed me. It wasn't a lover's kiss. It was a kiss of convenience with no passion; the release after a build up of emotions that the mind is unable to sustain. The meeting of our lips was alien to me. He wasn't Henry.

"I'm sorry, Jewels. I got caught up in the moment. I don't know why I did that."

"I'm pregnant."

I don't know why I blurted out such a stupid thing during such a momentous occasion. I guess it was a defense mechanism. I couldn't handle any complications in my already messed up life.

"I'm not sure what they taught you in Sex-Ed Jewels, but you don't get pregnant from kissing," he chuckled.

"Henry. He's the father."

"Oh."

Mattie tugged his dad's jacket and the moment was forgotten. Gabe picked him up and spun him around, finally demanding that the man prepare another blue cotton candy cone for his magnificent son. We sat, like a happy family, wondering what the future held for our precious Mattie. Gabe called his Mom who instantly cried. She was packing a bag and would arrive in the evening to hear her grandson's voice.

Gabe stepped outside to make his next call. I imagined that he was trying to reach Kate to share the good news. The call was quick. He must have had to leave a message. When he walked back in, he told me that he had to finish out his work shift and that he would probably be home after his mom's arrival. He hugged Little Man and we went our separate ways.

Mattie gave no indication that anything had changed, but I knew that he was smiling on the inside. After getting back to the main house, we painted in the sunroom, making a fantastic mess. He was quite a good little artist. We hung up each masterpiece and stared at them for a long time, side by side, in deep thought, as if we were the world's best art critics. He repeated the word blue as he pointed to the color on the paper. Connor didn't get his miracle, but maybe Mattie had.

14

⸻

We ordered a pizza for dinner and ate it down at the boathouse. Being there again brought back a heap of memories. The table still held melted candles and an empty bottle of champagne was turned over on the wooden planks below. I grabbed a few of the floor pillows from the back corner for us to sit on. Within ten minutes, I had eaten half of the pie, blaming it on the baby to make myself feel better. Mattie threw pieces of pepperoni to the fish, lying on his stomach with his head sticking off the dock to get the best view as they nibbled the morsels.

All I could think about, in this special place, was Henry. Well, Henry and now Tricia. Anger and jealousy seemed to go hand in hand. Tricia may indeed be the owner of a face that could shatter glass, but all I could imagine was Heidi Klum.

His jacket was still hanging on the hook above our invented bed. Walking over, I picked it up and held it to my nose. The smell of salt and fresh air had replaced his scent, but I put it on nonetheless, wrapping my arms around me, remembering his hold. Images played in my mind of our night together. The proposal seemed like just yesterday, but months had passed. When I relaxed into those distant thoughts, the sound of that horrid woman laughing over the phone invaded my mind. In my heart, I knew that Henry had crossed the line. Reality began to set in. Things were different now. The jacket slid down my arms and fell to the floor.

I gathered Mattie and we made our way home, using the old jars I'd found in the boathouse to catch the fireflies that lit the tree lined path. The day had been emotionally exhausting. After a quick bath for Mattie and a phone call to Tommy, we collapsed under the multiple layers of linens on my bed. We watched an animated movie he had chosen from my brother's old video collection. My eyes were as heavy as Mattie's as we both struggled to keep them open. I knew we'd never be able to stay up long enough to greet Gabe's mom. The house seemed cold. I tucked us in tight, just leaving our arms on top of the comforter. I placed my hand across Mattie's chest and we surrendered to sleep.

I heard the door creak open, but felt too sleepy to become alert enough to get up. I felt an arm over my waist, but the weight of it was too heavy to be Mattie. Slowly opening my eyes, I saw Gabe's face close to my own. Mattie was sandwiched between us. Gabe was still asleep. He probably lay down for a second, with the intention of carrying Mattie to the guest room, as he had always done before, but fell asleep instead. Startling him by moving his arm off my waist would wake Mattie.

Suddenly, I realized that I'd forgotten about Gabe's mom. The creaking of the door with Ms. Martin's expected arrival made me realize that she was here. I was thankful. In my tired state, moving her boys seemed like a big task. We'd have to get them situated before I could get her settled into a room for the night.

I carefully turned my head toward the door and surprise claimed every muscle in my face. In the doorway, Henry and Kate stood, mouths open, bewildered by the scene they were taking in. Kate looked furious and disappeared from sight. Henry stood a little longer with the most hurtful expression on his face. I didn't move. I couldn't say anything. He finally relinquished his stare and left. If I followed him, he'd know that I was pregnant. One embrace would divulge my secret. If I didn't go after them, I knew I was destined to lose them both.

The front door echoed its slamming throughout the house followed by the sound of two car doors shutting. Gabe and Mattie didn't flinch. My head retreated down to the pillow and silent tears wet my face. My decision was made without careful consideration, but with no remorse. Depression had become a fertile breeding ground over the past several months in which to cultivate my new apathy.

Two hours passed before Gabe's mom knocked on the front door. I was awake for every second replaying the events of the night. Had I made the right decision? My answer to that question changed continuously. The knocking intensified, even though I was sure that the front door was open.

Henry and Kate left in such a hurry that they certainly didn't waste even a second locking the door as they departed. I nudged Gabe. Opening his eyes, he realized that he was holding me and apologized while instantly removing his arm from my waist.

"I seem to be accosting you today. Sorry."

"No worries. I think your mom is here. It sounds like someone is knocking at the front door."

"What time is it?"

"Almost midnight."

"I'll move Mattie into the guest room."

"You'll wake him. It's fine. Leave him here with me for the night."

He sat up and ran his fingers through his hair, trying to wake up, before standing and leaving the bedroom. Reaching for the remote, I turned off the television that had illuminated the room. I sat up and pulled the covers off my side, stumbling to the bathroom in the dark. I waited until the door was closed to turn on the light so I wouldn't wake Mattie. It took a moment for my eyes to adjust. Turning on the faucet, I leaned down and splashed my face with cold water. When I stood upright, the reflection in the mirror scared me. My white gown was stained red. I decided that I wasn't actively bleeding, wasn't in pain, and I wasn't cramping. I needed to be calm and think.

Obviously, I needed to go to the hospital. After showering off and changing clothes, I called Dr. Brandon who told me that he'd meet me there. I'd thought about calling Tommy, but I really had no news to share until I was examined. While I was deciding what to do, a knock interrupted my thoughts.

"Julia, are you okay? I thought you were coming down to greet my mom."

I opened the door. Worry must have consumed my face. Gabe stepped toward me and took my arms in his hands.

"What's wrong?"

"Can I trust you?"

"You know you can."

"No. I mean really trust you to keep my secrets. I hate to ask you to be my confidant because it means jeopardizing your relationship with Kate; which is already tenuous."

"Julia. Kate was a dream- an awakening. You've become my family. My allegiance is to you. Your secrets are safe with me. I promise you that."

"Could you drive me to the hospital?"

"The hospital…? Why? What's the matter?"

"I've been bleeding. I'm not hurting at all, but I'm bleeding."

He turned off the bathroom light as he pulled me into the bedroom and toward the door.

"Of course. Let's go now. Mom can stay with Mattie."

"What will we tell her?"

"You can trust my mom, Julia. She's not too thrilled with Kate or Henry for that matter. We've adopted you. You're part of our family whether you want to be or not."

I smirked.

"Did you call the doctor?"

"He's expecting us. He told me not to worry. I hate when they say that…spoken like a man who has never had a baby growing inside him."

"Hey tiger, relax with the male bashing. Let's focus on getting you to the hospital quickly."

"Sirens?"

"You bet."

We made our way downstairs and told Ms. Martin what had happened. She hugged me tightly and reminded me not to borrow trouble. Who was she kidding? Trouble always found me. I tried to keep a positive outlook for the baby's sake and was comforted that I wasn't hurting and the bleeding had stopped. Somehow, I figured pain would come with a miscarriage. I would be starting my third trimester soon and anyway, I felt fine.

Gabe pulled up to the emergency department and insisted on getting a wheelchair that I dismissed as ridiculous. When he disappeared into the hospital, I simply got out of the vehicle and started walking on my own. I managed to clear the sliding doors before he rolled up with the chair. His look said it all. I think he'd grown accustom to my stubborn nature. He pointed to the chair and insisted that I comply with his request. I shot him my best-annoyed smile and conceded to his wishes. The nurse triaged me and took me back straight away. Gabe asked if I wanted him to remain in the waiting room, but I didn't want to go through everything alone so he willingly accompanied me.

We waited for Dr. Brandon who arrived shortly after us. He reiterated that I shouldn't panic and asked whether I wanted Gabe to stay for the ultrasound. I grabbed Gabe's hand and told him to proceed with the scan.

The baby's heart was strong. We smiled at each other as the thumping sound filled the room.

"Your baby girl looks strong," said Dr. Brandon.

"A girl," I said delighted, squeezing Gabe's hand tighter.

"Sorry. I forgot that you wanted it to be a surprise. It's the late hour," he offered apologetically.

"Why am I bleeding then?"

Dr. Brandon pushed the machine away as the nurse cleaned the gel off my abdomen. He looked serious. He looked like a killjoy- the deliverer of bad news. I wouldn't allow my fears to trespass on this happiness. My baby girl was alive and well.

"We need to talk about something. A complication has developed."

"What are you saying? You said she was strong. That's why my appointments have been less often."

"She is. I'm worried about you."

"What does that mean?" Gabe said as he sat on the bed next to me, putting his arm around my back.

"You've developed a complete placenta previa. Typically, we wait to diagnose a previa, hoping that the placenta will continue to migrate up towards the fundus of the uterus, with the progression of the pregnancy, but that hasn't happened in your case."

"English, please."

"Your placenta is completely covering the cervix."

"That's bad, then?" Gabe inquired.

"Having a vaginal delivery would be life threatening. You'll need a C-section."

"What did I do wrong?"

"Nothing, Julia. Your previous uterine surgery made you more susceptible to a situation like this. Your bleeding was the best possible thing that could have happened- it revealed the previa. If you went into labor on your own, the outcome would be poor. We know what we're up against now."

"What do I do?"

"The best case scenario would be to get you to thirty-eight weeks, but I'd be thrilled with thirty-six. We'll be doing more ultrasounds. I'm concerned about intrauterine growth retardation, which is just a fancy term for the baby's growth lagging behind. The tech will do a biophysical profile each time you come for a scan. As far as you're concerned, you'll be on strict bed rest for now. That means that you can do limited walking to the bathroom and around the house, but no more. I'd like you to limit the time that you're out of bed. As long as the baby is doing well, I won't order complete bed rest at the hospital."

"You might as well order complete bed rest, doc." Gabe knew me too well.

"Very funny," I shot back.

"I'm serious Julia. You have to do your part. Keep your stress level low. Take your blood pressure every day. As we get closer, I'll use steroids to help mature her lungs. You'll require a planned C-section and perhaps a transfusion."

"And? There's more. I can tell by your facial expressions that gloom and doom is on its way."

"And... I must also tell you that a hysterectomy is a distinct possibility, given the complexity of your current situation and past uterine surgery. I won't know until I open you up and see where we're at. I just want you to be prepared."

"Deliver my daughter in good health and I don't care Dr. Brandon."

"We'll cross that bridge when we get to it, but for now, strict bed rest. Do you understand?"

"Yes."

"Tonight was a saving grace. Go home and get to bed."

"A saving grace," I repeated. "I'm a lucky girl."

"Bed," Dr. Brandon reiterated.

"I will. Thank you for coming."

"No problem. I'll have my nurse call to schedule a follow up appointment. No driving, either."

"I'll get her there," Gabe firmly stated.

"Then I'll see you both in a week," he replied as he exited the room.

My head fell on Gabe's shoulder as he hugged me. A nurse interrupted us to take a final set of vital signs and give me my discharge papers. Gabe left to get the car as the nurse wheeled me to the emergency department entrance. I sat there thinking about what Dr. Brandon had said. Maybe this was a good thing. We were prepared now and could protect her. Bed rest was destined to get on my very last nerve, but I'd do anything to save her. I was never given that chance with Connor. This time, I had more control.

126

Gabe played the cheerleader during our trip back to the house, telling me that everything was going to be okay and reminding me how strong her heart was beating. I didn't share his enthusiastic attitude, but I was happy that this was a treatable condition. Gabe had called his mom to let her know that we were on our way home. She was waiting on the veranda as we drove up, opening the door as the car stopped.

"Let's get you inside and up to bed. I moved Mattie to another room in case you couldn't sleep and wanted to watch some television."

"That was sweet of you."

"I made some chicken soup."

"I'll bring it up," Gabe said as he walked toward the kitchen. "Help her get her pajamas on, Mom."

"I will. Take your time on the steps, Julia."

"You all are going to kill me with kindness."

"Don't be silly," she responded.

"No, really. You have to stop doting over me. We need to talk business."

We climbed the steps slowly; more so than necessary, but I was trying to placate the help. Gabe's mom had been a registered nurse her entire life and had only recently retired last year. She was still filling in some shifts at the hospital to supplement her income.

"What kind of business?" she asked.

"How would you feel about moving in here and taking care of me and then the baby until I'm back on my feet? I have to hire a nurse anyway so I'd rather hire you."

"It would be my pleasure to help you, Julia, you know that, but I couldn't accept money."

"Why ever not? That is the dumbest thing I've ever heard. If I'm going to pay someone anyway, why not you?"

"I'd feel uncomfortable being paid. I've grown to think of you as a daughter over these past months. You've done so much for Mattie. Taking care of you would be the least that I could do in return."

We made our way into the bedroom, closing the door behind us so that I could change. Ms. Martin helped me into a pair of guest worthy pajamas that would be suitable for Gabe's company. She tucked me into bed as our conversation continued.

"That's bunk. I take care of Mattie because I love him. Gabe has become a great friend to me and I look up to you. I won't shower you with money,

127

I promise. I'll pay the going hourly rate for a 40 hour week. No more. How does that sound? If you say no then I won't hire anyone and I'll be left to my own devices; which can only mean bad things for me with my stubbornness."

"Well, when you put it like that, I have no choice but to accept your proposal."

"Perfect. When can you start?"

Gabe walked through the door with a tray of food.

"Start what?" he asked.

"I've hired your mom to be my nursemaid or jailor depending on how you look at it."

"Good. I'll worry less," he said.

"The only condition, Ms. Martin, is that you not sit around this house all day watching me like I'm a guppy in a fishbowl. You have to leave and do things with Mattie. I'm sure that Tommy will be torturing me with his company very soon."

"Do you plan to tell anyone else?" Gabe inquired, with his mom elbowing him in his side to zip it.

"No. Do you all plan to tell anyone else?"

Two no's were spoken in chorus. My secret seemed safe. Now, I would have to rely on my brother's discretion. I was dreading the call that I knew I had to make. He'd never forgive me for keeping something like this from him and I wouldn't dare hurt him. Gabe and his mom left the room to get settled in, closing the door behind them. I decided to call Tommy since I couldn't sleep. Considering it was 3:45 AM, I knew he would be in bed, but I wanted to hear his voice. Tommy was always my rock.

"Hello?"

"Tommy?"

"Jewels? What's wrong?"

"Why does something have to be wrong?"

"It's 3:45 AM in the morning. What's the matter?"

"Don't freak out."

"Nothing good ever comes from those words when you speak them."

"It's not altogether horrible news. I had to go to the hospital this evening. I was bleeding."

"The baby?"

"She's fine."

"She?"

"Yes. Your niece is okay. I started bleeding, but it stopped."

"What caused the bleeding?"

"I have a complete placenta previa."

"A what?"

"My placenta grew over the cervix so the baby can't be born in the traditional way. I'm on strict bed rest now. The doctor will deliver her by cesarean section once she's at a viable age. We're shooting for thirty six weeks."

"Do you want me to hire some help for you?"

"No. Gabe's mom is a registered nurse. She's agreed to move in and help out until I get back on my feet."

"I'll be there tomorrow."

"That's not necessary. I'll be bed-ridden for several weeks. You have plenty of time to sit and stare at me."

"I'm coming."

"Whatever- just don't be dramatic. I'm going to be fine. You should wait a few weeks. Ms. Martin will probably need a break from me by then. You know that I don't make a good patient."

"Truer words have never been spoken."

"You're hilarious. Your talent is wasted on us sinners."

"So I'll come in two weeks?"

"How can you possibly get away at Christmas?"

"You let me worry about me. You have enough on your plate; what with having a child out of wedlock and complications to boot."

"Nice. You'll be getting coal for sure."

"All I want for the holidays is for you to abide by Dr. Brandon's orders. I'm scared, Julia."

"I'll be fine. Cover me with prayer. I'll do my part. You have my word."

"I'll hold you to it."

"Understood. Will you bring some things from my apartment?"

"Sure. What?"

"I had asked Henry to get rid of Connor's things, but I doubt he followed through on that. If the blankets and toys are left, will you bring them for Emma Grace?"

"Emma Grace?"

"It was good enough for Mom and Ms. Walker. She'll have their same strength."

"Mom would be thrilled. I love it, sis."

"I'm glad."

"Have you told Henry?" he timidly asked.

"No. I don't plan to tell him either. The doctor wants me to keep my stress level to a bare minimum. Arguing with Henry would be counterproductive. I will tell him...at some point. I'm not ready."

"What about John?"

"Father could care less, Tommy."

"Don't speak for him, Julia. He would want to know. Mom would want you to tell him."

"Oh, God in heaven, spare me the turn the other cheek sermon at this late hour. Maybe you're right. I'll think about it. Now, you should get back to sleep."

"You're really okay then. You've told me everything?"

"Yes. Don't be so paranoid."

"Don't be so you."

"I'll try. Love you."

"Love you too. Goodnight."

With that farewell, I decided to try some of the soup that had cooled off. No one could cook like Ms. Martin. As I finished, Gabe stopped by my room to tell me that he had called in for work. He was going to Tybee Island to pick up some of his mom's belongings for the duration of her stay. I thanked him profusely for his friendship and with that I collapsed and fell asleep.

15

⸺◦∞◦⸺

The morning had brought a bit more clarity regarding the battle ahead. In order to save Emma Grace, I would have to learn to love my bed. Christmas had snuck up on me and no preparations had been made. I hadn't ordered a tree or bought the first present. This year would be spectacular, sharing it with the Martin family. The thought of seeing Mattie open his gifts, with his new found emotions, made me excited. It was quite possible that this would turn out to be the best Christmas ever.

There was one task ahead of me that I was dreading. Gabe had the right to know that Kate and Henry stopped by last evening. The shock and awe on their faces only solidified my inclination that our body language had sent a deceptive message to our visitors. I could hardly blame them for rushing to judgment. If the tables had been turned, I would have been less forgiving, ranting and raving before leaving, though I would never admit that to anyone. Their silence cut through me like a knife. They weren't interested in discerning intent. They were sickened by what they saw and made haste to put as much distance between them and us as possible.

Mattie appeared in my doorway with Ms. Martin, helping to deliver blueberry pancakes. He was easily persuaded to stay and watch Saturday morning cartoons with me. Unless you rearranged his things, Mattie was the most peaceful person on the planet. His company had a calming effect. I could tell he was bored when he started rocking. Reaching into the night table drawer, I pulled out a satin bag full of treasures for him to play with. The bag was heavy, containing Tommy's old marble collection. He stared at the bag for ten minutes before placing it in front of me- a sign that I should open it and divulge its contents. When they spilled out on my bed, he became engrossed at examining their colors and sizes. He was thrilled which made my heart beat joyfully. As he methodically categorized his new collection, Gabe walked through the door.

"Here you are. Is he keeping you up?"

"No. I've been confined to bed for four hours and I'm already bored."

"Tough luck." He sat down next to Mattie, smiling at his own humor, and began fiddling with the marbles. "What's all this?"

"Tommy's old marble collection."

"Tommy may not want us to play with those, Mattie."

"I gave them to him. Tommy is a grown man who will be having no children. He'd be thrilled to know that someone was getting some use out of his old things. Really."

"Well let's see what you've got there, Mattie."

He separated all the blue marbles into a pile and spoke his new word for us again. I would never tire of hearing the word blue. It made me want to purchase every blue object I could get my hands on.

"We need to have a big person conversation," I said, hesitantly.

"That sounds ominous."

"Something happened last night."

"Yeah, I know. I was there."

"Not that. We had some visitors. Help me out onto the veranda so we don't disturb Mattie's cartoons."

"Is that a good idea?"

"The doctor said limited walking. The veranda is only ten feet. Give me a break."

"All right. Up you go."

Gabe pulled me forward from my reclined position against the mountain of pillows under me and helped me stand. The sun was breaking through the clouds in visible beams of light, but the air remained crisp. The comforter he brought out was tightly wrapped around me. I felt like a burrito. My feet were swept up onto a pillow which he'd placed on the coffee table.

"I'm warm enough. Relax. You promised not to smother."

"It's December, Julia."

"You're in the South, Gabe. I'm used to brutal New York winters. This is nothing."

"None the less…you're warm. I'm happy. What's up? Your talks are never good."

"Why do people keep saying that?"

"History, doll."

"Well, you may have a point. This isn't pleasant news."

"Spit it out. Be direct. I can take it."

He sat down next to me, tossing his feet up next to mine. I had qualms about telling him, but he had a right to chase down Kate and set the story straight if he so chose. He nodded his head as if egging me on to spill the beans.

"We had visitors last night."

"You said that already. Who?"

"Kate and Henry were here."

"In this house?"

"Yes."

"When?"

"I heard a noise and woke up to find your arm slung over my waist-"

"Yeah, sorry about that…"

"No matter, but when I looked toward the noise of the creaking door, Henry and Kate were standing there with an awful look on their faces, imagining that we were together, I suppose. I can't blame them really, considering our close proximity to one another and the fact that we were in my bed."

"Mattie was between us. What did they say?"

"It never came to that. I didn't have much time to consider stopping them. Kate ran off immediately and Henry only lingered for a minute at most. I was torn. I didn't want to startle Mattie."

"That's the real reason you didn't go after them?" he inquired with skepticism in his voice.

"Okay. No. The truth is that I didn't want Henry to know about the baby…not yet, but I realize now, that Kate must be thinking something dreadful about us…about me…and I think my decision has sealed your fate with her. I wouldn't be surprised if she were on her way back to London today. We're both runners."

"I see. Well, if she cared enough to fight for me, she would have stayed and made her stand. She left. Like you said, she doesn't care enough."

"Oh God. Did I say that?"

"Before, when you were explaining why she went to New York when her brother beckoned."

"I'm an idiot. That was a poor choice of words, Gabe. I saw the look in her eyes last night. She does care enough. The pain on her face was excruciating to witness. Don't form any opinions based on the observations of someone with my inept senses. Perhaps, you need to find her and have it out. Let your heart be the judge."

"I appreciate the back pedaling, Julia, but what would be the point? The bottom line is that she left. You don't do that if you love someone... you stay and fight."

"Not always. Some of us flee."

"Fleeing is for cowards."

"You won't get an argument on that point from me. Even still, you'll never have closure until you hash it out with Kate. You'll always wonder."

"Maybe. I'll think about it over Christmas."

"Do that...give it some dedicated thought."

"What's on tap for today?" he inquired, intentionally closing the subject of Kate.

"Are you trying to be mean? Rub it in, why don't you."

"What?"

"I guess I'll be holding down the bed today...and tomorrow...and the day after that..."

"Sorry."

"You are sorry."

"Have you thought about a Christmas tree? We'll be the only family having a Charlie Brown Christmas if we don't buy one soon."

"I was just thinking about that this morning."

"Mattie and I will go and pick one out," he offered.

"Mr. Burney, down at Burney's Nursery will deliver and set it up. I'll call ahead."

"I can afford to buy a tree, Julia."

"I know. I know, but Mr. Burney and I do business every year and we have a system. He relies on my financial patronage every season. He's probably waiting by the phone. He'll send a crew over to wrap garland on the veranda railings and they'll hang wreaths for me in the windows. You can buy a tree for the cottage if you're dying to spend your own money."

"Okay. Far be it for me to mess with tradition. We'll be back in an hour. Do we need tree trimmings?"

"Heavens no. I have enough in the attic for this tree and the one you buy for the cottage."

"Let's go. Get up. Back to bed," he insisted.

"Do I have a choice?"

"Not really. No."

Gabe pulled me up and held the back of the comforter off the ground as we processed inside. He was starting to feel like my lady in waiting and it was only the first day of prison. He needed a new occupation. He needed Kate.

"There's a wooden board in Tommy's room that has holes for separating and displaying the marbles. Would you get it? It's in his closet on the third shelf."

Mattie had all of the marbles in a particular order and I knew that I would disturb them with my moving in the bed. The board would keep them separated, orderly, and portable. Gabe returned and sat down next to Mattie. I carefully picked up one marble and put it in one section, waiting to see if he would become angry. Of his own volition, he picked up another and placed it in a different holder. We patiently waited for him to find a spot for every last marble. Gabe stood, holding the board and offered it to Mattie. He followed him out of my room and downstairs so they could leave for the nursery.

Time passed more slowly with my confinement. I spent the better part of the hour thinking about Kate. After calling Mr. Burney to make arrangements for our Christmas decorations, I finally decided to call her, in an effort to smooth things over for Gabe. She didn't answer her phone, which was no great surprise. She was a lot like me. We were the sort that required a cooling off period. If pressured, nuclear fallout would occur. The sweetness of her tone on voicemail certainly didn't match her current mood, after last evening. I plowed ahead, leaving a wandering message about what she thought she saw.

"Kate. It's me, Jewels. About last night...what you thought you saw, you didn't see. Mattie spends the nights with me when Gabe works late. That's all. They crash in Tommy's room. Last night, he must have sat down to watch television and ended up falling asleep next to us. There is nothing going on. If you would have stayed, you would have known that, but you left, jumping to conclusions...like always. Gabe's a brother to me, despite what your wild imagination has been dreaming up. You're too hasty...."

Beep. How dare that voice mail cut me off? Redial.

"I wasn't done. Furthermore, your secret is safe. Gabe has no idea that you are a big coward about Mattie's autism- a serious shortcoming on your part. Get over yourself. I mean, who gives a rip if people stare a little. You love attention. And by the way, I lied for you. That's the kind of friend I am. I put your future happiness first in the hopes that you would stop being a stuck up Brit and come back to Gabe. The fact that you would think that I would ever be involved with a man that you had even the least bit of feelings for, makes you a mean bitch. You don't deserve my friendship."

Beep. Redial.

"Your paranoia is making you miss out on one spectacular Christmas in Savannah with my new family, the Martins'. They could have been your new family if you weren't so damn ridiculous. Wish you were here. Hope you have a bloody good Christmas in New York with Henry and that twit Tricia. Yeah, I know about her. Be sure to send my best to your brother; me choosing me never felt so good."

Beep. Not again.

"Love you. Goodbye. And God save the Queen."

Click.

Wow that felt good. I hope it still felt good an hour from now when I had time to regret making the call. I waddled to the bathroom to take a shower before the boys returned. I knew that I would be banished to the couch to watch everyone else decorate the house.

A few more months had to pass before I would be able to hold my Emma. All of the excitement permeating through my mom's old house made me wish that she were around to take in my fat belly and guarded joy. She was a lover of the holidays. Mr. Burney had held a torch for my mom since they were in kindergarten. My grandfather was very particular about who she spent time with. He'd never let her openly associate with Ned Burney; the son of a farmer. An imprudent match would not be tolerated. The last Christmas I spent in Savannah, he regaled stories of my mom's kindness, generosity, and friendship. He told me that she once presented him with a check to expand his business when she heard that the banks had turned him down for a loan. She was inspiring. I longed to be more like her.

I made a bed on the couch in the drawing room, where we had always set up the tree. Just imagining the hustle and bustle created by watching my new friends trim the tree made me giggle with delight. No one could see the house from the road, but it always brought me great pleasure to drive up and see the Frasier Fir pouring light through the drawing room window. The front door opened.

"I'm in here Gabe," I called out.

"Julia?"

"Tommy?"

What was he doing here? My brother came around the corner and looked comforted to lay his eyes on me. Wearing his usual priestly frocks, he sat next to me studying my face. His own relaxed expression became pensive as he searched for words.

"I thought you were coming next week for Christmas?"

"I had to come early."

"Had to...what does that mean?"

Tommy started wringing his hands and looking back towards the door. He was obviously nervous. I grabbed his hand to try and calm him.

"Since Connor's funeral, Dad and I have been talking- a little bit."

"That's good...I guess. Has he been playing nice?" I moved closer to him, growing concerned about the internal battle that was betrayed by the expression on his face. He was purposefully hesitating and I was beginning to feel sorry for his anguish.

"He reached out, Julia, and I've been trying to meet him halfway."

"What's wrong, Tommy?"

"I've done something, albeit unintentional. You're going to be awfully mad at me."

"Why?" I leaned forward anticipating the worst, but hoping for the best.

"I told Dad about your bleeding scare and the bed rest. I let it slip that you called me at three in the morning and he became concerned. I swore him to secrecy. He won't tell anyone. He doesn't know the baby is Henry's. That bit of news I've left to you."

"Tommy," I chastised.

"I'm not done. That's not the worst of it, unfortunately."

"How could there be more?"

"He's here," he added with fear in his voice.

"Here, here?"

I felt the blood drain from my face.

"Here, here...in the car."

I winced. I wasn't ready for all of this. I certainly wasn't prepared for a Christmas with my father. I hadn't spent a holiday with him since I left for college over a decade ago.

"How is this going to fit in with keeping my stress level low?"

"He has promised not to be difficult. He's your father, Julia. He's concerned."

"Yeah, yeah."

"Bitterness doesn't become you."

"Call it what you will. I have a very long memory. I could refresh yours if you'd like."

"Look, he won't stay if you don't want him to. He just wants to see for himself that you're okay."

"Oh, you owe me...big time. Help me up."

As I uncovered myself, Tommy pulled me to my feet, exaggerating the effort it took to get me vertical.

"You're huge," he gasped.

"It's a good thing God predestined you to the priesthood because you'd never make it with women."

I gave him a well-deserved smack as I walked to the front door, trying to call to mind my mom's attributes; the kind Ned Burney pontificated about. Knowing I lacked her compassion and grace, I opted to shoot for civil. Ruining everyone else's Christmas with private family battles was unfair. I opened the front door and saw him sitting in the passenger side of the car. I turned back to Tommy and grimaced, belly aching in a low tone so he could hear my disgust and disapproval of his most serious screw up to date. Turning toward my father, I tried to appear congenial. When John saw me, he opened the door and cautiously swung his legs out. I moved forward to the edge of the veranda, trying to seem welcoming.

"Father."

He rose from the car and walked to me, slowly, as if expecting another onslaught of insults; the kind he endured leaving Connor's funeral. I suddenly became aware of how horrid I must look. Months had passed since my face was masked in make-up. My hair was still pulled up and I was in my pajamas. Similar attire had solicited a nasty response from him during his last trip here.

"You look good…nice and healthy."

He was carrying a bag that he held out as an olive branch.

"I brought you some pajamas, books, and movies to help pass the time on bed rest. I bought them myself. No one knows."

"Thank you. That was very thoughtful." I wanted to add that it was very unlike him, but I figured that was just the mean spirit of my hormones talking so I remained quiet. "How long can you stay?"

"For Christmas if I'm invited?"

"This is your home too. Should I move out of Mom's room for you?"

"No. No. Any room will do. It has been a long time since I slept in this house."

"Yes it has. Come in out of the cold."

As my father walked ahead of us, I gave Tommy that eat shit and die look; the one from our childhood that signaled to the other that they should sleep with one eye open. He snickered back in reply as if his evil plan was working

"Where is everyone?" Tommy inquired.

"They've gone to Mr. Burney's nursery to pick out a tree."

John seemed curious about my new friends.

"Who are the Martins'- these people you have taken under your wing? I've heard your brother and Henry talk about them."

"They rent the cottage. Gabe is the Sheriff and he has one son- four years old. John, Mattie has autism. He's different and amazing all at the same time. He's important to me. I hope you'll be nice to him- to them. They've become family to me."

"Of course I'll be nice. I'm glad you've found friends here. I'm apprecia- tive of the support they've given you in my absence."

-In his absence? My entire lifetime could cover his absence. Tommy interrupted my emotions that were on the verge of boiling over.

"Where is Ms. Martin?" Tommy asked.

"Ms. Martin? The sheriff is married?" John seemed confused.

"No. Ms. Martin is Gabe's mom. She is a registered nurse. I hired her to look after me and the baby once she's born."

As if heaven sent, the Martin family made their entrance, interrupting our contrived, heartfelt conversation. I must have had that disconcerting look on my face because Gabe flew into protective mode, unable to see Tommy sitting in the corner.

"We have a guest? Is there something I can help you with?"

"I'm Julia's father. And you are?"

"Ah, pleasure to meet you. Gabe Martin and this is Mattie. I didn't know you were coming for a visit. Hi, Tommy."

"Gabe. Thanks for looking after my sister so well. I owe you a large debt of gratitude; especially your mom."

"No trouble...except for the occasional mood swings and stubbornness."

"Watch it," I pointed at him.

Mattie walked over to me and held up his marbles.

"Look, Tommy. Your marbles have found a new home."

"I'm so grateful, Mattie. I have an entire closet full of good stuff for you. Why don't you and your dad come with me? We'll find some new treasures."

"Oh, you're about to surpass Jewels as his favorite person," he quipped.

"Not possible," I firmly stated.

"Mr. Spencer, would you be so kind as to help my mom with the groceries?"

"That would be no trouble. I would be happy to. Please call me John."

"Thank you. Let's go Mattie. Tommy has some toys for us to take apart."

I had a few minutes of silence to collect my thoughts. I had anticipated telling my father at some point, but not at Christmas, and not before I had prepared some grand speech to break the news. He didn't seem disappointed in me, which was surprising. He didn't comment on my appearance, which was shocking. He seemed different. I couldn't put my finger on the changes, but they were evident in his amiable words.

John entered the house loaded down with brown bags. I tried to take one from him but he wouldn't hear of it. He ordered me back to the couch and I was quickly reminded that he was still my father. His admonishment took me back to age six. Naturally, I complied. His tone was lighter and he bashfully smiled as he took directions from Ms. Martin. As they disappeared into the kitchen, another knock at the door brought me to my feet.

"Sit down," Tommy's voice ordered from behind me.

"Yes sir, Tommy sir," I sniped back irritated. Was this the army, or what?

"Better yet…go upstairs and rest. We'll call you when we're ready to do the tree."

Mr. Burney's crew had descended on the house. Within three hours, every interior staircase was wrapped with lighted garland and red and green ribbons. Electric candles were placed in every window and wreaths hung on the exterior. The verandas were magically illuminated with colorful lights; my gift to Mattie. I couldn't help but go against tradition this year. I was a white light girl, but Mattie lived in Technicolor. Smiles were painted on everyone's face- even my father's. Perhaps, this would be a Christmas to heal old wounds.

16

⊸⊷⊶

Calling ahead, I warned Dr. Brandon that the whole lot of us would be attending my appointment. The family had obviously convened a meeting on the need to be uplifting; a move to counteract my nervousness. My home had turned into a positive motivational convention. I half expected that Tony guy from the infomercials to waltz through the door at any moment. I knew there was no gentle way to ask them to let me go to my ultrasound scan alone. Tommy and John were aware that Gabe had accompanied me the last time. Ms. Martin was my nurse. If anyone needed to be there, it was her. Gabe was protective and already invested in the outcome, having been with me for every appointment thus far. Mattie was just a tag along, but perhaps would get a kick out of seeing Emma. There was no way to avoid the circus ahead.

We loaded into two cars. Mattie rode with Gabe and me. My dad had asked Ms. Martin to ride with them. I was starting to think that he was sweet on her, though that sentiment seemed so foreign to his genetic code. I had no memory of him with my mom. Not one time, over the past thirty years, had he presented a woman to us as his girlfriend. However, he was being too charming and attentive to Gabe's mom. I almost felt the need to warn her.

Our caravan made its way through the beautiful streets of historic Savannah. All of the old mansions were aglow with lights and decorations. I could just imagine what Mattie would say if he could comment on the world he was seeing. Finally arriving at the hospital, Gabe pulled up to the entrance and stopped. Tommy dropped off Ms. Martin and

John to keep me from walking in alone. My father left to get a wheelchair as we waited inside the sliding doors, out of the cold. Dr. Brandon was delivering two babies today. He asked that we meet him at the hospital for the ultrasound so he could see firsthand how the pregnancy was progressing.

After signing in, which felt like it took an eternity, and tried the patience of my father who never waited for anything, we were sent to an exam room in labor and delivery. With a complete previa, no exam was performed outside of the ultrasound, which meant that everyone could stay- lucky me. Dr. Brandon's eyes doubled in size as he entered and saw his audience. Gabe and Tommy were on one side and John and Ms. Martin on the other.

"You weren't kidding when you said everyone. Gabe, hello. Tommy, nice to see you again."

"You too, Doc. I have some more questions," my brother replied.

"I wouldn't expect anything less," he snickered.

"This is my father, John Spencer and Gabe's mom, Ms. Martin. She's a registered nurse. She's been looking after me."

"Great. Good to see you all. Ms. Martin, you've been doing a fine job and I'm sure it hasn't been easy, what with Julia's nature."

"Hey, I get enough abuse at home. Show me my Emma."

Smiling with reservations, Dr Brandon squirted gel on my belly and began taking pictures as if completing some mental checklist. I could really see her now. Her face was so fleshy and plump. She had Henry's chin and my nose. Since I had had so many ultrasounds, I'd become wise as to where to look to see measurement stats. Everything seemed to be appropriate for gestational age. The doctor pointed out the vital organs and commented that she had long legs- every girls dream; a Spencer trait. She was also blessed with my full lips. Emma Grace was a beauty. I looked over at my father and he was wiping a tear from his eye. In the dark room, no one was the wiser and I wouldn't give him up, but I was surprised to see him so touched. He had changed. Maybe he deserved the same chance with me that Tommy was affording him.

After all the oohs and ahhs, the nurse wiped my belly off and turned on the lights. You could have heard a pin drop if Mattie wasn't saying blue over and over again. Dr. Brandon quietly made notations in the chart before delivering his verdict.

"I'm cautiously optimistic that we'll make it to our target delivery date."

"In my world, that's not a win," my father replied stoically.

"We're planning for a difficult delivery, Mr. Spencer. In my world, preparation is winning."

John grabbed my hand. I gave his a gentle squeeze. He was out of his comfort zone.

"No bleeding, Julia?"

"No. I'm feeling good."

"I hate to say this with everyone present, but you need to slow down on the eating. Your weight gain is a bit much."

Gabe's smart-ass comment was expected. "I didn't know how to tell you, Julia. One more pound, you porker, and I'd be initiating an intervention."

He was given the necessary punch in the arm before I turned my sights on the good doctor.

"Well, what else am I supposed to do besides eat? I'm confined to bed."

"Whoa. Let me rephrase. Eat healthy."

"It's Christmas," I argued.

"After Christmas, eat healthy. Agreed?"

"Agreed. How is the placenta?"

"No bleeding and baby growth is a great sign, but I do have one additional concern. It appears that the placenta has grown into the uterine wall. Of the three types of this disorder, you have the least severe. It hasn't extended outside of the uterus or into the uterine muscle. We call this placenta accreta. Your previous surgery is probably to blame. The good news is that it doesn't alter our current course of treatment. You'll need to continue with bed rest. I see no need to keep you here in the hospital since you've been following my strict guidelines."

"What are the ramifications of it growing into the uterine wall?" I asked.

"This development makes a hysterectomy more likely. We'll be more concerned with managing your bleeding now. Hemorrhaging during the separation of the placenta from your uterus will be tricky."

"And if I just agree to a hysterectomy out of the gates?"

"A hysterectomy is the safest option with your history."

"Then do it."

"You should take some time to think about it."

"If trying to hang on to my uterus is going to put my life in jeopardy then there is nothing to think about. I want a long life with my baby girl. I'm blessed. There's no need for me to be greedy and tempt fate."

"I agree," my father chimed in.

"Me too," said Tommy.

"Your blood pressures have been good. You're obviously managing your stress well."

"So far."

"I'll see you in two weeks unless you have a problem. Call ahead. We may meet here again. Have a great Christmas."

"You too. See you in two weeks."

Gabe used our ride home to build me up about the new development. He also apologized for the crack about my weight. I responded by telling him that he couldn't take it back and that if he didn't hush it up, I'd eat him. Laughter elevated my mood.

We'd left the front gates open to allow for the delivery of packages. The porch was covered with brown boxes of various sizes. I went a little overboard with Mattie, but I couldn't help myself, with nothing to do but eat and shop online.

Two FedEx envelopes were tilted against the front door. One was from my lawyer and the other from Peru. I already knew what papers I had asked my lawyer to draw up so I skipped that envelope and opened the pouch from Chimbote. Asking Gabe to bring the boxes to my room, I carefully climbed upward and found rest in my bed.

Spilling out the contents from the Chimbote envelope made my heart heavy. Cards from all my families were strewn across the covers. As Gabe came and went leaving packages, I slowly read through each one of them, trying to recall my horrible grasp of the Spanish language. I saved Father John's and Sister Mary's letters for last. They were in English and contained several pages.

Father John's correspondence related good tidings for a happy Christmas. I had sent him a letter after I found out I was pregnant, requesting that the church pray for Emma's safe delivery. He thanked me for the money I sent to buy Christmas presents for the children. That priest was the best person I had ever met. No matter what the hour or type of problem, he was in the thick of it always; much to the detriment of his health. I admired him so much. He'd taught me a lot about myself during my short stay in Chimbote. He was the one man in my life that loved unconditionally. Tommy was a close second, but we were still brother and sister. I remembered the good old days of tattling and hair pulling. Father John quickly acknowledged the things he saw as flaws in his own personality and was just as forgiving of other peoples' shortcomings. He'd go out in the middle of the night to bring peace to a gang war, thinking nothing of his own safety. He was my hero. I wanted to be just like him when I grew up. I wish my own John was as good a man as my Peruvian Father John.

News of Hector Costelano was included in Father's letter. Hector was killed by the police in a stand off, when he went to Lima looking for his family. Surprisingly, I didn't feel happy. Justice had been handed down for Connor's death, but I had hoped for the opportunity to look him in the eyes and ask him why. I wanted the chance to see if he was remorseful. I wanted to be in a place to grant my forgiveness. None of that mattered now. I wasn't in that place yet. All I could do was continue to work on my ability to forgive him and hope that would serve to help me move on. My only joy came from knowing that the Costelano family could live without the constant fear of Hector's retribution. They no longer had to spend their days looking over their shoulders. For that, I was grateful.

Father closed his letter with a blessing for Emma and me. He accepted my invitation to bring the church choir to Savannah when they toured the States on a fundraising trip. I couldn't wait to accommodate all those fantastic kids in this oversized home. I was anxious to see my friends again.

Sister Mary described the preparations being made for the Christmas holy week. I wished that I could be there to hear the singing and sermons that always touched my soul so deeply. I always felt at home amongst the people at the mission. By home, I mean inside myself. I knew who I was there. The outside world didn't claim any pieces of me. My focus was on the people and my God. The influence of being back in the States always clouded my purpose. Mattie had become my Chimbote. He had become my spiritual compass. The good Lord must have known that I'd be right back to my old ways of selfishness and ego. Mattie was my angel. He kept me centered.

Sister went on to ask that I thank my father profusely for the large endowment he made in Connor's name. They were planning to use a portion of the funds to build handicapped accessible homes for the hundred or so men, women, and children that were wheelchair bound. Some money would be given to the hospice program and the educational funds to send the kids of the mission to college and university. I'd been trying to remain on an even keel, but tears gathered and flowed freely from my eyes as Tommy approached.

"What's the matter?" he inquired.

"Read."

I gave him the letter. He sat half way through reading. Gabe walked in and wondered what we were talking about. I asked him to close the door. I didn't want my father to hear us.

"I received two letters from the mission in Peru. Father John said the police killed the man that attacked me. The other was from Sister Mary who asked me to thank my father for the gift of money he sent in Connor's name."

"You're obviously on the good list this year. That's two big presents for Christmas."

"I didn't want him dead, Gabe."

"I know, but someone did. That was unexpected from your father, based on how you've described him."

"I'm starting to realize that I don't know my father at all."

"Then you may want to use this time wisely to reacquaint yourself. That's the last of the boxes."

Gabe gave me that look like I needed to take his words to heart, before leaving. Tommy folded the letters and handed them back, dumbfounded.

"That's a lot of information to take in."

"Did you know about the endowment?" I asked.

"No." Tommy shook his head trying to make sense of what he'd read.

"I'm speechless," I responded.

"That's a first."

"Sarcasm from a priest?"

"I'm still your pesky brother."

"Uh huh. What's on tap for this evening?"

"We are going to take Mattie to feed the birds on the beach."

"Ah. I miss doing that with him so much."

"March 22nd will be here before you know it."

"Hush your mouth. Dr. Brandon said that he'd be happy with thirty-six weeks- not forty. I'm shooting for February 22nd."

He shook his head and then kissed me on the forehead.

"Yes, may God have mercy on us all so that we can make it to February 22nd," he replied, palms together in prayer mode. "We'll be back in a half hour. Will you be okay?"

"Yes. Go. Throw some bread for me."

When Tommy left, I decided to make my way downstairs to enjoy the lights of the tree. I didn't expect to see my father sitting on the couch. He was casually sifting through the New York Times. There was a contemplative moment of me considering racing back up the stairs to avoid being in his company alone, but my feet inched forward before my mind could shut them down.

"Hi, John. I thought you were going with the gang down to the beach."

He folded the paper and dropped it on the coffee table in front of him.

"I'm a little tired. Are you feeling okay, Julia? Can I get you something?"

"No. I'm fine. I just wanted to enjoy the lights of the tree. The house seems so quiet when Mattie is gone."

I sat down with him on the couch, keeping enough distance to feel comfortable, but still close enough that he could see the banner of resentment that I was so vividly waving at him.

"He's a special little boy," he commented.

"Really?" I replied sarcastically.

"Is a kind word so surprising from me?"

"Yes... I'm sorry. That was mean spirited."

"Probably deserved."

"If you say so."

We both stared straight ahead, not knowing what to say next. Minutes passed before I broke through the tension, deciding to acknowledge the gift he made to the mission. It was either that or break into a rendition of *Silent Night*.

"John, I want to thank you for your donation to the mission in Connor's name. That was a really nice thing to do and it means a lot to me. Truly, it does."

"I didn't want you to know about that."

"Sister Mary was so thankful for the gift that she wanted to be sure that you received word of that sentiment."

"They must be very special for you to leave us for them."

There was the tone of disdain for my departure that I'd grown accustom to. If you gave him enough time, the real nature of my father always fought its way out. Immediately becoming defensive, I inched away from him toward the arm of the couch.

"It wasn't like that. I was trying to get away from Jackson. His affair wasn't his only shortcoming. He didn't want Connor."

"That man is an idiot. I've always thought that."

"You never said that. You supported the marriage- very vocally, as I recall."

"I was just happy that he wasn't Henry."

"That's funny because I was the happiest with Henry."

"He's not right for you. He's too much like me."

"He's nothing like you."

"Where is he then? Desertion is classic John Spencer, wouldn't you say?"

"He's in New York…with Tricia."

"Yes. I've met that one…a real ditz. She couldn't hold a candle to you."

Kindness wasn't his usual mode of operation. His behavior had become unpredictable and tricky. One minute he was stabbing me and the next he was stroking me. The many facets of my father were becoming tiresome. I cracked a smile, completely surprised.

"Thanks for that, considering I look like an orca whale."

"You look lovely, Julia. From the back, you can't even tell you're pregnant. I'd swear you were giving birth to a basketball."

"You never tell me I'm lovely. What's wrong with you? Are you unwell?"

"What does it matter? When a man gets to the end of his life, he has the capacity to understand just how much he's mucked it up. I'm sorry for being me- for being a lousy father. Your sweet mother must be so disappointed in my lack of effort. I failed her…and you. Be happy knowing that I spend my nights, alone in the dark, wishing that I could do it all over again."

"You pushed us away. You stopped loving us. We were kids, John. We thought we had done something wrong. Hell, Tommy grew up thinking that he killed his own mom. You never told him that he wasn't responsible. You allowed that way of thinking to become his reality. That's a lot for a young boy to handle."

"I was a monster. I know that now. I couldn't see it then, but I am painfully aware of it now. I wish that God would have taken me and left your mother."

My response flew through my lips before I could think of something more congenial to say.

"I used to wish that all the time."

"Wow," he said sadly as he sat back, a little stunned.

"I hear myself and I know I sound harsh and bitter, but you're trying to force this sense of familiarity between us that just doesn't exist. You've been an absentee father my entire life. I don't know you."

"I understand," he replied weakly.

"Don't do that. Don't play the role of the victim- it's so not you. Be the ruthless man you've always been. That man I can understand. I've worn your criticisms throughout the years as though they were my second skin. They're a part of me…every mean comment and disapproving glare. Those emotional beatings gave me my strength. So, don't you come here and act like the cruelty served no purpose. Don't come here and say that you did it for kicks. Have a reason for not loving us. Have a reason for scarring up our hearts. I think we at least deserve that after all these years."

"I didn't come here to upset you, Julia. I came here out of concern."

"Concern for whom?"

"For me. I'm dying. How selfish is that; when you're fighting to save your child? I'm here for me- not you."

"You always up the ante," I spewed out disbelieving.

"No. I'm really dying- pancreatic cancer. That should cheer you up. Christmas has come early this year, child."

"Cancer? I'm sorry. You're my father. My mother loved you. I am sorry. I don't know what to say." The clock chimed and we listened in silence. "Does Tommy know?"

"No. I'd like the opportunity to tell him myself, if you don't mind."

"Of course."

We sat quietly. I was ashamed of my ranting. Everything I said reflected how I truly felt, but John came here to make amends. I was too angry to hear him when he told me that he understood. One thing was for certain; regardless of who was right or wrong- it wasn't going to change a damn thing. My crappy childhood would forever be recorded in the history books as crappy and John was destined to die. Coming to terms with both was now a necessity. Time was of the essence.

"What are your plans?"

"I'm sneaking off to have the Whipple procedure performed at Emory University next week. I'll ask Tommy to go with me. Your prayers would certainly be appreciated."

"They're yours. What about work? Who knows?"

"No one. Effective next week, I am resigning from my position on the board. My shares will be transferred to Emma Grace. As her guardian, you'll vote her proxy until she comes of age. Tommy doesn't want the money and you've barely withdrawn any of your trust fund. I've also established a charitable trust account in Connor's name. You can allocate the funds as you see fit."

"How long?"

"Their best guess is six months...perhaps longer with this procedure. I would like to see my grandchild born."

I began to cry.

"I'd like that too."

"Don't cry Julia. Don't shed tears for your sorry old father."

"But you're my sorry old father."

"My greatest regret in life is that I didn't tell you kids that I loved you."

"It's not too late. You can start now."

John looked me in the eyes and pulled me to him. This would be the second time that he had embraced me during the span of my life, with the first being at Connor's funeral. The gesture was so foreign to me, but I couldn't remember needing that closeness as much as I did now.

"I love you Julia. You are an amazing woman and a top notch lawyer. I should have offered you the job I thrust upon Henry. We could have worked side by side together, all these years. I was wrong about so many things. More than that, you are your mother's daughter. You have the same strength, poise, and love in your heart that Georgia did. You feel things so intensely. I see so much of her in you. That's why I kept you at an arm's length. I couldn't bear to be around you and not have her. She was in your eyes...your smile...the way you tilt your head to the side when you want something. I was mad at her for dying. I wanted Tommy to die and her to live. Who thinks that about their own child?"

"I wanted you to die and Mom to live. Who thinks that about their own parent? Grief is a terrible poison."

I separated our embrace to make a request. He looked pained and worried about the future. We were both in the fight of our lives. We finally had something in common.

"Will you come here after your surgery to recuperate?"

"I don't want to burden you."

"We have a lot of time to make up for. It's the least you can do for your children."

"I'll think about it."

As I shook my head in agreement, the crew returned from their walk on the beach. Both Gabe and Tommy had a look of concern on their faces, probably assuming that John had been disagreeable. Little did they know that I was the bully this time around.

17

Tommy didn't take the news of John's illness very well. I woke to find him sitting across the room in my recliner. His face was solemn and distant. Though further along than me in mending fences with our father, he had born the brunt of his hostility over the years, never fully understanding why he was so unlovable. A sibling can't fill the void that a parent leaves behind. I did the best I could.

"You're up early," I commented, interrupting his thoughts.

"Can you believe it? After all these years, we only have six months with him?"

"Maybe more."

"Unlikely."

"You've never been the pessimist Tommy; don't start now."

"I'm being a realist, Julia."

"That's my role. You're the pie in the sky, everything's coming up roses, and God has a purpose type. Step off my territory."

Holding out my hand, I motioned for Tommy to come over. He lay down next to me, holding my hand as we always had as children, when we'd lie on our backs, staring up at the night sky. Gabe knocked on the door and slowly opened it to see if I was awake. We had made plans the night before to get cracking on wrapping the presents, with Christmas only one day away.

"Who forgot to tell me about the meeting?" he joked as he entered.

"Come here. Lay down. We have some news."

"That's never good," he chuckled nervously, wondering what predicament I'd gotten myself into.

"This isn't good," I answered.

He walked to the empty space in the bed, next to me, and threw himself against the pillows. I held my free hand out to him, which he immediately grabbed, interlocking his fingers in mine.

"Whatever it is, we'll fix it."

"You can't fix this," Tommy replied.

"Let's have it then."

Tommy didn't respond. The news was too recently given for him to be emotionally able to speak it out loud. I had more time to adjust and cleared my throat to announce what my brother wasn't able to.

"My father is dying. He has pancreatic cancer. He came here to have his last Christmas and make amends with Tommy and me. He's having surgery next week. The doctors give him six months to a year. I've asked him to move in after the procedure."

Sorry is the only word that Gabe could produce. The three of us lay there silently, watching my old comforting friend, the fan, turn circles above our heads. Mattie burst through the door and nestled his way between Gabe and me. Within minutes, John walked by, giving the four of us a very odd look, as we filled the entire bed. No one knew what to say. Finally, Gabe broke the silence.

"Those gifts aren't going to wrap themselves."

"I know. I know. Mattie, Tommy and Grandma are going to take you for some ice cream, okay?"

Mattie bolted from the room and Tommy quickly followed after him.

"You open the packages Gabe and I'll wrap."

"Deal."

He pulled my lard self up into a seated position and began tearing through the packing tape, box by box, placing each item on the bed in a neat assembly line formation. He enjoyed looking through the presents I had bought online, making little comments after opening each one and guessing who they were for. He probably wondered if a few of the gifts I'd purchased for Tommy were actually his. They weren't. Gabe's gift was in the FedEx pouch from the lawyer. I left it on the kitchen table with hopes of giving it to him this evening. He had no idea what was in store for him.

The morning and afternoon passed with only a short break to eat lunch. Cold pizza was on the menu, which seemed to awaken the alien within. Emma Grace was moving across my belly as if she were trying to claw her way out. Gabe loved to watch her hands climbing from one side to the other. She was becoming as impatient as me. We both wanted her out.

Tommy and Ms. Martin entertained Mattie for most of the day. After returning from their errands, they headed over to the cottage to allow Mattie to reacquaint himself with some of his most loved toys. They'd been spending so much time at the main house that the cottage had been all but deserted. My father was napping since the house was quiet, except for the soft lull of carols that piped through the intercom system. I'd talked Gabe into running into town to buy some candy canes for the tree. The edible factor was missing from the tall Frasier Fir. I had fond memories of Tommy and me swiping candy canes as we passed through the drawing room, back in the day. Nana never seemed to mind.

Gabe had moved all the presents under the tree. They filled the far corner of the room, leaving only a small path for Mattie to get up close and personal with his favorite ornaments. I made my way through the drawing room and into the kitchen to get busy accomplishing my other task for the day.

Much to the family's dismay, I had decided to try my hand at my mom's homemade apple pie recipe. After the expected arguments regarding my being out of bed, they agreed to allow me to sit at the table with my feet elevated while peeling and coring the apples. Gabe's mom premeasured the wet and dry ingredients for me and Tommy moved the kitchen table underneath the island before heading to the cottage. Every last detail of my cooking had been well planned out, except one. The apple corer was nowhere to be found.

Searching the bottom cabinets of the kitchen yielded no results. Knowing it had to be somewhere, I decided to look through the upper cabinets instead of waiting for help. No one was home except John and he was sleeping. The coast was clear. Time was not on my side, though; Gabe was expected home soon. The market was fifteen minutes away and he had already been gone just shy of an hour.

Pulling the utility ladder to the counter, I carefully climbed upward to the first cabinet. Rifling through the junk didn't turn up the tools I needed. I started to try and reach over to the second one, but good sense invaded my decision making process and made me think better of reaching for things at that height. I decided instead, to get down and move the ladder over to the next cabinet. After dragging it across the floor, I climbed up again and started with the bottom shelf, hoping that my previous lack of organization wouldn't hinder a good outcome. No corer. I reached blindly into the higher shelf. I felt the corner of what I thought was the peeler, but I couldn't grip it well enough to pull it forward. I stepped on to the countertop, allowing a better view, when I heard the kitchen door open. The noise startled me. Realizing I was caught, I hugged the open shelves trying to balance my weight.

"Thank God, Gabe. Am I glad to see you? Don't be mad. I couldn't find the apple peeler."

"Hi Jewels," said the unmistakable voice with the British accent.

Clearly, I couldn't speak. The orca whale was beached on top of the kitchen counter, trying not to fall from the shock and horror of what was about to take place. With the options of fight or flight, I only had one alternative. Maybe I could piss him off enough that he'd just leave.

"Hello pot," I delivered in my best bitchy tone, unable to turn around and show him the glare in my eyes.

"Hello kettle," he replied.

"Why are you here?" I asked in a more monotone voice.

"Merry Christmas to you too," he said.

"Did you sleep with her?"

"Her who?" he responded, acting dumbfounded.

"Her who? Were there more? Her who. Don't be coy. Tricia. I mean Tricia."

"What?"

"Did you sleep with Tricia? Is there something in the question you don't understand? I think I'm being fairly clear."

My feet were getting tired and my belly was hurting from pushing against the bottom shelf. Emma Grace was obviously getting aggravated with my body's positioning as demonstrated by her quick movements.

"Yes." His words were subdued. I could tell that he felt ashamed or at least caught.

"Yes what?" I inquired.

"Yes, I slept with Tricia," he said exasperated.

I didn't have a cunning bit of nasty words to toss back. I already knew the answer to the question I had asked. All the same, hearing the love of my life tell me that he shared a sacred piece of himself with a hussy like Tricia still cut me deeply. Men always say that they can separate sex from emotions and maybe that's true, but for women, we're typically all in. He might have sexed up Tricia to get back at me, but she was almost certainly attached to him now on an emotional level. Things were no longer neat and tidy, despite his resolve to be a player.

I had still not laid eyes on Henry. As much as I wanted to have this conversation face to face, to up the accountability factor, I was afraid to move. For all intensive purpose, I was arguing with a cabinet. The sound of the door opening again was followed by the voice of an angry friend.

"What the hell are you doing up there, Julia?" Gabe said disapprovingly.

"Relax, Gabe. She's looking for something," Henry interceded, with a twinge of jealousy in his tone.

"You relax. She is supposed to be on bed rest. Get down this instant," he ordered.

"Bed rest?" said a confused Henry.

By the time Henry echoed his words, Gabe was at my side, slowly helping my foot find the next rung down on the ladder. When my feet finally hit the kitchen floor, Gabe released his hold on me.

"You need to get upstairs now. What were you thinking? You should have waited for me or John."

"John? What's he doing here? I thought he was in Europe," he asked.

"My father is spending the Christmas holidays with us."

There was no reason to delay any longer. There was no escape route that would spare me the inevitable action of turning and revealing my pregnancy. Just like I had decided months ago, I'd get it over quick and dirty.

"Could you leave us, Gabe?" I pleaded.

"Are you sure?" he replied.

"She's sure," said Henry intensely.

He gave my arm a light squeeze, gave Henry the evil eye, and walked into the drawing room. I slowly turned around and sat back against the ladder. The long black dress I was wearing hugged my protruding belly. The look on Henry's face created a snapshot in my mind that would forever be engrained there. His eyebrows pulled together in the center and he scowled at me as I waited for his reaction. He said nothing, but I could see his mind racing a mile a minute.

"Let me save you the mental math, ace. The baby is yours. She was conceived at the boathouse. Remember me...the end of June?"

"Baby? Why didn't you...?"

"Call you? I tried. Tricia answered the phone," I said curtly.

"Tricia means nothing."

"How sad for her," I thought out loud.

"It's not like that...she practically forced herself on me," he said in his defense.

"Well, bless your heart. That must have been terrible for you. Poor Henry."

We stood in a face off, both of us unsure of how to proceed. Henry stepped toward me, but his movement was halted by John's entrance. I would have to thank Gabe later for tattle telling on Henry. No one man could intimidate Tru like my father. John walked over to my side and pointed in the direction of the staircase.

"Julia, go upstairs. You've exhausted your time limit out of bed today. The pie can wait until this evening. No arguments. Go."

Even though I was a grown Southern woman, more stubborn than most men, I was never so glad to be sent to my room. Climbing the stairs felt like emancipation from despair and humiliation. I did wish that I could be a fly on the wall to hear my father sock it to Henry. Getting me pregnant was criminal enough, but Tricia was the icing on the cake. Henry Truman Walker...rest in peace.

When I reached my room, Gabe was lying horizontally across the end of the bed watching the news. I sat back against the pillows, assuming my usual position while he rolled back to address Henry's arrival.

"You can't seriously be considering taking that snake back. He'll want the baby- not you. Isn't Tricia proof of that?"

"Ouch."

"Well, I don't want to see you wasting your life on someone that doesn't cherish you. You're a package deal- you and Emma Grace."

"We're not...a package deal. He can be a father without being a lover, Gabe. Trying to fake an apathetic attitude and happiness without him will tear me up for awhile, but it will get easier. Hearts mend."

"No they don't. They just scar. You better get your game face on. The longing is clearly evident in your eyes. You aren't the master of deception."

"You're worried about me? You better get your game face on. I'd expect the sassy Brit to join her brother by this evening. She'll hop a plane once she hears the baby news."

"You think she'll…"

"Absolutely. I'd say you have five hours at the most to lose the longing in your own eyes. Good luck with that."

"Yeah?"

Gabe shook his head like his mind was traveling in a million different directions. When I was about to give him a pep talk, his pager went off. After a quick call to the station, he was out the door and on his way to answer a domestic disturbance call on the other side of town. His parting words to me were to get some sleep. He would be back for dinner.

He'd thrown the covers over me as he left, but Emma Grace was an internal heater. I was hotter than a Southern bride in the summer. Tossing them to the side, I tried to quiet my mind and erase the events of the day. Every time I shut my eyes, I saw Henry. I finally envisioned a blank piece of white paper in hopes that thinking about nothing would make me forget everything.

The butterflies in my stomach took flight as I heard the bedroom door open. John had obviously not finished him off. I closed my eyes, pretending to be asleep, hoping that my acting abilities would fool him from trying to engage me in conversation. The mattress rippled with movement. I sensed someone moving toward me. An arm flew across my body and little fingers touched my face.

"Blue. Jewels. Jewels. Sleep. Sleep. Jewels sleep. Mattie sleep."

My heart soared and my stomach calmed.

"Hi Little Man," I said, rolling over to see his sweet smile. His hands were sandy. I could feel the grit rub my face as he touched my cheeks.

"Sleep. Sleep," he said as he touched my eyelids.

"Yes. I will. Jewels and Mattie sleep."

He pulled seashells from his pocket and dropped them between us. His head gently rested back on the pillows as he examined his new treasures. My lids grew heavy watching him sort them into distinct piles. I struggled against sleep. Mattie began to slow down and relax. Before drifting off myself, I saw his eyes finally succumb and close.

18

Gabe woke us for dinner. Mattie instantly became full on ready for play. He gathered his shells, jammed them into his pockets, and darted from the room.

"Any sign of Kate?" I inquired.

"Not yet," he responded with a great deal of apprehension.

"Henry gone?"

"Good luck with that," he replied, ever the smart ass.

"Kate hasn't come and Henry won't leave. What ever will we do?"

"You missed the fireworks. He and your dad had it out. He quit."

"Who quit?" I asked, astonished at the prospect.

"John ordered him back to New York so Henry resigned his position with Spencer Industries."

"Seriously?"

"Yeah. I'm no fan of Henry Walker, but that's pretty gutsy. He said that he would only leave if you asked him to go."

"Goodnight then. Have a great meal. Lock the door on your way out."

"Nice try. You can't hide out here forever. He's not going anywhere. If you want him gone, just tell him so. You won't hear any complaints from me."

"Where is he?"

"Tommy is taking pity on him. They're watching football."

"I'm starving," I said, hearing the rumbling coming from my stomach.

"I swear...you can eat through any emotion."

"True. That smells delicious, though. What's Momma Martin making?"

"Your favorites- fried chicken, mashed potatoes, green beans, and homemade buttermilk biscuits."

"And desert."

"Fruit," he cautioned, knowing I'd be disappointed.

"Because I'm fat?" I asked solemnly.

"Because you're fat."

"Okay, fair enough."

We made our way downstairs. Henry came into view as my foot hit the bottom step. He was in the drawing room, alone, reading John's newspaper on the couch. I walked by him, without acknowledging his presence and proceeded into the kitchen. John looked happy helping Ms. Martin fry the chicken in the cast iron skillet. Sounds of oil popping gave cause to locate Mattie. Tommy had him in the television room watching the History Channel. The program was on the space shuttle and it seemed to capture his attention. Asking if I could help was immediately dismissed. With the last batch of chicken draining on the brown paper bags and the biscuits removed from the oven, we were all called to come into the kitchen for a casual meal.

Gabe and I were already seated when the others made their way to the table. I quickly solicited Mattie to sit by me, which meant that Tommy and Henry would have to be paired across from us. John sat next to Mattie at the head of the table and Gabe's mom mirrored him on the other end. Ms. Martin called after Henry who entered sheepishly, looking around to determine his seating options. With only two options left, he practically pushed past Tommy to take the empty chair near Ms. Martin. Sitting next to my father would have been far too risky with their earlier squabble.

Ms. Martin took the lead in ascertaining food preferences and filling plates. Gabe and I had already piled on our food while we had to wait for Henry to grace us with his presence. She prepared Mattie's first, asking me to cut the chicken off the bone for him. I made steady progress cutting the meat into little pieces as she turned her attention to Henry.

"What piece of chicken do you prefer, Henry?" she asked.

Before he could answer, I opened my mouth, causing Tommy's tea to practically come out of his nose. He just about aspirated the drink into his lungs.

"He's a breast man, Ms. Martin," I interjected.

Henry wasn't amused. He shot me that belittling look of great disappointment that I sent back with, a bit of a cracked smile attached, proud to have gotten under his skin.

"Don't be cheeky, Jewels. I'll take the wings, please, Ms. Martin. Thank you," he answered politely.

"Some green beans?" she asked.

"Please," he replied.

"How about some mashed potatoes? They're a little looser than usual, but…"

"The looser the better for him, Ms. Martin," I spouted, unable to stifle my angst.

Before I knew it, my plate was being lifted above my head. Gabe was taking it out to the brick porch, knowing I'd follow the food. The fork I was holding was still full of mashed potatoes.

"We're going to eat outside," he said with a smile, trying not to laugh.

"I'll join you," John dryly added, lifting his plate and utensils to follow us.

"It's December. It's cold out there," Tommy cautioned.

"I'll turn on the patio heater. She'll be warm enough. Enjoy your meal," Gabe replied.

Even my father got a good laugh out of my commentary. I was on fire, for the time being. I knew Tommy would reprimand my behavior later as being unchristian like, but I planned on getting as much mileage out of humiliating Henry as possible. I wondered how he liked it- feeling vulnerable and wounded. The shoe was finally on the other foot.

Retreating to the drawing room after the meal, I laid back on the couch, closing my eyes as I enjoyed the songs of Christmas. Just as I was zoning out, he approached.

"We need to talk," Henry demanded.

"About?"

"About this entire situation."

"Why don't you open your Christmas gift first? We always used to open one on Christmas Eve," I said. "Remember?"

I leaned forward and took the FedEx pouch I'd brought downstairs for opening in the morning. The pouch contained one envelope. I'd left Gabe's envelope upstairs on my bedside table, assuming he'd join Tommy and me in watching our traditional Christmas movie. I pulled it out and handed it to Henry.

"What's this?" he asked, confused.

"It's your Christmas present- open it," I demanded as I pushed the envelope into his chest. I sat back against the pillows on the couch and put my feet up on the coffee table as he read its contents.

"You're giving me the deed to the cottage and its five surrounding acres, along with a cashier's check for $500,000? I don't understand."

"Oops, wrong envelope. That's for Gabe. They must have gotten switched. Your envelope must be up in my room."

"That property is waterfront Jewels. It's worth millions. What if he sells it and you have someone living on top of you that you don't like? You just can't give away expensive assets like that. It's irresponsible. You could easily get five million for that land."

"It all comes back to money for you, doesn't it?" I noted, waiting for an answer that would support his position.

"People don't throw away their assets like this. You've only known Gabe for a little under a year and you're essentially writing him a check for five million dollars. That's crazy. And the money..."

"It's crazy to someone like you who is chasing his tail trying to turn a penny into a quarter. Gabe cares about people. He has no use for my money. That's why it's a pleasure to give it to him because he doesn't want it. He doesn't expect it. He's just happy punching a clock and making an honest living. He's happy with his life, making a modest salary. He accepts his position with joy, placing importance on people rather than power."

"So, he's everything I'm not?"

"He was there for me while you were banging Tricia. When I was bleeding and thought that Emma Grace was lost to me, Gabe was my strength. He and his mom have waited on me hand and foot. They've become my family. Mattie is essentially my nephew. I love them. They love me. They'll still be standing at my side once you're long gone. Hard working, good-natured, Southern folk don't desert a friend in need. Giving them the cottage and land means that he doesn't have to worry about providing a place for Mattie to grow up. It means that he can put his money into treatments and specialists for his son instead of rent or a mortgage. Your envelope is upstairs. I'll give it to you in the morning. I'm tired. I'm going to bed."

"Well I can hardly wait to see mine, big spender. What did you get for me?" he quipped, trying to bait me.

"Oh I think you'll be pleased," I replied. "It's what you've always wanted."

Ms. Martin sent me packing to bed with a goblet full of fruit. Gabe was good enough to sneak some whipped cream and chocolate sauce up to me. He brought Mattie by my room to say goodnight. They usually stayed in the main house, but the addition of Henry as a visitor got under Gabe's skin. He also didn't want to stumble upon Kate without warning. The cottage provided a safe haven. He knew that I would call with any news, allowing him time to collect his thoughts.

Mattie and I talked about Santa coming in the morning. He didn't seem to understand, but I knew he would go nuts over the gifts; especially the telescope I had installed down at the beach. I gave him a big squeeze before he broke free and ran out of the room. Gabe slid closer to me.

"Are you sure that you can't stay and watch the Griswold's' with us- it's tradition?" I begged.

"I better get him home. Santa will not come if you're awake, you know?"

"Speaking of Santa, he left something here for you."

I reached inside the FedEx pouch and pulled out the envelope, which Henry had mistakenly opened. Handing it to Gabe, I decided to pre-sell the reasons why I was giving him the gift so I didn't have to stomach him declining the present.

"Before you say anything, I want you to know how special you and Mattie have become to me. You're precious jewels; family, just like Tommy. I want you to have a place to call home, without struggling to make ends meet. Mattie's medical expenses are huge. I've spoken to an architect about building a proper home for you boys- one with an environment that will help stimulate Mattie. He said that they can build your home and a guest house for your mom for the $500,000. You can pick out the plan that suits you best. The current cottage needs to be bulldozed along with the memories it holds. It's time to start fresh. Please say you'll accept it. It'll destroy me if you don't."

"I don't know what to say, Julia. No one has ever given me a gift like this. It's too much."

"Say yes. You're not even scratching the surface of my trust fund. The land is an asset. I have plenty more acres left. Please say yes. It will ensure that the next generation stays together. Emma Grace and Mattie are destined to be the best of friends- just like us."

Gabe looked shocked. He was smiling, but speechless. After a few minutes of staring at the documents, he shook his head in agreement.

"One more thing…" I added.

"No more, Julia. You're going to send me into cardiac arrest. This kind of stuff just doesn't happen to commoners," he said laughing in disbelief.

"Commoners? You're a comedian. It's for Mattie- not you."

I opened the nightstand table and removed some papers that I had drawn up myself. Being a lawyer and having passed the Georgia Bar had come in handy for times like this.

"You've done enough for him," he said.

"This is a trust account for Mattie. I don't want you to worry about his future and any surmounting medical expenses. Since I've been stuck in bed so much, I have read about some good therapies that might help him. Traveling and treatments take money. You'll have to pay doctor's fees, hotels, airfare, food, rental cars…You can't do it on a cop's salary. Mattie deserves every opportunity. Now you can search them out and decide for yourself. Now you have the money to find your miracle. He's starting to communicate. This is forward progress. I believe with all my heart that he'll keep the momentum going with the correct therapy."

Gabe's eyes welled up with tears. One single droplet escaped before he could man up and wipe them away. He pulled me to him and held me, thanking me profusely for the gift of hope; the kind money can't buy. We both knew that Mattie was perfect exactly as he was, but knowing he wanted to communicate had changed the game.

"I have to go before a Victoria's Secret model comes out of your bathroom wearing a red bow," he sniped.

"No worries with that. I hate those skinny bitches right now," I replied as I dug into my fruit.

He stood up and headed for the door laughing.

"Hey, what did you get Mattie for Christmas," I inquired.

"Just a dog," he said smiling.

"That trumps my trinkets. Thanks a lot."

"I know. Nothing beats a puppy; except maybe waterfront property, a house, and a trust account. See you in the morning my dear, crazy friend."

Gabe and Mattie leaving made the house seem eerily still and quiet. I went to collect Tommy from his room for our annual *"National Lampoon's Christmas Vacation"* movie, but he was fast asleep. I didn't have the heart to wake him. Life was changing for me at an alarming rate. Traditions were falling by the wayside and new traditions were being made. I was learning to be okay with that.

John stopped by to say goodnight before he retired for the evening. He was looking more tired than usual. We exchanged pleasantries and well wishes for a restful sleep. He hugged me again, and although it still felt awkward, I was getting addicted to his newfound desire to express himself through actions. Somehow, I knew my mom was pleased with both of us.

The addition of Henry to our family Christmas gathering had taken a lot out of me. My invisible wounds were starting to weep; the sadness was spilling out. With my father and brother asleep, I decided to follow their lead and rest before the excitement of Christmas morning captured my diminishing energy. After washing my face and changing into pajamas, I entered the bedroom. His reflection in the dresser mirror startled me. Henry was sitting in the recliner, staring.

"You scared me," I gasped alarmed and perturbed. "Don't you knock?"

"I didn't know where to sleep," he replied softly, realizing that the others were asleep.

"Not here. This house is full of couches- pick one. I'll give you some linens and a pillow."

Henry looked sullen and depressed. It wasn't a look he wore well. He had always been the poster child for control and self-assuredness, but no longer. His eyes were sad. He put his head down into his hands for a brief minute, before collecting himself to face me. He was lost.

"Sorry...about whatever I did to make you so angry- even to the point of keeping the news of our daughter from me. You're mad about Tricia. I get it, somewhat, but you asked me to leave, Jewels, or did you forget that? You didn't want to work it out. You sent me back to New York to live without you. I simply tried to do what you asked. Listen, I don't expect pity from you, but in the course of a day, I've discovered that I'm going to be a father, I've lost my job, something is wrong with our baby, and it's clear that you want nothing more to do with me. I need a bit of time to get my bearings- not pity, just time. So, do you think it's possible for you to withhold your insults and fury for one evening?"

When I go in for the kill, I typically forget to stop and assess the damage. I just plow forward until total and utter defeat is achieved. My aching heart had demanded his ruin, but the man before me was already a wreck. He was injured. I finally allowed myself to see that. Sitting down on the bed, I mustered up the empathy that the situation called for, answering his concerns point by point.

"I was wrong not to call you about our baby. There are other jobs out there for someone as talented and savvy as you. I'll explain the pregnancy complications in detail so you understand what we're facing. I don't know what to say about us."

He could tell that I was sending up the white flag of surrender. The baby's life demanded that a truce exist between us, and hope, though suppressed, remained a part of my being. His response was to rise from the recliner and sit down next to me on the bed.

"How is our daughter? Why are you on bed rest? No one around here will give me a straight answer."

"They're just protecting my privacy. Everyone has been sworn to secrecy."

"A job well done, I'd say."

"I started bleeding during the second trimester. Dr. Brandon diagnosed me with having a complete placenta previa..."

"A what-?" he interrupted.

"Let me finish and then I'll answer your questions as best I can. That means that the placenta has grown over the cervical opening- the birth canal. The baby's delivery has to be planned. Having her try to be born vaginally would be disastrous. She'll need to be delivered through cesarean section. During my last check-up, he said that the placenta had grown into the uterine wall. They will have to excise the placenta from the uterus very carefully to manage bleeding after they take her. Currently, we are just trying to get to thirty-six weeks to help allow time for her lungs to mature. That's why I'm on bed rest."

"What are the risks for you?"

"Hemorrhaging."

"How can we be sure that she'll wait and you won't go into labor at home?"

"My exams have been okay and my blood pressures have been good. By scheduling the C-section at thirty-six weeks, we should be fine."

"Should be?"

"Yes."

"Why aren't they keeping you at the hospital- just in case?"

"I don't want to be at the hospital, Tru. I'm more comfortable here."

"It's too risky."

"If I were at any great risk, Dr. Brandon wouldn't agree to let me stay at home."

"I can't lose you or her."

"Emma Grace will be fine. She's a fighter."

He grinned proudly. "My mom will be ecstatic to hear you named her granddaughter after her."

"I know."

"And us, Jewels? What's to become of us? Do I live here? Do I buy a house close by? I don't know how to be with you and be apart."

"I don't want to punish you. Yes. I did ask you to leave. I recall that night perfectly- every pain filled moment. I've thought of little else, confined to this bed day in and day out. We tried again and it didn't work out."

"You know, you have this insane ability to just move past people. Most others would drag around and be depressed, but you just pick yourself up and dust yourself off. You get on with it. You never wallow. There isn't one person you couldn't live without if you absolutely had to. Me? I've been a wreck, but you- one foot in front of the other."

"Always," I said proudly. "I run forward toward the next thing."

"You're not running toward anything. You're running away. Don't you realize that relationships are hard? It's not supposed to be all sweet smiles and smooth sailing. You and I are very headstrong. We are going to disagree. We're going to fight. Two passionate people together do not always equal peace and harmony. Where has this idea of perfection in relationships come from? You certainly didn't have the example growing up with John. Tommy is married to the Church. Jackson was a bust. Why would you think that we'd never experience adversity?"

He made a good point. I was a runner. There were no arguments to be proffered in my defense. Relationships were hard and sometimes messy. Getting through the difficult patches was what made the love enduring. In my heart, I knew that, but in my mind, I still had this crazy idea of obtaining perfection. I couldn't answer any of his questions. There were no adequate words. Instead, I just stared into his gorgeous eyes and became mute while he continued analyzing our situation.

"I've thought about this- a lot today, since no one except your brother would speak to me. In thinking about the words that were spoken that night, I was so wrong to imply that you were in any way responsible for Connor's death. I wanted to hurt you as much as you were hurting me. I'm ashamed for saying that to you. I hope you can forgive me. I truly didn't mean the words I spoke."

He grabbed my hand from my lap and squeezed it tightly. With his other hand, he tilted my chin to his face so I had no choice, but to look in his eyes.

"The real sticking point in our relationship has always been the fact that I was working for your father. You were more upset about my job with Spencer Industries than anything else. I really believe that this whole mess is born out of the animosity that you and your father share. It's a bloody game to you both. Our relationship became the casualty in this life long war with John. He wanted to take the thing you loved away to punish you and you sure as hell enjoyed knowing that I was forbidden fruit. Well...I don't work for your father anymore. I chose you. You win."

"You shouldn't have done that for me. I can't make you any promises. This probably isn't the best time for you to be leaving anyway."

"What does that mean?" he inquired curiously.

"It means that Emma Grace and I are not a package deal. You and I have trust issues. Regardless of how you ended up in New York, if you loved me so earnestly, Tricia wouldn't have found her way into your bed. You wouldn't have let that happen."

"Tricia was a mistake. She was the result of a broken heart and too many drinks."

"Alcohol isn't a defense...and you were so quick to condemn me when you thought Jackson and I had slept together that night. Oh how the tide has turned. It's not so black and white anymore, is it?"

"I'm a horrible person. Does that make you feel better?"

"Not really, no."

"Good. You know, you're every bit as horrible for not telling me about Emma Grace. Look, the bottom line is that I've chosen you. I'm choosing my daughter. Nothing else matters now."

"You will always have your daughter, Tru- you have my word on that, but you should probably consider alternant living arrangements for after the baby is born. I'm sure this isn't the time to house hunt with the business of the holiday season."

"That's it then?" he said frustrated.

"You need time to come to terms with all the changes in your life. I don't want you falling back into a place of comfort just because it's easy. My life has changed a lot since you left. I have a responsibility to Mattie- even if you don't understand that connection. Gabe and I are the best of friends. He accepted my gift. They'll be in my life forever. Our daughter and Mattie will grow up together. If you can't get past your misplaced resentment for Gabe, then you and I have no future- not even as friends."

"May I at least stay here, in this house, until Emma Grace is born?"

"Yes."

With those words, the baby kicked so hard that I lost my breath. I winced. Henry flew into panic mode, throwing his arm around my back and scooting closer to me.

"What is it? What's the matter?"

"Nothing. She's kicking. Emma Grace always finds that one spot in my upper ribs to pound me. Here...let me have your hand," I said sweetly trying to change the tone of our conversation.

Pulling up my pajama top and exposing my big fat belly took some bravery. I was huge. No matter how much cream I slathered on my abdomen night after night, I was still developing unsightly stretch marks. I grabbed Henry's hand and placed it on my side. His touch was so warm and loving. I'd forgotten how much I missed our closeness.

"Wait. Be patient. She never stops with one wallop."

He smiled and we sat with his hand on my belly waiting for her to answer her daddy's voice. He finally moved to the floor and knelt down in front of me to take it all in. There was a lot of me to take in.

"Wow. Did you feel that?" he asked. "That was amazing."

"Yeah. I felt that," I replied laughing.

Unexpectedly, he leaned into my belly and kissed the very place she had kicked. His lips sent chills up my spine, but I didn't let on. He watched as she performed all her tricks; crawling from one side of my belly with her hands, to the other. I finally realized how selfish my choice had been to keep him from all of this. My scorn had left me with regrets.

"Is Kate coming?" I asked interrupting his baby watching.

"She's afraid to see Gabe," he said nonchalantly.

"She should be."

"What happened with that?" he responded, never breaking eye contact with Emma's tricks.

"She didn't tell you?" I asked surprised.

"No," he replied.

"She was embarrassed of Mattie. When you called and demanded that she join you in New York, I suggested that she invite Gabe and Mattie to accompany her."

"I never asked her to come to New York, Jewels."

"What?" I said perplexed.

"She got spooked. Not everyone can handle trying times with the same grace as you," he said jokingly, pulling himself back up to the bed.

"I know. I'm one of a kind."

"You are."

He put one hand on my cheek and the other on Emma Grace as he leaned in, placing his forehead to mine. I could feel his lips in front of mine, his breath blowing gently over my face. My heart began to race. I finally got up the courage to speak.

"Good night," I said, breaking our intimacy.

He opened his eyes and retreated back, as his hand fell from my cheek to his leg.

"Can I sleep in your recliner?" he requested.

"Do you promise not to stare at me all night?"

He shook his head in agreement and collapsed back into the chair. Taking a comforter off my bed, I handed him a pillow and covered him. He smiled as if he knew we would be all right. I wasn't so sure.

19

Mattie pounced on my bed early. The sun's rays were barely breaking through the windows. A big lick demanded my attention. The smell of puppy breath in my nose alerted my eyes to search out the source. There in front of me was a beautiful black lab puppy with a large blue bow around its neck. Mattie grinned and his expression was recorded in my mind.

"Mattie. Dog, dog, dog. Black. Bark."

Pulling myself up in bed, I gave him a very tight Merry Christmas squeeze. He put his dog on the floor and they were gone in the blink of an eye. Gabe walked over and sat on the bed.

"Merry Christmas, Santa," he said laughing.

"Santa? Seriously…another weight crack on Christmas, of all days? Shame on you, Gabe Martin. You might get coal in your stocking this year?"

"Now, I wouldn't be so harsh as to make jokes about your weight on Christmas. I was referring to the ridiculously generous gift you gave us last night, or have you already forgotten?"

"Forgotten. I don't keep an account of things like that. I wish you wouldn't either. We have to remain on equal footing so you can tell me when I'm being an ass."

"No problem there. Merry Christmas."

Gabe gave me a soft hug and told me to get downstairs so Mattie could tear into the over abundance of gifts I had purchased for him. I wanted to have time for a shower, but I knew that the rest of the family was waiting on me. Henry's presence made me want to achieve some form of beauty. I hadn't felt that way in a long time.

Everyone was gathered around the tree awaiting my arrival. Mattie's new puppy was tearing at the bows that adorned the packages. His eagerness mirrored my own excitement on this beautiful morning. My entire family surrounded me. I never imagined a scenario that included my father in my home during the holidays. With my brother keeping watch and trying to navigate the healing waters, the Spencer clan had come full circle. Together, we were a fearsome sight to behold. The Walker family should shake in their boots- even if I still liked Ms. Emma, his mum.

John motioned for me to sit next to him on the couch. Henry was in my crazy chair in the corner- the one I always gravitated to when I felt the least bit unstable. When I finally made contact with the seat cushion, Henry disappeared into the kitchen, returning with a plate full of food for me. He obviously hadn't received the memo regarding the starve Jewels campaign. I was thankful. I could feel four sets of eyes scrutinizing my every bite. As quickly as he had placed the food in front of me, he retreated back to the chair, far away from my father.

Not to be outdone, Gabe brought me a glass of freshly squeezed orange juice. He knew that no real competition existed between him and Henry- at least in my mind- but I suspected he wanted Henry's gesture to be diminished as ordinary and common. In this house, I suffered from round the clock caregivers- like it or not. Gabe wanted to send the message that no brownie points were scored for such typical behaviors. The message was received. Henry shot him a dirty look and Gabe smiled back. He had gotten the better of the upper crust Brit.

Mattie's joyful affect made the tree seem even more spectacular than before. The lights were brighter and the ornaments took me back to early holidays with my mom. Angels I had made her and old dough ornaments still hung from the feathery branches. The smell of the tree and Ms. Martin's apple cider could make even the crankiest Grinch jovial.

Mattie opened gift after gift until the giving tree was exhausted. As typical with all children, he latched on to one gift- the least expensive- and was satisfied. He only had eyes for the marble maze I'd purchased for the collection he inherited from Tommy. The bike with training wheels, indoor basketball hoop, art easel, and Lionel train set couldn't hold a candle to watching the marbles roll down the ramps and around the curves to the bottom. No matter how hard Gabe and I tried to get him to look at his other presents, he was completely disinterested. Finally realizing that he was in his time of bliss, we grew content. This had been the best morning ever.

Tommy and Ms. Martin took on the daunting task of cleaning up all the torn wrapping paper and returning some of the gifts to the cottage. John and Gabe moved to the keeping room, off the kitchen, to try and put together the basketball hoop. Mattie was still mesmerized by his marble maze and the puppy was slap worn out from the excitement of Christmas morning. She lay quietly next to her little master as he played. Henry and I were left in the drawing room, side by side, on the couch, listening to carols in front of the tree.

"Where's my big gift?" he inquired. "The one you promised me today."

John's cancer and impending departure from Spencer Industries made me rethink the gravity of the gift I'd drawn up for Henry. His own resignation from the company meant that he was finally free. He had clear waters ahead to charter the course that would suit himself and his daughter. My gift would only muddy the waters and pull him under. Though he professed to be a changed man, Henry was Henry. The lust for power was still just beneath the surface. I did have faith that, over time, his need for power would decrease, as his daughter filled his life with experiences that business couldn't manufacture, but change demands continual good decision making opportunities. Henry needed time to become that man before I levied such a burden on him.

I grabbed my belly. "Here's your big gift. Isn't this enough?"

"-Of course. There could be no better gift," he said, embarrassed for asking.

"What are your plans?" I inquired, trying to change the subject.

"I'll go to New York and clear out my office for the replacement your father has hired. I need to get some things from my apartment."

"Are you going to sell it?"

"No. Kate is living in it. She's welcome to live there for as long as she wants while she's job hunting."

"Oh," I said surprised. "I figured she was back in London."

"I told her about the baby, this morning. Maybe I should have let you, but she's my sister and I'm excited."

"No. It's fine. How is she? I hate that she's alone on Christmas."

"Me too. She can't bear you being disappointed in her. I invited her, but she wouldn't come down for the holidays."

"Gabe's past it, you know. He's moved on. I think he's sweet on Dr. Brandon's nurse."

"And you? Are you past it?"

"She's a sister to me, Tru. She's my best friend. We both made mistakes. I was probably too harsh in my criticisms, but I meant what I said. Friends have to tell each other the truth- even when it's hard...like you telling me that you slept with Tricia. That couldn't have been easy."

"I don't want to talk about that again."

"Why? Nothing ever gets solved by just pretending and living in a false reality. The Walkers' should learn to face things head on and deal with the consequences."

"-Like you Spencers'..."

"You were right when you accused me of being the reason Connor died."

"No..."

"Yes. I was running from my problems with Jackson. Regardless of the evilness of Hector Costelano, if I had stayed in New York, and dealt with that cheating loser head on, I would never have been at that clinic. Connor would be having his first Christmas in my mom's house. One poor choice made me lose my everything. That's on me. I see that now. You were right. I was wrong. But I also know that I can't change the past. I've discovered, with Gabe's help, that losing Connor wasn't a punishment for being a coward. That's what I was- a coward. I'm not that person anymore. I'm done running."

"I can see that."

"Your sister should have told Gabe about her feelings- about being scared of Mattie's struggles. He could have helped her through them. She didn't give him the chance to be the voice of reason. Don't you think Gabe has had moments of being embarrassed or worn out to the point of giving up? Do you know how hard it is to love someone that can't show you love back? Gabe's no saint. He's human. The damaging part is that Kate did exactly the same thing to him as Mattie's mother. She broke his heart when she ran off to New York. If she had shared her concerns, and showed a little trust, Gabe would have gotten past it."

"She is sorry."

"Then she should tell him so. She should make it right- even if the apology doesn't lead to reconciliation. Besides, Kate's place is here. Her niece will be born soon. Surely, she won't miss that due to pride?"

"I'll talk to her. I'm leaving tonight."

"So soon?"

"Your father is not one to keep waiting. I need to conclude our business arrangement so I can start looking for another job. Your baby's father is unemployed, remember?"

"You'll find something."

"I have some ideas."

"Care to share?" I asked.

"Not yet. Let's get that baby born healthy."

"Agreed."

"Tommy said that Costelano was killed by the police."

"Yes. I wish I felt sorry, but I don't. I'm not that forgiving. The police said that they were sending back my belongings from the investigation. I hope my mom's locket is among the things sent. I must have lost it that night in the clinic during the struggle. I feel naked without it."

"Let's not talk about that night. I'm just thankful that you and Emma are okay. When is the next ultrasound scan? I want to be there."

"Three weeks. I'll be thirty-two weeks on January 22."

"I can't wait to see her," he said happy.

"She's going to be a handful. I can already tell."

"Just like her mother," he replied, laughing.

"Hilarious. Go pack. I wouldn't want you to miss your flight. And send my love to Kate. Tell her that I said to get over herself and come back home."

He shook his head, but it was restrained, like he dreaded the upcoming conversation with his sister. Before leaving, he kissed me on the forehead, rubbed my belly and went upstairs to gather his things. His fact-finding mission had turned out to take longer than expected. He had yet to discover the real reason behind John's visit. I was anxious for him to return to New York so that Tommy and I could sort out John's surgery at Emory.

20

⸺∘⸺

With Henry gone, a family meeting was called to discuss John's cancer. One by one, we filed into the kitchen, leaving Mattie and Dog watching television in the family room. As we took our seats, Ms. Martin set out coffee service, cake, and a bowl of sliced fruit on the table. Though I longed for the cake, I knew that she meant for me alone to have the fruit.

John was looking more tired than usual. The whites of his eyes had become a pale yellow color like lemon curd. He had barely touched his Christmas dinner and I knew that the disease was waging a nasty war inside of him. Knowing that he wouldn't be able to stomach the coffee, I quietly retrieved a glass of cold milk from the refrigerator along with a bottle of water for myself. He grabbed my hand as I placed the milk before him. He thanked me for looking after him. Acknowledging his kind words by stroking his arm, I waddled back to my own chair. Once seated, Tommy took the floor.

"Dad and I are leaving tomorrow to fly to Atlanta. The surgeon at Emory is expecting us in the afternoon to go over his surgery."

"Someone needs to explain this Whipple procedure to me," I demanded.

John responded before Tommy could speak for him again. He didn't like the role of the sick person. My brother would have to tread carefully.

"The surgeon will remove the head of the pancreas, the distal stomach, gallbladder, common bile duct, duodenum, jejunum, and some surrounding lymph nodes," my dad spoke calmly and efficiently.

"Well, you lost me after stomach," I said smiling, trying to lighten the mood.

"Will you have to undergo chemotherapy?" asked Ms. Martin.

"I'm not certain of anything yet. The doctors in New York told me that there was no evidence that the tumor had metastasized, but that was two months ago. The doctors at Emory will do a PET scan the day after tomorrow to determine if that still holds true."

"How long do you have to stay at Emory after the procedure?" I wondered.

"Patients usually stay about two weeks. I suppose it will depend on how things go in surgery and the results of the PET scan."

"I'll pack a bag tonight and come with you. I can rest there just as easily as I can here."

"Julia, the hospital is no place for you, considering your condition. I appreciate the gesture, but you need to protect my grandbaby."

"Don't worry, Jewels, I've taken a leave of absence to be with Dad. He won't be alone. I'll keep you updated twice a day, okay?"

"Do I have a choice?"

"Not really," Gabe interjected.

"I want you and your brother to understand something, very clearly. My lawyer has drawn up a living will. I expect the both of you to honor it to the letter. Do you understand?"

"That will depend on what it says," I said skeptically.

"I do not want any heroic measures to be taken on my behalf. If things go badly, I do not want to be placed on life support..."

"This meeting is adjourned. I'm not going to entertain any thought that has a bad outcome. You'll have the procedure and you'll be fine. That's it. I've had enough loss this year. Do you understand?"

"Julia, you have to be prepared for all possible outcomes- not just the one you want. For me, you must promise to adhere to my wishes. Please."

"Let me see the papers. You know, I'm a lawyer. I could have prepared them for you."

"This isn't the type of thing that a daughter completes for her ailing father. Tommy, do I have your word?"

"Yes. I'll respect your wishes," my brother replied.

"Julia?"

"I'll think about it…and that's all I care to hear tonight. Mattie and I are taking Dog upstairs to watch the History Channel. He'll be up all night and I'll be asleep in five minutes. Anyone care to join us?"

"Will there be popcorn?" Gabe asked.

"No. I'm a fatty, remember? All I can offer you is boring television," I replied, laughing as I made my way into the family room. Turning back to my father, I said, "I love you, John. Wake me before you leave."

My father nodded in agreement and walked out onto the veranda with Tommy. I was trying to stay positive, but the living will dialogue threw me for a loop. The very discussion made me feel like he was giving up- that he was resigned to death. Life was going to be the theme in this upcoming year. I wasn't going to prepare for any other outcome. He better fight the good fight.

Mattie ran up ahead of Gabe, with Dog following closely at his heels and me. She was a beautiful girl, all furry and lanky. Her legs were the biggest things about her and she had the sweetest disposition. Gabe had done well when picking her from the litter. Mattie didn't even seem to mind when she tried to gnaw on his fingers. He'd simply shove a toy in her mouth and turn her body in the opposite direction as punishment. She'd met her match in every way. Mattie loved repetition. Where the rest of us would give up correcting her, he could go on for a good fifteen minutes until he proved his point. He was a born animal trainer. We all piled on the bed. Gabe was talking to Mattie as I drifted off to sleep.

John woke me in the morning to say his goodbyes. He seemed to have a renewed vigor despite his frailty last evening. Perhaps this was for my benefit, but I chose to accept his demeanor as the gospel. He was fine. I was fine. The surgery would be a success and he'd be back before Emma Grace was born. That was my reality.

The day passed slowly, waiting to hear of their arrival at the hospital. Gabe was back to work and Mattie and Ms. Martin were at the dreaded horse therapy. Dog and I were the only two left in the big house. She was good company, following me around like a shadow from one room to the next.

For a few weeks now, my heart was being drawn outside to the cemetery to visit with Connor. The holidays were hard, knowing that, under different circumstances, he'd be here, taking his first steps. Dog needed to be walked and I needed time alone with my son. I latched on her leash and opened the door slowly, trying to see if anyone was in sight. While I was a grown woman, capable of making good decisions, I was still made to feel like a prisoner being watched. After scanning the yard for people and cars, I decided to make my escape.

Their graves seemed bare without the summer flowers. No one had bothered to rake the fallen leaves that covered the ground. The beautiful grass that we laid in June had become brown and dormant. The fountain was drained and the birds were gone. Dog didn't seem to mind her stark surroundings. She dove in and out of the leaves and walked along the ledge of the fountain while I sat and thought of my boy. Seeing his name chiseled into the headstone made it seem so final, but I could remember his every feature. I could recall his thick dark hair and sweet cheeks; even the memory of his weight in my arms as I rocked him. Even still, the tears were just hiding under the surface to answer the broken heart that still didn't beat quite as loudly as it should.

"I've been missing you so much, Connor…wishing you were here. Tommy says that you don't feel the constant ache that plagues me; that you're happy where you are. I wish I knew that to be true."

Dog dropped a stick at my feet and sat wagging his tail, until I complied with the request. Tossing the small tree branch, I moved closer to Connor's grave. Crying was therapeutic.

"Let me pull it together. I didn't come out here to be a downer. I'll tell you about Christmas. My friend, Mattie, got a new puppy that you would have loved. He licks everything his tongue can find. We also had visitors. Uncle Tommy and Grandpa John came down to check on me. Your sister should be along in a few weeks, but you must already know that. We've named her Emma Grace. She's a fighter-reminds me of Sissy. I'm sure she's hunted you down by now and is smothering you like a mother," I said, laughing in remembrance of my former shadow. "Your little sister kicks me all the time, day and night. You were so calm compared to her."

My hands found my belly as I thought of him, once growing where Emma Grace now thrived.

"I need a favor from you- from Mom. Watch over Grandpa John during this surgery. He needs protection and strength for what he's facing. I'm not ready to lose him. Saying good-bye to you used up every ounce of grief within me. Tell your boss upstairs not to overestimate your mother's spiritual capabilities. I'm weak and broken. Tell God that."

Rising to return home, before my absence was discovered, I drew closer and traced his name etched in the stone. Goodbyes were never easy.

"Know that I love you more than I can put into words. There are no words for this type of longing. You'll always be my first child- my precious boy. God brought you so far just to take you away. I'm trying to understand this cruelty. I tell myself not to be angry. Oh, what I wouldn't give for just one minute with you, alive in my arms- one recognition in your eyes that I was your mother."

The tears wet my face and clouded my vision, but Emma's kick brought me back to the present, reminding me that the future was right around the corner. Knowing that Gabe would return at lunch to check on me, I decided to make my way back to jail.

When he arrived, he brought a cheeseburger and fries and was now my new best friend. The only thing missing was a tall chocolate milkshake, but beggars can't be choosers. He made it abundantly clear that if I told anyone, he'd never sneak food to me again. God bless greasy fast food joints. After Gabe's lunch delivery, Tommy called to say that they'd made it all right and that John was getting acclimated to his new hospital room- poor nurses. Henry who asked me a host of questions regarding my state of health and Emma's activities for the day followed his call. By the time Mattie and Ms. Martin had made it home, I was ready for peace and quiet. I was all talked out. Sensing my exhaustion, she presented me dinner in bed and took Mattie to the cottage to wait on Gabe's return from work. The phone rang as I was preparing to bed down for the night.

"Hello."

"Cheers," said my too distant friend in New York.

"When are you coming home?" I asked with a big yawn.

"I didn't think I was welcome. We didn't exactly part on good terms, jerk."

"No, we didn't, crazy, but my house is your house. We're best friends. We are going to disagree. You can't be running away at every bump in the road, Kate. I'm sorry for calling you a mean bitch. That was rude. You aren't a bitch."

"And I'm sorry for calling you a redneck hick with no taste," she replied.

"You didn't call me that," I said, defending her apology.

"Yeah, I kind of did…to Henry. Sorry."

"It's okay. I accept your apology. Go ahead and ask."

"Ask what?" she replied.

"About Gabe. Go ahead."

"How's Gabe?" she said, playing along.

"He's great. Gabe's tearing down the old cottage in the spring to start building a forever house for him and Mattie. Ms. Martin is moving too. He's building her a guest house."

"Henry mentioned that you gave him the land and money for construction. And Mattie...how is he?"

"He's talking now. He's putting together words and is responding more to us. Ms. Martin is looking into special diets and other lifestyle changes to coincide with the mainstream therapy he's getting now. We're hopeful. Oh, and he got a puppy for Christmas."

"A black lab? Henry told me."

"What hasn't he told you? What do you really want to know, Kate?"

There was a long pause. I was sure that she was trying to gain the necessary courage to ask the question that lay deep in her heart.

"Does he ever ask about me? Has he moved on?"

"You mean with another woman?" I inquired, trying to discern her motives.

"Yes. Is he seeing anybody? I mean, it's okay if he is. I would just like to know."

"The truth?" I asked.

"Nothing but..." she replied anxiously.

"He seems sweet on my obstetrician's nurse, but I don't think he's acted on it yet. At least, he hasn't mentioned anything about it to me. We've become pretty close. He would have said something. I doubt he's gotten up the nerve."

The line went silent and I felt bad for her. Gabe had made it pretty clear that she had lost her chance with him, but I didn't have the heart to tell Kate. Besides, who can ever tell what a man is truly feeling when their pride is at stake. For all I knew, he was still interested. He seemed awfully nervous about her showing up at Christmas. If he weren't still madly in love with her, why would he care? The two of them would have to get in a room together and sort it out. I planned to steer clear of it.

"Come home Kate. You can't hide forever. Eventually, you'll want to come and visit your new niece. Why wait? I need a birth partner. Can you imagine the boys in a delivery room?"

"Okay, okay. Twist my arm. I'll come back for her big entrance, but I don't do blood. You should warn Gabe that I'm coming."

"I will. I love you. I'm glad you called."

"God bless America, redneck," she replied.

"God save the Queen, jerk."

21

⟨⟨⟩⟩

The weeks passed with only bits and pieces of information from Tommy, regarding John's condition. No doubt, this was purposeful due to my challenged pregnancy, but filtered information was better than no information. The surgery was a success and the PET scan was clean. The cancer had not metastasized to any of his major organs. He would be home tomorrow and I would be able to assess the situation myself.

Henry slipped in during the night without me noticing. Occupying the same recliner in the corner, he didn't even budge as I fumbled around the bedroom looking for my bathrobe in the morning. His travel clock was next to him on the table. The alarm appeared to be set so I didn't wake him.

Gabe was looking over the paper, wearing his cop get-up, as I made my way into the kitchen. The house had become an organized mess. A laundry basket of clothes that needed to be folded adorned the kitchen bar along with a mountain of correspondences I needed to answer. Ms. Martin had been busy with Mattie over the last several days and I'd been camped out in my room thinking of my father.

"Leaving for work?" I inquired. "Where's the Little Man?"

"He's sound asleep, upstairs with my mom. I have some time. Eat breakfast with me."

"Henry's back," I informed him as I searched the fridge for something to eat.

"His car in the driveway was a big tip off," he replied smirking. "Yes. England's finest has returned. We are saved."

Giving him a look of disgust, I walked over to the sink to rinse some juicy, red, ripe strawberries. My eyes were drawn away from the fruit, out the kitchen window, to a car that was coming down the drive.

"Who in the world is coming here at this hour? Are you expecting someone?" I asked.

"No," he replied as he left his seat to take in my view.

We watched as the silver Porsche slowly came to a halt. The woman inside didn't exit the car immediately. She took time applying lipstick and brushing her hair before opening the door. Her long leg was bare, due to the small swatch of black fabric constituting a skirt that clung to her hips. A black stiletto heel was attached to the slender limb. After the first mile long leg, another followed. Her hand slid out into view, pulling her tiny torso out of the vehicle. The biggest thing about her was the thick, blond mane that fell down past her shoulders. Slamming the door closed, she paused briefly to admire her reflection in the car window. After rubbing her teeth clean of any lipstick residue, she confidently strutted toward the front door. In awe of her perfection, I mirrored her movements through the drawing room and into the foyer, opening the front door before she had a chance to knock.

"May I help you?" I asked curiously.

"Maybe," she replied. "I'm looking for Henry Walker."

"You're looking for Henry?" I said coolly.

"He's expecting me," she retorted annoyed.

"Funny, he didn't mention it," I replied, pausing to see if my intimidation tactic worked.

"I'm sorry. Who are you?" she asked, turning her head to the side as she scanned my body top to bottom, and back up to my face.

"The mother of his baby," I shot back, rubbing my belly and smiling innocently.

"Funny, he didn't mention it," she spewed with delight.

"He's asleep, but feel free to wait," I responded, motioning to the drawing room.

"No, thank you. I have some calls to make. I'll just wait in my car."

"Suit yourself."

"I usually do."

She turned, just as I slammed the front door closed. Gabe stood in the doorway of the drawing room trying to hide his amusement.

"Well done," he said.

Ignoring his jab, I walked back to the kitchen, with him following closely behind.

"Who do you think she is, Julia," he asked, standing at the kitchen window, staring at our visitor as she shoved those gangly legs back into her small sports car. "Do you think he is seeing her?"

"I doubt it. She's so..."

"Thin?" he replied, laughing.

"She is, isn't she?" I leaned further toward the pane of glass to improve my view. "I could snap her like a twig, that one."

"You're pregnant, Julia. You're not supposed to be thin. You're beautiful," he said in a reassuring gesture, smashing down parts of my hair that were obviously in their own zip code.

Realizing that his appearance intervention had not stopped, I reached for the silver platter, removed its contents, and gazed upon my unsightly reflection

"Why didn't you tell me I looked like this? You shouldn't have let me answer the door in this state of disrepair," I said, smacking him on the arm. "Turn around."

"What? Why?"

"Turn around. I'm going to change into this black dress." I reached for the most attractive apparel I could find in the laundry basket.

"What's the point? She has already seen you," he said throwing his arms up, confused.

"I don't care. Just turn around," I demanded.

Turning his back to me, as ordered, I proceeded to slip off my robe and nightgown. The black, belly-hugging dress just barely fit.

"Okay," I said, signaling that I was clothed.

"Okay, I can turn around?" he asked.

"Yeah. Will you hand me that hair clip on the counter next to you?"

He complied with my request, tossing it to me. I twisted my long, dark curls up and clipped them tight.

"There. How do I look?"

"Good. Great. Better than her- definitely."

"Don't you patronize me, Gabe Martin. I'm not in the same league as her right now, but I look presentable, right?"

"-Better than presentable. Why are you doing this? You don't even want Henry. That's what you said. Hold up, wait a second. You want Henry?" he decided, acting surprised.

"This is news to you? You're a cop for crying out loud."

"But you said…"

"I'm a woman. We say a lot of things we don't mean. I couldn't let him back in my good graces so soon after Tricia. You men have a lot to learn."

"Obviously. Look, if I didn't comprehend your master plan, Henry hasn't gotten it either. He has been following you around like Dog since Christmas, waiting on you hand and foot, and you've given him absolutely no encouragement. Do you know that he stayed up late last night doing your laundry-even the girly stuff," he giggled holding up a pair of huge grandma panties that were on the top of the laundry pile.

"Give me those. They're comfortable. I can't wear sexy stuff right now," I replied, embarrassed to learn that Henry was washing my intimates and leaving them out for others to see.

"All I'm saying is that you can't expect the guy to wait around forever, Julia, in some strange holding pattern. You told him it was over. You said welcome to fatherhood, but goodbye to you. What's a guy supposed to do?"

"When did you become a fan?"

"I wouldn't say fan. I do, however, appreciate the effort he has put forth to try and sway your decision. It's down right admirable. If this has all been a ploy to play hard to get, you better rethink your strategy- quick."

"Or else?"

"Or else, legs for miles is going to ride into the sunset with your prince," he said with certainty.

"You think?"

"I'm a guy and this may sound weird, but Henry is a hard person not to like, if you're of the female persuasion. He's good looking, as far as I can tell from the stares the women give him. He's athletic. I doubt there's an ounce of fat on his entire body. It's disgusting, really. He's obviously smart, wealthy, and that accent seals the deal. Women love the accent. Hell, I love the accent. Kate stole my heart at our first meeting when she said Sheriff Martin. She could have been reading the phone book."

Gabe became distracted and seemed to lose his train of thought, no doubt, thinking of Kate.

"Anyways, I'm not a fan of his- after Tricia. You can't shine shit. But then again, what do I know? I'm a simple country boy who enjoys deer hunting and turkey calling. I'm not worldly. If you think your evil plan to make him pay is working, keep up the ice queen persona. I'm sure mini skirt out there isn't interested in Henry at all," he said, giving me the thumbs up sign.

"What do I do?" I implored, with worry written across my face.

"Here's what you do. Put back on your nightgown, rough up your hair again, and tell him you don't feel good. Mission accomplished. He won't leave with the twig if you're under the weather. That's how you snap her- use good old Southern drama. Girls raised in the South don't accept defeat. You've been in the big city way too long. That's your problem. Remember your roots. As much as I would absolutely love to see how this thing plays out, I have to go to work," he said, taking a small bow. "You're welcome."

"You're a genius Gabe Martin- positively diabolical."

"Thanks. I think. Stop selling yourself short. Big or little, you're still better than her on your worst day. You're Julia Spencer. Start acting like it," he replied, kissing my forehead and handing me back my tent like nightgown.

"Love you," I responded sweetly.

"What's not to love?" he said, running his hands up and down his form.

"That's my line."

"So it is. See you tonight. Give Mattie a kiss for me."

"I'll do it."

He shook his head, giggling like a schoolgirl, mumbling, "Ah…good times," as he walked out the door.

With his departure, I quickly took off the black dress. Placing it in the laundry basket, I put back on the tent. I pulled my hair out of the clip and gave it a good toss, as Gabe suggested. Grabbing some blush from my purse on the counter, I intentionally rubbed the rose hue onto my cheeks, throwing it back in my bag and sitting down just as Henry entered the kitchen.

"Hi love. How are you?"

Tru was wearing khaki shorts and a navy blue knit polo. His hair was still wet from the shower, as he approached to stroke my belly and say good morning to Emma Grace. Leaning down in front of me, his eyes stared at my face.

"A woman is here for you- outside. I asked her if she wanted to come in, but she refused."

"Yes. She's a realtor. Are you unwell? Your cheeks look flushed." His hand found its way upward to my face, concerned.

"I don't feel so good today. A realtor?"

"Do you have a fever?"

His hands cupped both my cheeks then gravitated to my chest and back.

"I don't know. I don't think so. Why do you need a realtor?"

"Emma Grace will be here soon. I need to find a house. We should get you to the hospital."

He started to pull me out of my chair.

"No. No. I probably just picked up something from Mattie. He's around all those other kids at therapy. It's no big deal. I'll just take some Tylenol and drink lots of orange juice. I'll be fine. You have plans. Go. Don't keep Tricia waiting."

"Her name is Callie. I'll reschedule. I wouldn't feel right leaving you today."

"If you're sure?" I replied, trying not to smile.

"My girls come first. Let me go explain the cancellation. I feel bad she drove out here for nothing."

I followed closely behind him to the door.

"Tell her that I'm so sorry for screwing up your plans."

"I will. You don't worry about that. Sit down. I'll make you a ham and cheese omelet. Be right back."

With that, the door closed. My plan had worked. Gabe was the puppet master. I had become his evil apprentice. After feeling a very small tinge of remorse, I promptly decided that the ends justified the means. I tried not to be too obvious, staring through the window, watching them converse. Callie looked truly disappointed and I relished in my victory. Baby trumps big hair every time. Thank you, Emma Grace. Operation GET YOUR DADDY BACK was commencing.

When Henry returned, he dragged me back up to bed, insisting that I get more rest. If there was one thing I didn't need, it was more rest. I was the most rested person in America. There was little for me to argue, considering that he had bought my little rouse. I made my bed and now would

194

have to lie in it- all day. Lucky me. Tommy would call that justice, but I preferred to think of it as falling on my sword for the greater good.

"Here you are," he said, placing the tray of food down in front of me.

"I am really sorry for messing up your day."

"It's no trouble. We rescheduled for tomorrow."

"I think I'm going to be sick," I realized looking at the omelet.

God was zapping me. Maybe it was Henry's news that I didn't stay off the house hunting search or maybe it was heavenly retribution for lying, but my stomach began to churn. I motioned with my hand to the trash can beside the nightstand, which Henry grabbed and presented to me in the knick of time.

"Sorry. I don't know where that came from. My stomach was fine when I woke up this morning."

"She's really doing a number on you. I can't wait for the next ultrasound."

"You're in luck. We have one scheduled this week."

"Perfect. I'm the only one who hasn't seen her. Now, let's get you a shower. Come on, then, follow me."

Being in the bathroom with him was like old times. He turned on the water as I disinfected my mouth with Listerine, brushed my teeth, and then deposited a piece of mint gum on my tongue to settle my stomach. When I was done, he stood behind me and pulled off my robe. He turned to leave as I grabbed his arm.

"Don't leave. Stay and talk to me while I sit perched on my shower chair. I'm tired of my own company."

"Are you sure?" he asked surprised.

"Yes, unless you have better things to do. I'm having your baby. I think we're way past modesty. It's not like you don't know every inch of my body anyway- right? Just because we're struggling, it doesn't mean that I don't love you, Tru. There is no one else in the world who I feel more comfortable with than you."

"Okay," was all he could muster by way of a response.

"Okay. Help me out of this tent," I said, smiling, referring to my old lady nightgown.

Henry assisted me and stood staring at my naked body, which revealed itself one inch at a time. I couldn't read his thoughts. That bothered me immensely. Self-doubt became my clothes, cloaking me, and weighing me down.

"I know. I'm huge," I said, figuring that's what he was thinking.

"You've never been more beautiful," he replied, placing his hands on my belly.

"Thanks. A girl needs to hear that occasionally; especially when she looks like a whale."

"I love you," he said out of left field.

Panicking, I said the only thing that came to mind.

"Could you get rid of those eggs before I get out? Emma Grace and eggs obviously don't mix."

He looked disappointed. I was disappointed. I had the perfect moment to remedy my own sad situation and I didn't have the courage. There was no acceptable excuse. He'd already gone out on a limb in declaring his love; someone save me from myself- anyone.

Henry left and returned as I was stepping out of the shower. He walked towards me with a towel, outstretched. With his body against mine, he wrapped the white cotton towel around me. Feeling his hold, I exhaled slowly to steady myself. As he prepared to take a step back away from me, I found my courage, closing my eyes, and kissing his lips ever so gently.

"What was that for?" he asked.

"We should talk. Will you hand me my robe?"

Henry looked stunned. I was nervous, but I felt reassured knowing that he kissed me back. After tying my robe, I grabbed his hand and led him to the bed, where we sat.

"I've missed you... a lot. I know that you've been trying to mend fences with me and I haven't made things easy for you. I'm sorry. It's just that I was so hurt."

"Tricia was a big mistake, Jewels. We both agree on that, but the bottom line is that you sent me away. You gave up on us."

"I know. I did. I realize now that you had every right to see whomever you chose; but it was just Tricia?"

"Yes."

"I'd be lying if I didn't tell you that I'm still of the opinion that our love...our history... should have kept that affair from happening."

"I don't want to go back over all this. I slept with Tricia. That can't be changed. Whether or not you think that I didn't have a long enough mourning period over the loss of our relationship is really none of your concern. You left me- not the other way around. You don't get to decide how other people handle their heartaches and disappointments. People in your life are allowed to feel any way they want to, even if it doesn't match up with your own thoughts on the matter."

I pulled back, stunned at his frankness.

"Look, I've been making an effort because you are the mother of my child. We are going to be in each other's lives for the long haul. Like you said, that doesn't have to be together. I'm tired of forcing myself on you. I think I'm finally prepared to move on, officially."

"Oh… well that makes my kissing you rather embarrassing, doesn't it?"

"Jewels, we will always love each other. I do love you. That's why I told you so. We have a child to raise together; it doesn't mean that we have to be in love with one another, right?"

"Sure. Right. That's a good point. One request though, in light of this new understanding; would you please stay in the house until we get through the infant stage? I don't think it's in Emma's best interest to be carted between houses, especially with me breast-feeding. You can move into the room next to the nursery. The room is bare, but I can order some furniture for you."

"I'll stay. I agree; it is best for the baby," he said in a matter of fact tone.

"Okay, then it is settled. I'm getting kind of tired. I think I'll take a nap. Would you mind closing the door when you leave?" I asked, trying to disguise my disappointment.

"Sure," he replied. Looking concerned, he added, "Are we okay?"

"Absolutely," I responded pulling the covers over me and turning on my side, away from his field of view.

"I'll wake you for lunch."

"No. Don't. I'll set my clock to get up before Tommy and John arrive."

"Okay. Have a good sleep. I'll be here if you need anything," he said as the door closed.

When I heard his footsteps on the stairs, I got out of bed to lock the door. The last thing I needed was for him to walk back in and see me crying. I still had a small amount of pride intact. Dog snuck in as I swung the door shut, jumping up on my bed. Claiming the spot near the footboard, he responded to my neck scratches with tail wagging.

Trying to stifle the sounds of my discord, I plunged my head into the pillow. Crying seemed to upset Dog. She marine crawled her way up to my face, licking my wet cheeks. My mind was filled with images of girlfriends and step monsters caring for Emma while Henry was away working. A tart like Callie was destined to be in my sweet girl's life and there wasn't anything I could do about it.

When I calmed down enough to speak clearly, I called Gabe who informed me that he would be home in a flash with a chocolate milkshake. Thank God for true friends.

22

Trying to seem unaffected by his rejection, I did my best to make small talk with Henry as we waited for Tommy and John to arrive. They called from the limousine I had sent to collect them saying that they would be home momentarily.

I'd managed to take a shower and get dolled up just as Gabe had suggested during his pep talk earlier in the morning. He'd said that it was time to make Henry jealous. I was drowning in a sea of hopelessness, but agreed to play along. Gabe warned that he would be overly helpful and touchy during the course of the next few days. He was always helpful, but the touching would seem weird; although, after the events of the day, I was game.

Gabe arrived and brought me a big bouquet of flowers. They were hydrangea blossoms- my favorite. He kissed me on the cheek as he placed them in my hand.

"Hi beautiful," he said as he rubbed my belly. "How was the rest of your day? I enjoyed the time we spent together this morning. I'm glad you agreed to consider exploring the possibilities we discussed," he added as he gave me a pat on the backside.

Henry's expression was priceless. His jaw almost touched the floor and his eyes grew in size.

"I bought some tickets to that concert you wanted to go to. Maybe Henry could watch Mattie for us; give him some practice for Emma Grace. What do you say, Henry?"

"I say that Jewels is on bed rest. She can't be going to any concert," he said irritated.

"True. However, the concert is in March." He turned his attention back to me. "I could only get tickets for the Atlanta show so I thought we could spend the weekend painting the town. I'll check into suites at the Ritz Carlton."

"Sounds good?" I replied, not having the script to Gabe's mind game in front of me.

"She's breast feeding. She can't be away from the baby so soon after giving birth," Henry firmly stated, rather annoyed, but proud of his argument.

"You're right. That's why we're going to take Emma Grace with us. My mom said that she would come and watch her while we're at the concert," he said to Henry as he slapped him lightly on the back. "I've worked out all the details. You don't mind; do you Henry- just a quick trip to the city? Julia deserves it after all these months stuck in bed, don't you think?"

"I guess," he responded bewildered.

"Good, then it's settled. I can't wait," he said, grinning from ear to ear as the front door opened.

Tommy was standing in front of John. Anxious to see my father with my own eyes, I charged the door. Before me stood a sickly old man, devoid of the vigor he once had. John's eyes were still a light yellow and his skin was pale. He seemed a little short of breath which was concerning.

"Hi Father. How are you?" Without waiting for a reply, my nervousness kept my mouth moving. "Come in and sit down. I've had Gabe move a bed into the study for you so you don't have to climb stairs. Are you hungry? I could fix you some food? Do you need to take medicine? I could get you a glass of water."

"Julia, child, take a breath. I'm fine- just a little tired. It has been a long two weeks."

"Come on Dad," said Tommy, "Let's get you to the couch. I'll bring in your suitcase."

Tommy walked past me, asserting control over John. It was apparent that they'd grown close through this ordeal and I was happy for my brother.

"Stop fussing over me Tommy. I can still walk."

"Now you know how I've felt all these months. Sucks, doesn't it?"

"Don't talk like that Julia. Ladies don't use those words."

"Yes sir," I said mocking him.

"I'm still fit enough to take you to task and don't you forget it."

"That's it. I'm sold. John is fine," I said, adding my estimation of his health.

Tommy walked back in carrying a package. Henry grabbed the suitcase and disappeared to place it in the study. I sat down next to my father on the sofa and Gabe sat on the arm, next to me, with his hand on the small of my back. This was obviously for Henry's benefit. When he returned, he sat in the chair across from us- the sad chair. My father broke the tension with questions.

"How have you been, Henry? I heard that you helped your replacement get adjusted to working in our New York office. Thank you."

"I'm fine, sir. I was sorry to hear of your illness. Your new hire is quite versed in the Spencer portfolio. He'll be a great asset," said Henry, acting congenial.

"Thank you. That's good to hear. Any job prospects for you?" he quizzed.

"I'm considering some opportunities."

"You know you have my highest recommendation."

"Thank you, sir. I know."

Tommy walked over to me and held out the brown paper covered package.

"This came for you. It's from the Peruvian police department. What could that be?" he asked.

"Father John said that they would be posting my personal effects after the investigation was closed."

"Are you sure you want to relive that event, sis?"

"No, but I want Mom's locket and my pictures," I replied.

Henry stood to walk over and intervene, but Gabe beat him to the punch.

"Come on. You and I will open it together. Let's put the past in the past."

Henry and I looked at each other. It was clear to me that he wanted to be the one to get me through it. Maybe Gabe's plan was working. Regardless of who helped to open the package, it was going to be difficult. I hadn't thought of that night for a very long time. Henry's unhappiness was apparent as he stormed out the front door. After hugging John and discovering that he didn't need or want anything, Gabe led me up the stairs to my room. He took out his pocketknife and cut through the police tape, exposing the contents to light.

On top was an official letter with attached documents from the police, which I laid to the side. Under that was a plastic bag with my dress in it. The garment was still covered in Connor's blood and mine. Gabe became upset.

"What kind of crack pot police force sends these items back to the victim? Do you have a number for these people?" he said angrily.

I stood motionless holding the torn dress, remembering Hector shoving the knife into my belly. Gabe noticed my emotional distance and unclenched my fingers from the plastic bag. He walked to the door and tossed it out into the hall.

"Are you sure about all this? I can go through this stuff and find your mom's locket," he said concerned for my mental health.

"No. I'm okay. I'm not a victim, Gabe. I'm a survivor. There's a big difference in the two. Let's keep going."

I pulled out some of my books that were left at the mission, along with pictures and correspondences from the States. Below the letters was another plastic bag containing my blood-drenched shoes. Gabe immediately took them and placed them next to the dress in the hallway for disposal. Returning to my side, he took the box and shook it, rattling its final contents.

"Is there anything left?" he asked as he peered into the box.

Reaching in, his hand swept the inside of its cardboard walls.

"Here's something," he commented as he pulled an object from the box. "What's this?"

In his hand, was the black, death amulet that Hector's acquaintance had given me during my birthday party. My own hand rose to hold the object again, grabbing it out of Gabe's grasp. Without delay, my mind was transported to the events of that night and the tragedy in the clinic. The memories flooded back with warp speed in a schizophrenic fashion.

"Julia?" he said, waiting for some type of response. When one wasn't forthcoming, he became concerned. "What's the matter, Julia?"

My hands rubbed across the smooth ceramic surface, surprised that it had survived the long journey intact. I stood and walked out onto the veranda, leaving the door open behind me. Suddenly becoming paralyzed with fear, I began to cry, scanning the yard for the evil that was certainly lurking behind the magnificent magnolia trees.

"Julia, talk to me. What is this thing?" he questioned, grabbing my arms, and shaking me gently to try and break my trance.

All I could do was sob louder. I heard the sounds of someone below, scurrying to the front door. Within minutes, Henry was at my side.

"What's the matter with her, Gabe?" Henry asked.

"They sent the blood drenched clothes back and this thing seems to have upset her a great deal. I don't know what it is," he replied, confused.

Henry stood in front of me, taking my head in his hands, forcing me to make eye contact with him. Tears rolled quickly off my chin and down my neck.

"Jewels, it's me, Tru. Talk to me, love. Why are you so upset? What is this thing you're holding? Tell me so I can help."

I held up the amulet in front of his face.

"This thing...they gave it to me at my birthday party...to warn me that they were coming for Connor...to kill him...it means death for who-ever holds it...I'm marked...again...they want Emma Grace...they want my baby girl..."

Grabbing me, the amulet still in hand between our bodies, he held me tightly, stroking my hair as I cried out in agony.

"You're safe here. No one is coming for you, love. I'm here. You're safe. Gabe and I won't let anything harm you. Right, Gabe?"

"Absolutely, Julia. Henry and I will protect you. You're safe here. This is Savannah. They can't get to you in the States."

My body became weak and I slid down Henry to the ground, finding support from the veranda railing. The commotion drew Tommy and John to the scene. They both looked at me, unsure of how to help. I couldn't see anything past my own experience- the experience of that night.

"It's just that he promised to get me and the baby...and he did. He lured me to the clinic and I was so stupid for going. I should have stayed and waited for my guards, but I wasn't scared. I should have been scared. They tricked me. He punched my face and I fell." I recalled the attack so vividly that I grabbed my cheek, once black and blue. "...and my hair; he pulled it so hard," I said, running my hand over my curly locks. "The knife was so big. He waved it around and around. I could barely see him... there was so much blood coming from my head. I should have left...the door was right there, but I stayed and fought him...that's why my Connor is dead. They'll get me again...that's what this means," I said, holding up the amulet, paranoid. "This is a warning. They're coming for Emma. We're not safe. They'll find me," I said seriously, looking out into the dark night.

Just as Henry was about to talk, John stepped forward and knelt down behind me. He waved the others off and they obeyed, moving to the veranda door. He pulled me back against his frail body and wrapped his arms around me.

"You let it out my sweet girl. Daddy's here. You're not alone anymore. You're not alone," he repeated as he rocked me back and forth. "We're fine. You all go in the house. Close the door."

John held me for what felt like an eternity as I sobbed. Every ounce of pain that had claimed my existence had surfaced. He reached into my hand, demanding that I release the amulet, which he laid to the side.

"You are Julia Spencer- a remarkably strong woman. I don't know how you've carried this alone for all these months, but I'm here now to carry it with you. We'll share the weight. Do you hear me? Let it go. You did nothing wrong. You're safe."

I lay back in my father's arms for a long time, unable to move. He was patient and kind; the father I had always dreamed of having when I was growing up. Now, at the end of his days, he'd become my daddy.

With things quiet, the boys couldn't contain themselves in my room any longer. The door creaked open and they cautiously entered on to the veranda. John motioned for them to come near and help get us vertical. We were both frail. With Henry and Gabe on each side and Tommy steadying my dad, we rose, still defeated, but living to fight the good fight.

Once erect, I asked Henry to give me the amulet. He didn't comply at first, but I insisted. With my family behind me, I held the amulet over the railing, and let it fall from my fingertips. I quoted a passage from Psalms, chapter six, which I'd repeated many times since Connor's death. "*Pity me, O Lord, for I am weak. Heal me, for my body is sick, and I am upset and disturbed. My mind is filled with apprehension and with gloom. Oh, restore me soon. Come, O Lord, and make me well. In your kindness save me.*" As it shattered into small pieces, I stood resolved that history would not repeat itself. Hector's life had been taken to pay for Connor's death. We both lost. It was over.

I turned around into my dad's open arms. Gladly finding an escape in his tight hold, I asked the others to leave me alone. I was tired and beaten. Gabe emerged with my mom's locket; the last of the items in the box.

Opening it to find her picture made me and my dad smile. We said our goodnights and Tommy carefully led John downstairs to rest.

After a long, hot shower, I exited the bathroom to find Henry sound asleep on my bed. The recliner was begging for his companionship, but I didn't have the heart to wake him and take a stand. I dressed in my old lady nightgown and got under the covers, taking care not to cross the imaginary line I'd drawn down the middle of the bed. With Tru spouting that he had moved on, I didn't want to be the one that broke the understanding.

Try as I might, sleep did not come easy. As usual, Henry had the ability to doze through any crisis. He lay beside me, on his back with a peaceful smile on his face. While he was enjoying some jovial fantasy, I had difficulties blocking out the thoughts of Hector Costelano. The arrival of the death amulet did little to banish my fears. Every time I closed my eyes, the images of Hector charging me with the knife and it plunging into my uterus, played in slow motion. The images looped, showing me the door and then the fallout from my choice to stay. I could still hear the sounds and taste the dirt clouds as they rose from that dusty clinic floor.

Without making a conscience decision to do so, my eyes opened wide, halting the montage of horror. Dreams had become anything but sweet for me. Turning my attention to the fan above, I began to count.

The sounds of glass breaking interrupted my coping exercise. With Gabe and Mattie away at the cottage, the old fears resurfaced. I tried to calm myself and control my panic, but the anxiety began to choke me. I finally nudged Henry who barely moved.

"Tru, wake up, someone is downstairs. I heard glass breaking."

He groaned and mumbled, "It's probably just Tommy or Dog getting into something. Go back to sleep."

Surely, he was right, but the crashing sounds didn't make any sense. As Henry turned over to escape my nervous chatter, I decided to go downstairs and see for myself. The house was dark except for a small lamp that sat on the round table in the foyer. The light bounced off the glass shards that were scattered across the floor, throwing a rainbow against the wall. The front door bolt was still locked, making an intruder less likely. I relaxed until I stepped in a puddle. The water that had once sustained the hydrangea blossoms glistened below me.

A moaning sound demanded my attention. Beyond the destruction of the vase, I noticed two feet in the doorway of the drawing room. Hurrying around the corner, I saw John lying on the ground, clutching his chest.

"Daddy? No," I whispered as I knelt at his side. "No."

"Julia Grace?" he panted.

"Yes, Daddy. I'm here. I'm here."

"I'm cold," he uttered weakly.

Crawling to the couch, I retrieved a throw from the sofa and the telephone off the side table. I dialed 9-1-1 and tried to cover him. I frantically begged the operator to send help quickly. My dad closed his eyes and his breathing became shallower. Scared, I pulled his head onto my lap and told him to open his eyes.

"Tommy," I yelled. "Henry."

My brother arrived first, running to our side as he caught sight of us on the floor.

"What hap-," Tommy began to ask only to be interrupted by John.

"I can't breathe, son. My chest hurts."

"An ambulance is on the way," I added, trying to remain calm for my dad's sake. "You're going to be fine."

Henry raced in to see what situation accompanied the noises that woke him. As he and Tommy conversed about opening the security gate for the police and rescue crews, I pulled myself off the floor and stood to join them. My head felt dizzy and I began to stagger forward, off balance, toward Henry as he was turning on the overhead light.

"Where's all this blood coming from? Did you cut your head on the broken glass, Dad?" Tommy inquired as he began to search the back of John's head for wounds.

Henry stood in front of me, moving his lips, but I couldn't hear him. The ringing in my ears was overpowering. I'd felt this once before. My face became flushed and my knees weak. My mind became cloudy and the room started to spin.

"Jewels, are you okay, love?"

Continuing to walk towards him, I felt warm liquid running down my legs, leaving a trail behind me on the floor. My dress was covered in my own blood. I was losing her.

"You're bleeding. It's you," he screamed as my body began to fall horizontal.

Henry dove for my head, catching it before it smacked against the ground. My shoulder hit hard and pain ripped through my body. Hearing returned with this new positioning. My face looked upon John, who was staring back at me through his own discomfort. His hand reached out to meet my own. With our fingers barely touching, he smiled at me with his eyes.

"I have always loved you. A father could never be more proud of a daughter than I am of you," he said through his strained breath. "I should have told you more. I'm sorry. You are your mother's daughter."

"I am my father's daughter."

"I'm tired baby girl. I'm so tired."

"I know. Let's sleep for a little bit," I said as my eyes unwillingly closed. "I love you Daddy," I mumbled.

"I know," John said smiling. "I have always known."

Henry began to cry, pulling me up against him. "No, love, no. You have to fight. Open your eyes. Keep your eyes open. Fight," he said over and over as he stroked my hair. "Help is coming. Hold on. You hold on. Don't you go to sleep, Jewels"

I pushed against the heaviness of my eyes and wiped his tears.

"Promise me something."

"No."

"You promise me, Tru. Save her. Choose the baby. You save Emma. Let me go. Promise me," I demanded through my own tears.

"I can't do that," he replied, destroyed.

"You have to...promise me, now. I'm so tired."

Gabe, who must have heard the call go out over his scanner, came into view.

"Oh, you'll just do anything for attention, won't you?" he grinned trying to seem less concerned, for my benefit.

"Gabe?" I responded, closing my eyes.

"You remember who you are. We've talked about this before. Fight for us. We need you. Mattie needs you. I need you," he admitted.

"I'm tired, Gabe."

"I don't care, Julia. Don't you be a quitter. Don't you dare quit on me."

"Tru? Do you hear that?"

"No, love, what is it?" he said, trying to pull himself together.

"My mom's here with Sissy…and Connor. He's grown. They're here for me. Do you see her, Dad?"

"Don't you do that, Jewels. You stay with me. You hear me. I can't lose you. Don't you go with them."

"I love you," were the last words I could muster.

With that, death called. The amulet demanded satisfaction.

23

———— ∞∞∞ ————

The black slip clung to my swollen frame. I stood searching my closet for the appropriate mourning dress. My belly was sorer than it had been when I lost Connor. Pushing hangers past me, one at a time, I looked for the same black elegant dress that had worn my misery before. With each hanger, I recited a line of that scripture verse that had been my prayer for months: *"Pity me, O Lord, for I am weak. Heal me, for my body is sick, and I am upset and disturbed. My mind is filled with apprehension and with gloom. Oh, restore me soon. Come, O Lord, and make me well. In your kindness save me."*

Things were different this time around. I was left to make the funeral arrangements and invite the guests. Much to John's dismay, the list was limited to close friends and family. The ridiculous flowers of the past were replaced with my favorite hydrangea blossoms. A simple lunch would be served and then we'd leave for the hospital. Some of our hearts were torn and already absent from the happenings of the day.

Sensing Tommy was too emotional to serve as the pastor, I contacted a family friend to say the funeral mass. My brother had been down this road before with me. The difference was that now, he'd experienced the entire journey. This time he was more deeply attached.

Henry's mom, Emma, flew in from London. Emma Walker intended to meet Emma Grace, but not this way. Kate traveled from New York to lend support to Henry and me. Having my best friend back to lean on filled a void. She was the person I could most be myself around. My feelings, whether they be anger or inappropriate humor, were always acceptable. The argument that sent her packing seemed to have taken place decades

209

ago. There are some people in your life whose importance defies time and circumstance. She and I always had the gift of picking up just where we had left off- minus the hostility. Emma Walker and Kate had instantly taken on the task of managing things at the hospital for me, while I took on the unwanted job of planning another burial.

With Henry's heart broken, Gabe remained the rock at my side. He attended the meeting with the funeral director, helped me to choose a burial outfit, found someone at the church to sing, and hired a local caterer to provide food after the Mass.

Mattie and Dog provided my moments of sanity and comfort. Little Man obviously knew that something terrible had happened, but he couldn't comprehend the specifics. All he understood was that it was time for marbles and painting. Those activities gave me the necessary distraction, allowing me to make it through the hours in the days preceding the loss. Mattie's innocence and inner dignity uplifted my spirits. His actions had their own love language. No words were ever needed to convey his feelings. He was God's messenger and my angel.

Ms. Martin never left my side, administering medications and changing my surgical dressings. She'd taken to sleeping in bed with me in the event that I needed even the smallest thing. Her closeness and care was of the kind that a mother shows a daughter. She was selfless and resolute that I would make it through this trial. Gabe was one of those rare sons that didn't take his mom for granted. He knew how lucky he was. This woman, giant in character, had instilled those same values in her son. I was blessed to have the Martin family in my life.

Same scars. Same cemetery. Same faces. Same sad dress. Same sad chair. The morning was filled with a punch list; get dressed, go to the chapel, try not to breakdown, bury my heart, push food around my plate, listen to people's mundane small talk, and wish them well as they left me to my pain. I curiously wondered what they would speak about as their cars cleared the Spencer gates. Would they talk about the latest movie they saw or the weather outside? Were they altered in any way? Did life just continue? Would anyone comprehend the fact that something important was taken from me- again? Could they understand that no sentiment would bring me comfort or fill that space in my heart? These are the things I pondered as their voices mouthed their condolences.

Henry was a wreck. Sadness consumed him. I had never seen him so broken and lost. His confidence was replaced with anxiety and fear. Where I had come to a point of acceptance, he was angry. Our views on fate and faith divided us. Throughout the week, we had spent very little time together, taking turns going to the hospital and coming home to sleep. He still showed love, but his actions were habit driven instead of genuine affection. The one discussion we had about the death ended badly. My faith had become my life preserver. I began to understand more definitively, the views that Gabe had shared with me after I lost Connor.

With the departure of all our guests, Henry and I retreated to the bedroom for a private moment of grief. When we cleared the door, we just held each other. The only sounds heard were sniffles and muffled sobs. We held on to each other as if our own lives depended on it, afraid to let go and move on to the next difficulty. Pushing him back slightly, our tear filled eyes met.

"We can persevere or we can surrender," I said, trying to be a motivator.

"You're so strong," he replied sweetly, but a bit annoyed.

"I'm not strong because I've had the courage to choose perseverance. I'm persevering because I genetically don't know how to surrender. I'm a Spencer. We'll make it through this, one second at a time, if need be," I said, trying to sound encouraging.

"Why aren't you angry? This is twice. None of this is fair."

"Who said anything about fair? I wasn't supposed to be able to get pregnant and I did. God doesn't play fair. He exceeds our limited expectations and bestows far more gifts on us than we deserve. If you're asking for things to be fair, I hope you're prepared for the outcome. You pray for fairness and I'll pray for mercy."

"You're just too resilient; it's not natural to be so brave. You let people go so easily," he criticized, embarrassed for not having it together.

Henry collapsed down into the recliner. His top shirt button was undone and his tie hung loosely around his neck. I approached and knelt down slowly, still mindful of the recent trauma to my abdominal muscles. My hands gravitated to his knees, which I used to pull myself up between his legs.

"I can't change who I am, Tru. I'm the little girl who lost her mom in this house all those years ago. I went from wearing her jewels and playing dress up to having her erased from this place- from my life. I am still trying to find those jewels- those pieces of my mother- myself, so I can remember a time when I felt secure and unconditionally loved. My dad locked me away- maybe not physically, but in every other way that makes a child know who they are in the world. I was lost and alone until I realized one day that there was only one person, on this earth, that I could count on. I walk forward, one foot in front of the other, because I have no other alternative. What do you think made me peel myself off that dusty clinic floor in Chimbote to fight for my life? My mind is wired for survival. God put that scrappy, annoying, resilient nature inside of me."

"Since when did you become all spiritual?" he asked, disbelieving my dogma.

"God doesn't make mistakes, Henry- of that, I'm certain. Sometimes, the lesson in our suffering isn't meant for us. Sometimes, our suffering brings others to a better place. When I stopped being so generally pissed off, I discovered that He always sheltered me in times of sorrow and sent his comfort, by way of people, to minister to me. Connor's death put me on a path back to you. The Martins' came into my life. My dad initiated reconciliation. I have no doubt that God collects every one of my tears. He cries with me."

"You seem so sure..."

"The night of the storm, when you found me in the cemetery, I was screaming every kind of blasphemy at Christ. That was a turning point in my faith. What resulted was an immense thirst to understand my heart- breaks- a thirst that He gave me. A dialogue opened that evening between two people who really loved each other. There was no agenda. He patiently waited for me to return to Him. I was the prodigal son and it didn't mat- ter what I said or did. He greeted me with love and joy. I was the lost sheep. He never gave up on me. That's how I can stand this heartache. The cracks are allowing His grace to pour in and heal me. He's given me peace. His strength, displayed through me, is what you criticize. I don't want to return to the angry person I was after Connor. I would like to think that I've grown somewhat since then."

"Well, I'm still angry," he said with assurance.

"Then be angry- for a little while."

"Maybe you should be wearing a loin cloth and screaming in the desert like that bloke John the Baptist?" he replied, poking fun at me.

"Maybe you should be screaming."

"I don't want to fight with you. I just want to get to the hospital, okay?"

"Sure," I said quietly. "I would like to change out of this dress- it's suffocating me."

Kneeling back to prepare to stand, he grabbed me and gently kissed my lips.

"You are the single best decision of my entire life, Julia Spencer- prophet or no prophet- loin cloth or no loin cloth, though the loin cloth sounds hot," he smirked. "I love you."

"What's not to love?"

He laughed and the emotion was a gift. That laugh told me that everything would be okay; that we would grieve and move past the misery. This tiny amount of joy was something to build on; it was heaven sent. The blessing wasn't lost on me.

The house was empty when we made our way downstairs. The family probably realized that we needed some time to be alone. I was relieved to have discarded the dress for some sweats. Henry changed into a pair of jeans, a gray Henley, and a skull cap to hide his messy hair. He went out ahead to start the car as I lingered at the front door. Looking back, I realized that with the loss, the house wouldn't know the memories I had planned for it- those were buried.

The ride to the hospital was quiet and thoughtful. Both of our minds were racing in multiple directions. As we traveled the streets of Savannah, I remembered thinking how odd it was that the world looked the same, despite out recent tragedy. Life truly does go on.

Henry reached over and grabbed my hand out of my lap. We didn't smile at each other in response to the comfort the touch brought us; we just interlaced our fingers and held tight to one another. The weight of our despair would not pull us down. Despite Henry's assessment that it was easy for me to let go of people, I was still, very much, the scared little girl who lost herself when her mom died all those years ago. Certainly, time had proven that my survival instincts were ridiculously strong, but I never claimed to be immune to the weariness; it was contained, but still ever present.

Preparing to pull into the hospital, I was reminded of my blessings. Today, I stood with Tommy and Gabe and experienced a brother's protection and fierce loyalty. My insane sister Kate reminded me to fall back on humor as a source of strength; a theory demonstrated as she provided distasteful commentary about our varied funeral guests. Little Man and Dog reminded me to be open to the possibilities of miracles. Ms. Martin reminded me of a mother's love. Henry now held my heart, gingerly, in the palm of his hands, finally learning to keep them open, allowing for growth and the fine mess that always ensued. My dad taught me that respect comes from within. The approval I had yearned for over all those years was lurking inside of me the entire time. This enlightenment made me understand that no one can give you what you already own and no one can take away what you don't freely give. A spirit has but one owner.

Henry offered to drop me off out front, but I wanted to make this walk with him- together. Being away from the hospital was easier, knowing that the family was holding a constant vigil. As we got off on the fourth floor, I saw Tommy and Gabe in the family waiting area outside of the intensive care unit. The others had gone to take Mattie to the cafeteria to scrounge up some ice cream.

"Hi, sis," Tommy said as he held out his arms for a hug.

"Have you been in yet?" I inquired, hugging him back.

Tommy moved on to Henry while Gabe and I shared our own embrace.

"Yes. Things are stable. The nurse said to call once you arrived."

"Okay. Thanks. We'll go get washed up and put on the gowns. Can you call while we get ready?"

"Absolutely...go ahead."

We had participated in this same cleaning ritual for five days. After scrubbing our hands, we would put on yellow gowns. Only then, would we be admitted into the unit. The nurse was waiting for us as we approached the door. She led us to the room. Henry pulled a rocker over for me to sit in. There she was, so tiny and fragile. The big girl I was sure to deliver in four more weeks only weighed a mere 4 lbs. 5 oz.

The neonatologist stopped by to explain the results of her brain ultrasound and her current prognosis. Surprisingly, she had not experienced a brain bleed that was common at her premature age. The staff expected to wean her off the ventilator soon. Her heart was strong. She was a fighter. She was my daughter.

When the doctor left, Henry fell to pieces. He couldn't take seeing her so vulnerable. I could tell that he was preparing himself for a forced good-bye, which wasn't an outcome that I would accept. I reached in the isolette, stroking her precious little arm, and began to sing her a lullaby. Tubes and wires overwhelmed her small frame. Monitors echoed sounds of life. Henry stuck his hand through the other portal, using his other to wipe away the tears of fear and the unknown that overwhelmed him. Emma was fighting to hold on and her dad was fighting to believe she could.

"She'll be fine," I declared, interrupting my melody. "You just have to believe. With God, you have to show faith. She'll be home in no time. Just wait. You'll see."

All he could do was stroke the back of my hair and rub my back. I knew he was trying to placate me, but it didn't matter. My Emma was coming home. Of this, I had no doubt. I spent the rest of the afternoon by her side, entertaining family visits, one by one, only leaving her once. I entrusted her to Kate and Gabe while Henry, his mom, and I went to the cafeteria. Ms. Martin had taken Mattie back to the cottage

When night fell, Henry took his mom home. The truth of the matter was that he couldn't hack seeing his baby girl in such a state. Knowing this, I suggested that he stay there and get a good night's sleep. He jumped at the opportunity. Kate thanked me for not making him feel inadequate. She sensed the same fear and detachment that I had. The remaining three of us camped out in the waiting room with the other mommies and daddies, desperate for good news. When I woke in the middle of the night, out of discomfort from trying to sleep on a couch fit for a four-foot person, I noticed that Gabe and Kate had disappeared.

The morning brought many changes. Gabe was holding Kate in his arms. They were both sound asleep. She was obviously ready for steak. Tommy had materialized with a cup of hot tea and a croissant from my favorite downtown bakery.

"Can I see her?" he asked like an impatient toddler.

"You still have ten minutes before they allow visitors."

"It'll take me that long to scrub up and get gowned," he insisted.

"True. Okay. Tell her I said good morning. I'm going to talk with the doctor after rounds and then wait for Henry."

The neonatologist came out and sat with me in one of the counseling rooms. He said that she was out of the woods, was off the ventilator, and if she continued to have a good morning, I could hold her this afternoon. Jumping out of my chair, I practically French kissed the man, before screaming out in joy. Gabe and Kate came running in and we shared the news, high fiving and hugging. I had my miracle; in His kindness He had saved me- again. There would be no more broken glass to choke down.

When Ms. Walker and Henry arrived, Kate gave them the great news. I wished I'd been there to see the weight fall from his shoulders, but I was already back with Emma Grace counting the minutes until she was in my arms. Ms. Walker accompanied Henry into the unit, carrying a blanket that once belonged to him. This was her first heirloom and I felt its significance.

When the nurse finally came by after lunch with the doctor to assess her vitals, we got the go ahead. She instructed me to sit down in the rocker and Emma would be handed to me. As I prepared to sit, I paused and then stepped aside.

"You should hold her first," I said.

"No, I couldn't. You've been waiting for this."

"And you finally believed. Your tears were collected. Your suffering meant something. Hold your baby girl, Tru. Besides, once I get her, I'm not likely to give her up," I added with a smile.

The nurse suggested that he open his shirt and allow for kangaroo care- skin to skin- which would give her human contact and help keep her warm. There sat Henry, with his tiny princess on his chest, snuggling close. She was saving her father without even knowing it. This was an important moment of bonding between them. I would never get her back now.

After hours at the hospital, Gabe and Kate came back to relieve us. They offered to sleep at the hospital while we went home for the night. Making them promise to call if anything changed, I went home to enjoy a much-needed rest in a real bed. Once we arrived at the house, Henry led me up the stairs and into my bedroom, insisting that I cover my eyes. With a manufactured drum role, I opened them to find a beautiful crib where the recliner used to be.

"I don't think you'll fit in that. Where are you going to sleep?" I said laughing.

"You're hilarious."

"When did you have time to do this?" I asked as I admired his handiwork.

"I haven't been sleeping well with you gone," he replied, reserved.

"I thought you were over me. I recall that your exact words were that you were finally prepared to move on."

"You're not going to make this easy, are you?"

"No," I said, smugly shaking my head back and forth.

He came up behind me, moved my hair to the side, and began kissing the back of my neck.

"How about a shower? We do our best thinking in the shower?"

"No, actually, that's where we get in the most trouble," I replied.

He spun me around.

"You have a dirty mind. I love it. Though, you do have a belly full of staples and I'm exhausted."

"Don't flatter yourself," I said, giving him a look like he was totally off base for assuming. "Truth is... I'm not sure I'm still interested."

"Julia Grace Walker," he replied enunciating every syllable.

"Julia Grace Spencer," I clarified.

"Julia Grace Spencer-Walker," he retorted.

"Maybe?"

Over the course of a long hot shower we found conversations to laugh about again. We found solace in just being- not doing. As my head hit the pillow, my mind drifted to memories of my daddy. The blood clots that claimed his life were quick. Instead of suffering a long and debilitating battle with pancreatic cancer, God had, in His infinite mercy, called John back to Georgia Grace-if he could get past Sissy. Of course, I wished that I'd been given more time to rediscover who my dad was, but deep down, like he said to me, as we were both collapsed on the drawing room floor, I had always known. His harshness had served a greater good in forming my character. My childhood suffering had served a greater purpose. The lesson wasn't just for me.

Henry had lingered downstairs after our shower, returning calls, and preparing documents for the reading of John's will. We all knew what it contained since he had advised us of his wishes several weeks ago. I had left Henry's Christmas envelope on the vanity in the bathroom, in hopes that he would read it before coming to bed. His declaration of love and a life together was an answered prayer, but I wanted to be sure that the prospect of running Spencer Industries would not bring him greater happiness. I fell asleep before being privy to his reaction.

Mattie rushed in and jumped on our bed in the morning with Dog. Henry was happy to see them both. The distraction kept us from talking about the documents, but I did notice that they were gone, when I went in to wash my face. We all hurried to get ready and then piled into the vehicle for our trip to Emma.

Gabe and Kate looked like they had spent the night in the broom closet. They were all messy- not the kind of sloppy you get from squeezing into a small chair or on a four foot couch. We made time for girl talk as I walked her to the elevator. They had made amends. She was eating steak. All was right with the world and I was thankful.

For I am convinced that nothing can ever separate us from His love. Death can't, and life can't. The angels won't, and all the powers of hell itself cannot keep God's love away. Our fears for today, our worries about tomorrow, or where we are- high above the sky, or in the deepest ocean- nothing will ever be able to separate us from the love of God demonstrated by our Lord Jesus Christ when he died for us. (Romans 8:38-39, TLB)

24

Weeks passed and Emma Grace was making great strides at the hospital. Our daily visits allowed us to bottle feed her and conjure up ways of sneaking our princess out of the unit. We were all tired of leaving her behind. With her weight steadily increasing and her tests normal, we were finally given the green light to take our baby home.

Ms. Walker had remained in Savannah. She was no Georgia Grace Spencer or Ms. Martin, but she was a respectable third. I had enjoyed getting to know her better and finally understood the sickness that is Kate's raunchy humor. Despite her fine apparel and lineage, she was very much a sailor at heart. The apple didn't fall far from the tree. I was left wondering how Henry turned out so proper.

Emma's homecoming enjoyed much fanfare. Mattie decorated blue welcome home signs with blue artwork and blue streamers. Dog had taken up residence by her crib as defender and protector. Kate, it turns out, had reluctantly taken a job in New York while she was mad at me last summer. Until she could sort out a better circumstance for herself, she was restricted to flying down every weekend. Gabe, Mattie and Ms. Martin had moved into the main house in anticipation of the cottage demolition to make way for their new construction. I had managed to salvage bits of the old place in order to share a piece of history with our daughter some day. I would just have to be judicious with the information I released. That cottage held some scandalous memories of her parents.

Henry never mentioned my Christmas gift and spent the better part of his weeks in New York finalizing my dad's affairs. When he was home, his days were filled with endless phone conferences or drafting documents and memos on his computer. John had left me everything with the exception of a trust account to take care of Tommy in his retirement and a surprising loot of money for Ms. Martin. She had cared diligently for him in the end. I now owned controlling stock in Spencer Industries. I never wanted to be a part of his world, but I now understood that he was creating a legacy for his family- for his grandchild. I would do my best to respect his life's work.

Bringing Emma through the front door of my mom's house and past her picture made me proud that she was a third generation lady of good Southern stock and technically of Royal British line; which made her sound a lot like a horse instead of a little girl. Henry was beaming, and for now, he could wear the coveted good dad award. I continued to hold out hope that business wouldn't skew his priorities. After cake, blue ice cream, and fried chicken, Henry left again to tie up some final loose ends and pack his apartment in Manhattan. His mom left on the same plane as him and Tommy. The house was back to its semi-quiet state; if you didn't count the addition of a baby crying, Mattie upset about the crying, and Dog barking at them both in response.

Henry's stay in New York was longer than expected. Visions of him sitting at John's desk and soaking in the power scared me. I plowed ahead taking care of the daily tasks that an infant relies on like clean diapers and bottles. The events of the past year reminded me that other people's destinies were out of my control.

After receiving a call from a law firm downtown, regarding Dad's estate, and being the only lawyer in town to handle the questions, I dressed for the appointment while trying to come up with an excuse for getting out of it. I called back, suggesting that the meeting be put off until Henry could attend it for me, but the paralegal was insistent that the matter was time sensitive and be handled quickly. Leaving Emma Grace with Ms. Martin, I headed to the address she gave me.

The building with that particular number was in a ritzy part of town. I knew that I must be at the right place. The historic structure had John written all over it. There was brown paper covering the door logo, but the address numbers matched. Proceeding in, I hoped to expedite the issues quickly and be back to Emma within the hour.

A nice older woman greeted me at the front reception area and showed me to a conference room on the second floor. I waited and waited until becoming impatient and annoyed. Walking to the windows, I opened the shutters. The room overlooked a beautiful courtyard with a magnificent fountain below. Fumbling through my purse, I found my cell phone and called to check on Emma Grace. As I connected to Gabe's mom, I heard the door close behind me.

"Sorry to keep you waiting, Mrs. Walker," said the familiar British voice.

"That's Julia Grace Spencer, Mr. Walker," I replied turning to see the most handsome man I'd ever laid eyes on in his Hugo Boss suit, five o'clock shadow, hair messy, but with every strand still perfectly in place. "What are you doing here?" I asked, astounded. "You're supposed to be in New York."

"This was our dream, remember?"

"That seems like a lifetime ago."

"Yet, here we are."

He walked to me, holding out the white envelope I'd left for him.

"Rescue me," he said, the words spoken boldly and with sincerity.

"Maybe I've moved on…" I replied coyly as he took a few steps forward before halting, playing cat and mouse.

"I can give you what you're asking for, but you have to give me the opportunity to show you that. Don't just shoot me down based on speculation. Give me a chance," he added as he approached again slyly.

"A chance?"

"That's all I'm asking for."

"Okay…one chance. For the next week, and I mean seven whole days, you can not do any business. No phone calls. No emails. No quick trips. If you can make me a priority for one week, I'll give you an answer."

"No business for one week and you'll be my wife?"

"No business for one week and I'll give you my answer."

"One condition. You have to wear the ring this week. You need a reminder."

"Agreed. Do you need a reminder?"

"No Jewels. I promise."

"Your phone, Tru. Give me your phone," I demanded.

He reached into his pocket, flashed his devastating smile, and handed it over. The first window was painted shut, but the second opened with ease. The cell made a small splash after it left my hands and found its rest in the fountain below.

"You are one fine mess," he offered before he kissed me. "Julia Grace Walker."

"You mean Julia Grace Spencer-Walker."

"Of course that's what I mean."

www.ingramcontent.com/pod-product-compliance
Lightning Source LLC
Chambersburg PA
CBHW031954240626
47153CB00003B/979